# Touch Me Softly

## Book One of the Reawakening Series

# KELLY VIOLET

Touch Me Softly

Published by Pump Up the Violet Publishing, Los Angeles, CA.

Original Photo by Tanja Heffner on Unsplash

Cover Design by Kelly Violet

Cover content is for illustrative purposes only and any person depicted on the cover is a model.

Library of Congress Control Number: 2017962590

ISBN-13: 978-0-9997048-0-6

First Edition

Printed in the U.S.A.

Pump Up The Violet
Publishing

*This book is dedicated to the strong women in my life: my mom and two sisters. Although my mother passed away this year, she taught us girls to follow our dreams and we thank her for that every day. And because of you, maman, I get to follow one of my dreams of publishing my first novel.*

*To my sisters: Always in my corner, you believed in me when I didn't even believe in myself. I love y'all so much.*

*Thanks to all of my family and friends who believed in me. This first book is for and because of all of you. Special thanks to Tum-Tum, SG and MBT for giving me feedback and encouragement throughout this long process. Friends for life!*

# Chapter One
*Wynter*

*My heart pumped fast and furious in my chest. His calloused hands turned rough on my skin. It was no longer fun or exciting.*

*I whimpered, "No." The pressure overwhelmed me, hot and stinging in its intensity. His muscular body dwarfing me. It terrified me. He terrified me. I asked him to stop before it got this far. It was all happening too fast. I wasn't ready. We just met.*

*Making out in the beginning was nice, and then something shifted. A little out of my comfort zone, I wanted to keep it light. I liked being fun and flirty for a change. I found freedom in that, but everything went horribly wrong in an instant. His touch gentle at first. Then it wasn't.*

*He held me down, and I was drowning in the dark. With no way out.*

*Confused and broken, he ruined me.*

"Wynter Renee Simmons! Hey, you doing okay over there?" The voice of my best friend, Darcy, boomed through my headset. She never used my government name unless she was angry with me. Her voice snapped me back to the present.

Yikes! She must've called my name several times. I rubbed at my eyes, banishing the memories and berating myself. Time to refocus. Stop remembering. I lifted my gaze back to the computer screen. I noticed she'd put her vibrant, red hair up in a ponytail.

With the orientation of her laptop, I had a wide view into her apartment, or loft as they called them in Scotland. One of Darcy's stuffed animals sat on the desk, just within the webcam's scope. Fish, even of the fluffy variety, surrounded her no matter her location.

Darcy Williams was a unique girl and I loved her to bits.

While we chatted on our weekly video call, I probably seemed dazed staring into space for however long. I forgot what we talked about, but from her tone, she'd tried getting my attention several times. I pushed up from my slouched position, answering her question. "Dar, I'm fine. Just stuck in my head, I guess." *And that night a year ago still haunts me.* I didn't dare say the last part aloud.

My best friend had no clue what happened all those months ago. The timing never seemed right for the conversation. And it was okay. It had to be. I let her believe nothing much had happened. It was better this way.

Once we got back to our motel room, a mile away from the band's hotel, I stood in the shower for what seemed like hours bawling my eyes out. They were so red when I stepped out of the bathroom Darcy assumed I hadn't slept well the previous night. Sleep was the furthest thing from my mind. I refused to tell her why.

I forced myself to give more attention to our current conversation even though memories dragged me down deep into the darkness. More and more.

"So, what's going on with your fish friends?" Although I never understood the details of her job as an aquatic veterinarian, I loved hearing the passion in her voice. My friend had accomplished so much and at such a young age. It always brightened my day to listen to her adventures since she now traveled abroad consulting with aquariums and other organizations working with marine animals.

"Mm, I operated on a sea turtle the other day…" After a few minutes listening to Darcy's story about the latest animals in her care, I tuned out again. The list of tasks for work already piled on my desk for tomorrow played like a Rolodex through my head. Two of my clients needed the assignments completed by Friday.

As a virtual assistant, I worked mainly from home. On a normal day, I handled everything online with a conference call or video chat and limited face-to-face meetings for local clients. The nature of my job helped in my pursuit of becoming a hermit. I wasn't comfortable in my own skin anymore. Everything about that night haunted me. "I don't want to continue boring you," I heard Dar say.

"Oh, you're not. I like hearing about your work. Even if half the time I have no clue what the hell you're talking about." That I wasn't listening made me feel like a bug at the bottom of a shoe. The circumstances of my existence were crappy and not getting better. I

2

comforted myself in the fact that she knew me extremely well after our twelve-year friendship. My brain wandered sometimes. Darcy had a fifty percent chance of success if she guessed I was list making right now.

"That's why you get paid the big bucks to be my friend. To say statements like that to cheer me up." Her lips formed one of her patented smiles and I shook my head at her. Darcy joked about this all too often, yet nothing would make me give up on our friendship.

"On another note, I have news plus a question," she hedged. Why she continued to act as if I ever told her no, I had no clue. I put up a good fight even though she won ninety-nine-point one percent of the time. *I'm proud of my point nine percent success rate, dammit.*

Her suspenseful pause made me antsy. "Well, out with it!"

"I'll be coming back to the states for several weeks starting next month. Can I stay with you?" She asked every time. My response was always the same. I worried more about how I'd pull my life together before she came home and less about her coming home. She hadn't stayed with me for a long stretch since last year and any personal life I had was so non-existent now.

"Yes, Dar." I aimed a strong side-eye her way through the webcam. "You don't have to ask me every time you come back. I have a two-bedroom apartment for this very reason. We're roomies for life. Just tell me when you're arriving at the airport. Cru and I will scoop you up."

"Why are you still driving that hooptie around?" I refused to forgive my grandparents for teaching her that word. Most people called her worst names though, but she was my baby. The 1999 Volvo had been with me since I turned seventeen. My first and only car. She had several thousand miles on her when I got her, but we'd been through some tough spots together.

I called her Cruella because the black Volvo turned heads with her white hood. The story was that a tree fell on the hood during a storm and the previous owner only found a white replacement to fit the make and model. I never had the heart to change it once I got her. The car was my other best friend. End of story.

"Listen here, friend, don't talk bad about Cru. She still runs fine." *Just barely.* I'd been told many times mere stubbornness didn't describe me well enough because I did everything in my power to keep her running for as long as possible. *I brought her home seven years ago.* And I'd keep her around for seven more if I could.

Also, I knew full well I'd have big problems if too many parts needed replacing all at once. I kept putting a visit to my mechanics off, hoping she'd continue to run for me. I circled back to the previous topic before Darcy badmouthed Cru again. "When are you coming in and what gifts are you bringing me?"

"What makes you think I have any goodies for you, huh?" I almost saw her in my mind's eye with a fist on her hip. Her desk blocked my view, so I wasn't certain. The image made me smirk. "You're lucky I'm still willing to let you pick me up in that deathtrap you call a car. That'll be my gift to you, our continued friendship." She busted out laughing.

I shook my head, fake pouting to the max. Dar didn't buy it for a second. "You always bring me presents from your work adventures." The whiny tone oozed out of me in full effect. I was almost myself again, bantering back and forth with Darcy. It hadn't felt like this in forever. I'd become isolated, pushing myself down a deep, dark hole. I needed to dig myself out of it now.

"You better bring me presents or your ass can find your own way home from the airport." I said, lifting only my right brow. The feisty move was perfected years ago. Darcy noticed it right away and took my threat for what it was, empty.

"Ha! You wouldn't dare, Wyn. You love me too much." I hated when she read me so well but teasing her had always been a favorite pastime in our friendship.

"Dare would I," I mimicked in my best Yoda voice which was pretty horrific. She snorted which was the reaction I wanted. I did my patented funny face where I puffed up my cheeks and bugged out my eyes.

"You're too much sometimes." Darcy's eyelids shuttered, muffling her words in exaggerated slow motion.

"Um, your yawn was epic, Dar. You sound like you need rest. Listen, keep me posted on your travel plans, okay?" Darcy was stubborn too, staying on the line for extra minutes even if she seemed way past exhausted. One of us had to wind down the conversation or else we'd chat for a few more hours.

"Yup. I'll send you my arrival information when I book." Darcy stretched and patted her messy ponytail. "Well, okay. I'm fading fast. We'll talk soon. Love ya."

"Back at you, Dar! Tell the fishes I said hello." I clicked on the red icon to end the video chat before she could get another word in.

My joke ended each of our video calls lately, knowing for a fact, she talked to the animals in her care like they understood her. But who am I to joke? *She may know something I don't.* Darcy cracked me up all the time. Still, I admired her because she got to do what she loved, taking care of marine animals.

I glanced at the bottom of my screen for the time: fifteen past seven. No wonder Darcy almost fell asleep on her keyboard. Midnight crept up on her in the UK. I clicked a few keys, closing several open windows, and putting my laptop to sleep by closing the lid. My workday had been relatively light, finishing up what I needed to get done a few hours ago.

My makeshift work area, or what I called my corner office, had all the supplies I needed to handle anything my clients threw at me. The L-shaped desk was my pride and joy, only second to Cru. My laptop, headset, and a neat pile of folders full of paperwork sat perched on top of the expensive looking wood finish. To the left of me sat a used small office cabinet I got for a steal at the surplus store near the college for ten bucks a few months back. Getting it up the flight of stairs had been a struggle, but I got it done with little to no injury to myself. There were no new nicks or scuffs on my furniture or front door either. A huge accomplishment.

I pushed in my office chair and walked to the kitchen for a snack. Watching television in the living room then heading to bed early sounded good. *Get a few hours of peaceful rest.* A rerun of a sitcom played. I sat back and got comfortable on my patchwork sofa.

*We weren't alone in the hotel room. My best friend lay snuggled in the arms of the band's lead singer behind the door of the bedroom just a few feet away from us. The thought distracted me from the calloused hands of his friend scraping over my body for only a moment.*

*I told him earlier I wasn't getting undressed. He'd obviously taken my words as a challenge. They weren't meant to be. His rough hands were under the material before I realized his intention. He pulled my shirt up to reveal my bra. I had always been self-conscious about my body, but he dove right in, kissing my breasts over the bra cups. Fists at my sides, my hands clutched the threadbare comforter straddling underneath me on the sofa bed. He tore at the fabric of my shirt, the sound of it ripping echoed in my ears, shoving his hand under my bra, squeezing at one of my breasts.*

I woke up with a start, squeezing the throw pillow under my head. Another dream about that night. More like a nightmare. But I was at home on my sofa. Safe. I panted, out of breath, like I'd run a half-marathon. The terror following me scared me most of all.

A mix of sweat and tears saturated the throw pillow and section of the sofa I fell asleep on. Light and a low hum emanated from the television, where an infomercial was airing. It was after midnight. I pushed onto my hands and knees, sucked in some air then forced it out. My heart rate slowed, almost returning to normal. Sleep eluded me on nights like these. I walked down the hall to the bathroom, washing my face and brushing my teeth.

It was hard to hold my own gaze in the damn mirror. I didn't recognize the person staring back at me. I appeared ashen, which should've been nearly impossible with my dark complexion. The dark circles under my eyes didn't bode well either. I must've hidden it all well enough because Darcy never commented on our video chats.

The nightmares consumed me. I woke up in a cold sweat most nights. Fear. Disgust at myself for what happened. Not stopping it when I had the chance. The hurt inescapable even now. Those memories haunted me every single day.

He ruined me a year ago. I tried burying everything from that night, hiding it from the few people closest. It hadn't been hard to do. My grandparents lived several hours away, and I only visited a few times a year. With Darcy returning next month, how was I supposed to keep her from finding out about these nightmares? I had a few weeks to figure it out.

The Sandman didn't return fast enough, so I headed into Darcy's room to see how much damage I'd done. I used it as storage space when she left for one of her projects, stowing random items in her bedroom. I took stock of the room, moving and organizing a few items around the cramped floor space. The distraction shut my brain off. After an hour, my mind and body got tired again.

I walked back to my room down the short hallway, my feet dragging. Near exhaustion set in, but I knew a peaceful slumber would be too much to ask for. No doubt about it.

The comfiest sweatpants I owned sat in the bottom drawer of my espresso-colored dresser. I pulled them out, wanting the safety and comfort the sweats provided. Even though I spent most of my days at home, a typical wardrobe was worn jeans and a nice blouse. There was always a slim possibility an unexpected video call with a client would arise or I'd need to run an errand.

Shoot. That reminded me. I needed to go grocery shopping to stock up on Darcy's favorite foods. A surprise for when she got home. I threw my comforter off and sat up in bed. My mind fretted over other stuff beyond my immediate control. Rest too far off. I jotted down notes in my phone, a task list to get done before Darcy got back into town. I expected the sun to rise in several hours. Sleep was a lost cause now.

*Ha. Sleeping means dreaming, so at least I won't have that in my immediate future.* I had other thoughts filling my mind now and was thankful for the short reprieve.

# Chapter Two
*Rafael*

"Hey, Colt. How's it going?" I worked up the nerve to talk to the frontman about the setlist for our upcoming show. Although the band had several great songs under its belt, I had a few suggestions. I thought switching things up would liven up the band's overall sound.

Doug and Berto, the lead guitarist and drummer, were out picking up lunch for the four of us. I considered this opportunity as good as any other to bring up my ideas to Colton Strong, the lead singer of the band I joined up with a couple months ago. I shuffled my notes around, glancing up and noticing his expression. He wore a smirk that froze me in my tracks. His amused look wasn't for me though. I hadn't yet humiliated myself by sharing my ideas.

New to the band dynamics of Country Blue, I was observant enough most days. Colt wore two perpetual expressions when not playing up his frontman act: brooding and irritable.

He seemed like a nice guy and all, but I didn't notice him smile much about anything. The rare smirk caught my attention. It brightened up his dark demeanor, showing a slither of light. Whatever caused the look, it was an interesting change.

Country Blue selected me as their new bass guitarist, and I considered myself a lucky S.O.B. They were an up-and-coming band. Colt's best friend and bassist, Nick Ferrara, left for greener pastures when another band's bassist got injured in a bad car wreck. Their star was rising a lot quicker than Colt's band, so word was that Colt encouraged Nick to leave.

Mine and Nick's paths crossed a few times around town. The prick never became one of my favorite people. He talked too much. Said even less. Something told me he saw his chance with Devil's Tea and took it without thinking about his friends. His brothers.

Either way, the bassist opening came at a perfect time for me. Fucking this up wasn't an option. Neither was Nick waltzing back in if he wanted to. I had something to contribute to the band's sound if given half a chance. I just had to speak up and see what came of it.

"I'm doing all right, Rafe. Fantastic, actually. Heard from my girl. She's coming back to the states soon." I didn't know Colt had a steady girlfriend, but I was out of the loop. *It's the cards I'm dealt as the newbie.* I had dues to pay before getting into their close circle. I sure as hell took it as a good sign he let that much slip. The dynamic duo were out running errands, so we had the space to ourselves for the moment.

"Cool, man. Where she been?" I rifled through my backpack, looking for my notes. I stuffed them in my bag after practice and even worked on them more when I got home last night. *Where the hell are they?* I usually transferred the daily scribbles into my notebook, but time had gotten away from me.

My brain never stopped working on my music. I excelled at it, this one thing. It kept me going through all of life's bullshit. People told me I was a worthless piece of shit. Too much of a pansy. I tried not to listen, but two voices from my past managed to break through. No matter how much I pushed the words down, they still tried to break me.

Music remained the one positive in an ocean of negatives. It gave me purpose. This opportunity with Colt and the guys gave me a chance to prove them wrong. I'd make a living playing music. Be successful at it. Happy even.

*I have to prove it to myself too.*

"She's in Scotland on a project for work." I kept up my search for those missing sheets. "Darcy's kind of a genius," he continued. I glanced up at him. High praise from Colt. *Interesting.* He shrugged his shoulders, the sappy expression disappearing from his face the next moment.

I searched the bottom of my tattered backpack, my fingers touching a rounded edge. I opened the compartment more and dug out the crumpled pieces of paper. *Yes!*

Colt had moved on. Some OCD reared its head as he continued moving the wired microphone stand a few inches back and forth in the center of the cramped room. His charisma showed onstage and even at practice. I guessed it was part of his frontman persona. I hadn't commented on the shrug; it was none of my business anyway.

I hoped to meet this Darcy. She had to be damn special to have that effect on Colt. I bet any money she'd be a riot in person, if for no other reason than how Colt might act with her around. I couldn't wait.

My strides were long as I walked over to him. A man on a mission. *A death wish more like.* The room reminded me of other independent studio spaces. It was small as hell. With the furniture and various equipment lying around, the place looked like a disaster zone. At first it surprised me just how much shit they'd shoved into the compact room. In a few short weeks, my stuff now contributed to the chaos. Berto's drum kit sat between the tight corner of the two back walls, his extra sticks hanging out of a messenger bag. A shabby couch took up another wall near the door.

"Hey, Colt." I wiped the sweat from my palms across my pant legs, wrinkling the papers even more and almost tripping over my damn guitar stand.

*I'm a fucking nuisance.*

*Shit, just get it over with,* I prodded myself. *Tell him your ideas and be done with it. If he doesn't like 'em then fuck it, at least you tried. Pull up your big boy pants and do it.* The internal pep talk did little to ease my apprehension. I dove right in anyway. "I wanted to talk to you about some stuff I've been experimenting with. About the newer songs. I have a few ideas for the rhythm section and hook on 'Save Me from Myself.'"

The fact I'd been working on a new song, I kept to myself. 'Runaway Girl' came from a personal place and it wasn't finished yet. I didn't know if I had it in me to finish. I'd wait to see how this all panned out before I put myself out there, shared my lyrics. Hell, it wouldn't surprise me if the guys didn't even like the damn song.

*Bastard. Worthless piece of shit.* The old insults slammed into me unbidden. One main voice echoed in my head on a loop since childhood, shaking my confidence right when I needed it most. I shoved the first few sheets of paper at Colt. Before I got the balls to open my mouth to translate my chicken scratch writing, a loud bang sounded from the hallway, rocking our equipment and my already shaky equilibrium. Another bang followed, rattling the closed door. *What the hell?* Our practice room was at the end of a long corridor. A gust of wind wasn't the culprit since we were at the back of the building, far away from the front entrance. And hardly any air came through the damn vents.

We weren't in the safest part of town either, thousands of dollars' worth of equipment in the room with us. Not to mention the rest of the building. Whoever it was fucking with us better prepare themselves for a battle because I wasn't going down without a fight. That was for damn sure.

We had few options for weapons. I grabbed the nearest piece of replaceable equipment, picking up a guitar stand. Doug's, going by the pornographic stickers he plastered all around the damn thing. Colt had been too quiet since the bang, so I glanced in his direction. His movements were stealthy as he inched closer toward the door, a small blade in his grip. *Where the fuck did the weapon come from?* Realizing I knew shit-all about Colton Strong, I moved toward the door, backing him up anyway.

Colt had his hand on the doorknob when the sound of snickering stopped us short. He leaned back, put his switchblade away and cursed under his breath. He grabbed the knob again, swung the door open and stared at the other half of his band.

"Fuckers! What took you so long anyway?" He yelled as I held the stand like a baseball bat.

Doug and Berto, the fucktards, hung on each other laughing their asses off. The bags full of our lunch forgotten at their feet.

"You two assholes have a few years on both of us, yet you still act like ten-year-olds. How does that work with the ladies?" I shook my head at the amateur pranksters. I backpedaled, putting Doug's stand back with his other stuff.

"Works great for me, mano." Berto winked, grabbed his junk and thrusted the air. *Great!* No common sense. Doug picked the bag of food off the floor and followed his partner-in-crime into the practice room.

All the action Berto received after one of our gigs dumbfounded me. But only because he acted like a little shit when it was just us. Yeah, he was one hell of a drummer. The best I'd seen in a long time. His charisma on stage explained why ladies flocked to the funny bastard. He sometimes left with one woman on each arm. His charm won over the ladies, I guessed. He had swagger too. Like most drummers, he capitalized on it. I had my hands plenty full with one woman at a time and had zero interest in Berto's the-more-the-merrier antics.

Doug seemed to do alright for himself, proving to be more selective in choosing a bed partner, unlike his randy friend. His whole demeanor screamed laid-back California guy. Growing up in wine country, but *not* Napa Valley, he'd often share hilarious stories from his childhood. Ignorant about other parts of the big state famous for wine, I listened and learned with every story.

Still didn't explain their appeal to the ladies when they acted like fucking adolescents, though.

Colt stayed behind the scenes after our gigs. It wasn't always possible with him being the lead singer and all, but he managed it.

I did well for myself even though I sought more substance. The crowds at Country Blue shows were a lesson in contradictions. We got all types there. Women on the prowl looking to bed a musician. A few grabbed my ass at gigs since I joined up with the fellas. It boggled my mind how bold people were nowadays. When he hung around, Colt got the brunt of the attention. Whether he wanted it or not.

On a good day, the lead singer had a formidable presence with his tall and broad build. Everyone gravitated to the brooding man. The guys wanted to be him, and gals wanted in his pants. Most guys in his position considered that a definite perk of the gigs. Not Colt. Like me and Doug, he seemed to be more selective as well.

For me, relationships were important. I wasn't a little boy anymore. I learned some hard truths growing up. So often, friends and girlfriends—even family ties—came and went. Few things lasted forever; I knew all too well. Still, I preferred getting to know someone. I liked to learn about and from them.

I sounded like a damn Hallmark card for Christ's sakes. Point blank, I wanted a more substantial relationship. Something resembling all the stories I heard from my mom about her parents. God forbid I had a relationship like my mom and dad's. Because theirs crashed and burned on an unending loop that I was forced to watch.

I had little hope in finding it at one of our gigs, though. *Never say never*, right? We were getting more attention with each new booking. The road got lonely even with bandmates. I wanted to share this journey—the successes and failures—with someone special.

*Ugh,* even my own sugary musings made me want to puke. "You're an asshole, Berto."

"I know," he chortled. I shook my head, thoughts circling back to finding those damn papers and shoving them in my bag for another time.

With the two knuckleheads back, my chance at a private conversation with Colt was long gone. But I'd lost track of my notes again. They weren't near the mic anymore. The dipshit twins milled around in the center of the room, chowing down on their food. I glanced at my sandwich still in the wrapper. It held little appeal at the moment. In all honesty, adrenaline still pumped through my body from all the excitement a few minutes ago.

Colt sat in a chair by the corner near Berto's kit, faced away from us. "Hey Colt, have you seen—"

"You got any other ideas, Rafe?" He tossed the question over his shoulder and it caught me off guard. Turning around in the chair, he raised an eyebrow and waited for a response. *What the hell am I missing?* Colt then lifted the sheets of paper in his hand. Berto stopped smacking and snatched them out of his loose grip.

*Well damn.*

I tamped down my first instinct to shout *hell yes!* and instead said, "Yeah sure, I have a few more."

"Well? Let's see 'em then." I walked over to my backpack, squeezing the strap with a tight fist and pulling out my other composition books and the last few scraps of paper at the bottom. I wrote on whatever I came across. Napkins worked in a pinch. I used apps on my phone too and transferred the good ideas into a notebook on the regular. Berto snatched the books out of my hand and started flipping through the filled pages.

The guys studied my notes for a while, throwing grunts and short phrases back and forth. Muttering to themselves mostly. It scared the hell out of me. Frayed nerves weighed me down as they took their time reading my ideas, ignoring me. I left the room to grab a can of soda from the old school vending machine at the end of the hall.

Doug brought back energy drinks with our sandwiches, but I never touched the stuff. Most of my energy came from coffee or my constant state of anxiousness. My feet dragged down the hallway. I dug deep in my pockets and scrounged up the coins for my

13

carbonated sugar fix. I hadn't considered the sandwich waiting for me in the room, which never happened. Not much came between a man and his next meal, but I left it near my backpack before leaving the room.

The resounding pop of the aluminum can's top calmed me, after taking a long sip. The cold drink slid down my dry throat. I took a deep breath and turned around, strolling back to the room for the final verdict. Just as I crossed the door's threshold Doug's words hit me mid-center. "Well shit, Colt. I love Nick like an annoying, younger dipshit brother and all, but we hit the mother lode with this quiet fucker."

Berto chimed in, "I like the choices he made on these notes. It'll change up our sound for the better, I think. And he writes lyrics too?" He peered back down at the papers in his hands.

*Guess I have nothing to worry about.* I smirked. It sounded like Doug and Berto approved. Although Colt remained quiet, his silence hadn't wrecked my temporary buzz.

*Hold up, what lyrics?* Oh shit, I forgot about the lyrics to 'Runaway Girl' in my composition book.

"You put it down to music yet, Rafe?" Doug looked up, asking, his eyes meeting mine. Colt reached for the notebook in Berto's hand. The answer was no. I shook my head at his question. *What the fuck is happening right now?* For a while now I'd thought about showing the guys my ideas. Maybe down the line sharing my other stuff. But their response was unreal.

As musicians, we expected suggestions for the music. My lyrics, though? The words on those pages were beyond personal. It wasn't even my story to tell. *Dammit!*

"I say we table this for now." Colt lifted it up. Still a few feet away, I knew what pages his eyes fixed on. "This is an edgy, dark song. It could work on our EP, make it stand out. Where'd 'Runaway Girl' come from, Tapiro?"

"Um, you know," I stalled. "From life and shit." My distracted answer was all they were getting from me today. Damn, I hadn't expected their interest. Not like this. They seemed to take my response for what it was: a vague non-answer. Talk of my best friend and his kid sister was off the table. God only knew where she ended up. I prayed she found safety and happiness wherever she settled next. My friend deserved peace after all she endured.

Doug and Berto put their heads together, still discussing my notes. A weird sensation of being watched skated across my senses, my skin tingled from it. I looked up to Colt's stare trained on me. His eyes questioned. Assessed.

I clapped too loud. Awkward and obvious as hell. "How's about we start practice then. Let's hammer all this out in the hours we have left, yeah?" Colt nodded. Like well-oiled machines ready to work, they moved to their gear. Me included. I wasn't ready to answer the questions in Colt's eyes or to share the story behind my lyrics with them yet.

Shit happened. I needed to get it down on paper and out of my system. Did I ever intend to share that song? I didn't have an answer.

Something told me Colt understood.

Berto suggested we incorporate some stuff from my notations and the other guys agreed. We got to work, figuring out our set for the show in a few days.

A few hours later Colt's phone pinged with a message. With a distracted glance, he checked it. That damn smirk made another quick appearance. This girl, Darcy, had our broody leader wrapped around her little finger, it seemed. I hoped she had no clue about her power over him or else we were all screwed.

"Okay. Let's go!" Colt wiped the sweat off his brow, grabbed the neck of the microphone with one hand and put the other on the center of the stand. Our cue, we got back to business. Berto counted us in and our instruments flowed into a perfect sync. The music cascaded over me. Eased through my fingertips, taking most of my cares away.

I loved playing with these guys. *And I think I'm finally where I need to be.*

# Chapter Three
*Wyn*

Darcy came home three days ago, and it was great to have her back. Shame swallowed me whole when I realized how alone and lonely I'd been these past months. Our video chats were not the same as having my best friend home. Done for the day, I pulled one of the spare comforters off the back of the couch and snuggled under it.

My big plans for the night included a nice, quiet evening watching movies with my homegirl. Even planned on giving her first pick as another welcome back gift.

The clock in the kitchen read half past seven and for the last thirty minutes Darcy was MIA while I finished up my work for the week. No one was happier than me that it was finally Friday. My two current clients were start-ups requiring a ton of attention and my specialized anal list making. I put the finishing touches on my to-do list then shut down my laptop, placing it on the coffee table.

"Hey Dar. How about we have a movie night?" I yelled from my cozy spot on the couch. Buttery popcorn sounded fantastic right about now.

Our two-bedroom, one-bath apartment was spacious. A creak of a door alerted me to activity in the hallway. I hoped Darcy heard me. I was ready to get our low-key weekend started. She peeked around the corner, her red hair creating a halo of loose curls around her pale, round face.

"Let's go out, Wyn." I studied her, squinting from my position several feet away. She was wearing makeup! Darcy finally came from behind the wall, revealing her outfit. She looked great, but her curls would fall by the end of the night. *Damn, I'm snippy tonight.* Her hair never stayed tightly curled without a boatload of hairspray and my help. Served her right too. Darcy thought she'd get her way with the half smile she perfected over the years. I got it. *She's punishing me for what I did at the airport on Tuesday.*

Darcy's homecoming was everything I wanted it to be. Her projects usually lasted for several weeks. This last one took her away for the better part of a year. She told me not to make a big deal about her at the airport. As her best friend I knew what was good for her, so I ignored her statement about being fine with a curbside pickup.

I arrived at the airport twenty minutes before her scheduled arrival time just in case the international flight got in early, parking Cru in the nearest short-term lot for her terminal.

My surprises in tow, I toted a dozen balloons with messages like *welcome home, congrats* and several smiley faces. The *pièce de résistance,* the object that made the moment so over the top, was the oversize stuffed turtle carried precariously in my arms, waiting at baggage claim. The damn plush toy dwarfed me by a few inches, so I knew the scene was beyond comical.

Fort Wayne airport bustled Tuesday morning with crowds of harried travelers. Like me, some people stood around baggage claim waiting for their loved ones to arrive. Others jostled their way out of the airport terminal for their final destinations. While waiting, I wondered about the traffic getting out of here. The drive in hadn't been so bad since our apartment was only twenty minutes away.

When she saw me, she stopped and gaped. Darcy stood a few feet away, her mouth opened then shut. No sound came out, just like one of her fish friends. It was beyond perfect. She stayed there stunned with a sprinkle of mortified thrown in. I couldn't help myself. I laughed, hard and loud.

We were a team, Darcy and me. My grandparents still called us the dynamic duo. Of course, I made a big deal about her coming home.

The damn stuffed animal was a bitch to lug around the airport, along with the unwieldy balloon bouquet. I remembered Darcy's embarrassment with a smile. She hated attention and all the fanfare even if she deserved it. As her best friend, it was my job to show her how much I cared. Mission accomplished.

After she stopped being pissed at me, we hugged for a long time, unable to hide wiping her eyes on her long-sleeved shirt. I smiled from the recent memory. She knew someone loved her. That's all that mattered to me.

"You know how I am when I'm on a job: no play and all work." Darcy put up two fingers as she listed the facts. "Scotland was fun, and the history's amazing, but I didn't go out much there."

In Darcy-speak that meant her projects consumed all her time. When working with her fish, she became the biggest geek the world over. She stayed late, started work early, and had fish on the brain all day long.

*Yeah and we scheduled our video chats on weekend nights, mostly. Prime nightlife time. So, what did that say about my social calendar?* We both desperately needed this outing.

"I told you about visiting my relatives at the beginning of the trip. They were elderly." She shrugged. "I sat around, chatted with them and ate a bunch of stew." So yeah, a chance to go out on a Saturday night was an obvious no-brainer for her. Me? I was still on the fence and desperately clinging to this hermit lifestyle I'd been cultivating.

"Ugh. Okay, okay." I steeled myself against the idea of going out tonight. It was a long time coming for me too if I were being honest. Since that night. *Best not to go down that dark path right now.* My ever-present rain clouds hovered over Darcy's grand plan for the evening. I pushed them away. "Where are we going anyway?" A night out with a fruity drink or two. And dancing. Both of us needed this, I guessed.

*What the hell am I going to wear?*

I focused on taming the long braids I had done a few weeks ago while Darcy went through my closet for an appropriate outfit. "What the hell happened to your wardrobe, Wyn? I'll be right back!"

We almost wore the same size, so she ended up getting one of her short sleeve sweater dresses for me. I'd put on pounds these last few months. The dress fit great, especially paired with black jeggings. I was glad for my penchant for buying comfortable, stretchy clothes now.

Layers of makeup was never my style. Instead, I focused on accentuating my eyes and adding color to my lips with a few swipes of shiny gloss. It didn't escape me that Darcy never answered my question about tonight. I'd fake it like a pro even if I wasn't up for surprises. I tried to let my growing anxiety go, focusing on the finishing touches and putting on my game face.

*Here goes nothing.*

The car ride was quiet as Darcy handled Cru, exiting the freeway and navigating the busy streets. I admitted to myself my game face was never solid anymore, a few cracks on the surface made themselves known. We finally turned into one of the public lots in the heart of downtown.

Our downtown had several restaurants, bars, lounges, and other local businesses. It was no match for one of the larger cities a few hours away, but it had its own vibrancy about it. Most places overflowed with patrons even though it was only nine thirty. Some probably had reason to celebrate the start of the weekend.

With our destination in mind, Darcy led the way, hustling the two blocks before coming up to The Satin Cradle. The Cradle was a popular music venue boasting up-and-coming bands from the area and beyond. They sometimes had themed dance nights too. I hadn't come here in several months. Now that we were here, though, I didn't expect many changes from the venue.

*Please, please, please let it be a dance night.* We stood in a short line outside of the downtown club. The weather seemed warm for mid-May, so we decided against jackets. Before leaving she assured me that we didn't need them where we were going.

We inched closer to the bouncer who checked IDs at the door. Darcy's lips remained sealed about why we were here, but there was this bouncy energy about her. *She loves dancing as much as me,* I reasoned, hoping that was her plan for tonight. My nerves frazzled, I needed liquid fortification ASAP.

The bouncer finally waved us forward with a finger, checking Darcy's ID then mine. The tedious process always took seconds too long because both of us appeared younger than our age. It annoyed the hell out of me when people thought I was underage. I was already in my mid-twenties, for Christ's sake. The rough looking bouncer handed back our IDs. Darcy forked over a twenty-dollar bill and didn't wait for change.

*Guess it's a band then since there's a ten-dollar cover charge.* He opened the door and we walked into a dim, cavernous hallway. A red curtain swung closed at the other end. As we strode down the long passageway, I heard the swell of noise, the sound of our heels swallowed up by the dark carpet, on the other side of the curtain.

Darcy reached the curtain first and drew it aside. My eyes swept across the mass of people. A wall-to-wall crowd. *Damn, this is so not good.* I stared over at the bar. Near it, on the left, were several small circular tables with chairs. Those seats were for people not bothered by a limited view of the stage. I didn't care that much myself, but I knew my bestie. She had other plans for us.

The crowd swelled with high energy tonight, so I figured the slate of acts were fan favorites. I stopped in my tracks. *Oh no!* An overwhelming fear took hold. There was only one band—one guy— Darcy bounced on her toes for, expelling red-hot energy like a rocket ship. One guy she'd be excited to see after coming home, which only meant one thing for me.

My best friend screwed me over and she had no clue. Shit.

"Ya know, Dar, you're devious sometimes." My quivering lips escaped her notice. She had eyes only for the stage up ahead. I smiled to hide the fear seizing my entire body. What if he was here? *Of course, he's here,* the pragmatic voice offered in my head. What the hell was she thinking dragging me here tonight? I looked forward to a few drinks with my friend but this, this was too much all at once.

My eyes whipped around the room then the stage, believing unequivocally that he'd sneak up on me. My heart worked double time. I was having a damn coronary. The breath in my lungs stalled, stopping in the middle of my chest, and I couldn't breathe. Couldn't tell my friend I was shattering to pieces.

If I dropped dead now, at least I'd go without seeing his face again. The morbid thought provided little comfort. A small saving grace was the hordes of people ahead of us, blocking a path to the stage. *We'd never get up front.*

A few dozen milled around with their drinks and others crowded together, jockeying for closer view of the stage. We were at the far back of this madhouse. It was so hot that beads of sweat pebbled across my skin, taking up residence along my hairline.

Maybe I'd talk Darcy into leaving. The whimsical idea popped into my head and I promptly whisked it away to where unicorns and other fairy tales lived.

The now too-warm sweater dress clung to my skin, making me itch. I was panicking. My brain knew it was a worthless reaction. Control was out of my hands though. Darcy headed straight into the depths of hell… I meant the growing crowd of people waiting for

,the band to start. Backing out now wasn't a viable option, so I inhaled, blew out the breath and followed behind her.

"What are you talking about? It'll be fun." Her smile was all teeth. "We'll hang out with the guys after their set like last time. No big deal." The final nail in my coffin. Her words confirmed my worst nightmare. *She doesn't know. She doesn't know.* I wasn't stupid or anything. Sooner or later, I knew this day would come. I just wished hell had frozen over first, trapping him deep within its depths, before ever having to lay eyes on him again.

Darcy mentioned Colt Strong, frontman for the newly renamed Country Blue, during some of our chats. They were more than friendly, I thought. She'd talk about him and his bandmates for a few minutes before I changed the subject, not able to handle hearing about any of them for long. A few weeks ago, Darcy even shared songs they had been working on to get my opinion since she knew I loved music just as much as her. It took a long time to get back to her about the tracks. I had to separate myself from what happened before I listened to the songs. It was the most difficult task I'd done in a long time. Almost impossible.

Darcy took my hand, forcing her way to the front of the venue. She moved like the slickest sports car, weaving her way between bodies, the sticky floor not slowing her momentum even a little. She excelled at maneuvering to get ahead in situations like this. Height challenged as we were, even with our heels, she still preferred being at the front of the action.

If I were alone, I'd stay in the back, away from all the craziness. She tugged me along behind her. Just a few years ago, we attended at least one concert a month. The smaller venues, and under twenty-dollar shows, were how we found some of our favorite bands. A few moved on to bigger venues and record deals while others faded into oblivion. Their music still lived on my playlist though.

"How the hell did your hand get so sweaty, Wyn?" Darcy dropped the loose grasp to wipe hers on her jeans. My panic took a back seat while I focused on not tripping or stepping on people's toes.

As we got closer to the front, it jumped up to the passenger seat and grabbed the 'oh shit' bar. My subconscious was a dramatic bitch sometimes. The stage was ahead of us now and the crowd parted one last time as Darcy nudged her way the few remaining feet, getting to the front of the stage.

We got there just as the stage lights came on. And there they were. The men of Country Blue. The opening chords of their first song reverberated through the speakers, striking my eardrums. My ability to breathe or speak, in that moment, fled.

My eyes darted to the floor because I refused to look up at the stage for fear of his beady eyes finding mine. I glanced over at Darcy, noticing the full wattage of her smile, and seeing just how close we were to the stage. To Colt and the other guys. A foot or two away from where they stood.

Close enough even for his sweat to hit us during their set. *Something else to look forward to tonight*, my snarky voice returned.

When we first met the guys a year ago, they were the Colton Strong band. A memory of Darcy mentioning their name change came back to me now. I must've suppressed the pivotal information, along with all the other comments about them. I glanced over to Colt's left and my right, releasing the breath I held in. My eyes watered, a single tear falling. I wiped it away quickly.

Darcy looked over at me, a big smile across her face. I returned it with a version of my own. I knew how excited she was to see Colt. If I were a better friend, I'd have noticed how Darcy bounced around since coming home. She vibrated with all this energy. Like a dumbass, I didn't get it at first. Now, I did.

My eyes found the bassist again. The reason for my unexpected but profound relief. Seeing him standing there was like taking a breath of fresh air after being trapped underground. Resistance was futile. Something about him called for all my attention. He wasn't who I expected. No words could explain how elated the fact made me. The debilitating fear from moments ago no longer held me captive, so I looked my fill of the mystery bassist. My eyes not straying far. *Who was he?*

I thought back to past conversations with Darcy where she might've mentioned this new development. Nothing came to mind. Mysterious was an apt term for the guy. His long hair obscured his face. He paid little attention to the crowd as he focused on his bass guitar. I assured myself I'd merely be a blip on his radar, he'd never look my way. The thought relieved some of the tension racking my body but also left behind a wave of misery. I refused to dig too deep into those conflicting emotions.

Their first song ended and went straight into another one. I remembered Colt wasn't much of a talker when he was on stage, preferring the music speak for itself. I considered the other guys. They all had a certain appeal about them for sure.

Colt's deep musical drawl evoked so much emotion in just one note. His brooding demeanor masked hidden depths I knew appealed to everyone in the audience. Berto played up his role as drummer, the heart of the band. His medium height, deep-tanned complexion, and stocky build spoke of his Latin heritage. And Doug a few years older, played lead guitarist and added some background vocals. He was scruffier than I remembered, yet still good-looking with shaggy blond hair. I recalled how friendly they'd all been when we met last year.

Their music flowed over me and I settled in to listen. I hadn't let myself relax and *just be* in a long time. I appreciated the complexity of the band's evolving sound, the emotion I heard in Colt's vocals and in the music itself. It'd changed in subtle ways, obvious right off the bat. I looked to Darcy, wondering if I dared ask about *him*. She'd probably get ahead of herself and try pushing us together. That was out of the question.

Something drew my gaze to the new bassist again, though. I examined him closer. His thick, dark hair settled just past his shoulders. A few stubborn locks escaped from behind his ears, hiding dark features.

Like most musicians, his body was in constant motion, his feet tapping as he played. This subtle action drew me. I noticed his lithe build first. The jeans he wore were snug, emphasizing his strong, muscular thighs. The dark-colored bandana wrapped around his right wrist grabbed my attention next. A long-sleeved denim button-down shirt covered a black T-shirt with writing on it. It was too dark to read what it said. His rolled sleeves sat halfway up his elbows. The outfit made him look like a rebel. A good reason for me to turn away, stop all this staring and get a damn grip on myself.

I didn't.

This guy appealed in a way I didn't understand. It was like the universe asked me to take a closer look. But that was one rabbit hole I didn't need to fall down again. *The clusterfuck of what happened the last time you let a guy in your bubble for half a second scarred you irrevocably.* No, I stopped the wayward thought right in its tracks.

I so wasn't his type, anyway, I told myself. A few pounds overweight, I always had a hard time talking to guys my age. Flirting was out of the question, especially now. He had so many other options here. Women probably offered him up anything and everything after a gig.

Best to stay clear when we joined the band after their set. It was an eventuality, not a guess. With Darcy and Colt in the same room, it'd be impossible to keep them apart. I wasn't sure how long she'd want to hang around, but suggesting we leave early was on the tip of my tongue.

If it got to be too much, I'd fake a headache or an ulcer. I let my imagination wander for a bit.

The house lights came up after another song ended. Colt's deep voice rumbled through the microphone as he talked to the cheering crowd. His tone welcomed and quieted the audience in equal measure, his muffled words escaping me.

With the house lights up, I stole another glance at the bassist. He adjusted his guitar strap, lifting his head to peer at the illuminated crowd. I noted his olive tone which made me think of the Mediterranean. He placed his guitar pick between thin lips, pushing his dark, shoulder length hair behind his ears.

The guys finished tuning up for the next slate of songs. The new guy glanced over his shoulder at Berto. With a quick nod, he signaled to him then turned back around. Our gazes clashed and held. Time slowed to a crawl. I flashed hot and cold, his smoldering eyes drinking me in as I'd done to him only minutes ago.

*You're imagining things, Wyn.* Berto tapped his sticks together, the spell between us breaking. A big lock of hair escaped and fell back across his face. I released my breath, relieved his extreme focus left me. Darcy bopped her head to the next song, one of her favorites. I peeked up at the stage, my gaze zooming straight to him.

*Shit.* He was gorgeous. And dangerous. I had to stay far, far away from him.

# Chapter Four
*Rafe*

*Fuck.* She was beautiful. Gorgeous. I loved women with curves and from my vantage point she wasn't lacking in that respect. Ample hips and curves made her the perfect image of a woman, in my humble opinion.

We were finishing up on stage. Berto had the floor, extending the hell out of his solo. The crowd tonight ate it up. I turned away from him, shaking my head at his antics. They screamed even more once the *showoff* settled down and cued the end.

My gaze returned to my dream girl off and on during our set. Now, I faced the crowd again and she no longer stood at the front of the stage. I didn't see her friend either.

*Just my luck she disappeared on me.* The frenzy from minutes ago quickly turned to an impatient hum. Colt thanked the crowd as the last chord faded out, murmuring goodnight. We broke down our setup with little fanfare.

After we finished, there was downtime to sell and sign merchandise while the venue techs got the stage ready for the final act. Our set had been a quick forty-five minutes. Once the headliner came on, they'd have a little more than an hour.

I planned to enjoy the next band uninterrupted. Most folks wanted the original band members' attention, not mine. Being ignored tonight worked out great as I had quite a few items on my mind. Colt also appeared preoccupied, unable to stand still while he mentioned hitting up another spot. They talked about continuing the party at a nearby bar. Most likely jonesing to spend time with his lady who was here somewhere, no doubt. I didn't blame him. The woman who caught my eye earlier barely left my mind.

Berto and Doug went along with Colt's plan. Several people stood on the periphery, wanting to know about the after-party. I wasn't in the mood to bar hop. The guys didn't do it often after shows, so I'd consider tonight an exception.

With Colt's girlfriend back in town, the night could only get more interesting. We played an amazing set. I'd hang out for a while and see if that girl ended up at the next bar.

Our brief exchange committed to memory, I recalled several details about her, and prayed luck would be on my side tonight.

*The house lights came up after our third song. My eyes recovered from the quick change in the lighting and there she was at the front of the stage. Our gazes locked. Her face was full and round. Smooth, dark skin drew my immediate attention. My eyes drank her in. No one and nothing else was around as far as I was concerned. Everything Colt murmured into the mic was indecipherable. The enthusiastic crowd a blur.*

*She wore long braids, an all too familiar hairstyle. The style reminded me of my best friend's little sister who had braids all the time. I noticed this girl's hair arranged in one large, neat braid of braids resting on her left shoulder. It lured my eyes to her neck. One light caught on the shiny jewelry hanging from her ear, sparkling bright. Pretty. Like her.*

*Her mutual stare was just as intense. It held me hostage for what seemed like an eternity, although I knew it lasted only a moment. Either way it ended too fucking quick for my liking. Before I could do anything else, Berto cued up our next song with the crack of his sticks. I tilted my head, a lock of hair falling into my face and blocking my line of sight. My mask while I played. I pushed visions of the voluptuous beauty from my mind and focused on the rest of our set.*

*A damned hard thing to do.*

The last band finished up, their set damn entertaining. August Crush knew how to keep the crowd revved up. Blue and the first opener deserved credit too. It'd been a good night of music.

We'd rocked our set even with all the changes we hashed out in the past week. And I was still finding my footing with the band. It was getting better, more fluid. More natural. That had to do with all of us, not just me. The direction we were heading was good. It made me optimistic about my place in the band. My voice had value.

Chatter about going to a different bar persisted among the guys. I listened passively. Berto mentioned this place just down the street. We finished packing up, storing our equipment in the van parked out back. Doug said he'd leave it there since we were only hanging out a few blocks away. As long as it was safe, it didn't bother me none.

We made our way inside and to the front entrance. Colt had settled our take from the door tonight with Cradle's owner earlier. A small crowd followed behind. Not the least bit surprising. Blue had a loyal and growing fan base and they wanted to hang with us.

The bar we walked to was in for a ton of extra business tonight. Someone should've called to warn them, I had half a mind to say.

Colt strode ahead, his long legs eating up the asphalt. *Someone wants to get to this place quickly.* I chuckled to myself. Arriving within minutes, I held the door for a few people close behind me. The competing conversations from the new venue swallowed up the ones I listened to with half an ear. The muted, red interior of the place had a chill vibe about it. As I walked in, my eyes found Colt. He beelined for the bar. And it finally hit me why.

His friend must already be here.

And if that was the case, I was one lucky S.O.B. tonight. Colt stepped up to two women who stood at a corner of the bar counter, nursing drinks. One of which was my girl from the concert.

*Thank you, God in Heaven.*

I knew deep down she wasn't his girlfriend. Too much heat and mutual attraction sparked between us with the one look we shared. My gaze went to the pale, freckled woman next to her. Like day and night, the two friends complemented each other. They had subtle similarities yet looked like complete opposites. I tried not to laugh, a smile breaking out anyway. A redhead.

*Man is he in for a world of trouble with that one.* Colt was a big boy. He probably already knew and didn't care.

Both women were about the same height. And curvy. I stood too far away for a better look. Her red hair, coupled with pale skin, was unmistakable and drew second and third glances. But my gaze returned to her friend. It just couldn't be helped.

I needed to mosey on over there and introduce myself. *Stop being a wimp*, I berated myself. Despite my Italian heritage, I was *no* Casanova. And this situation called for some finesse. Her stare earlier spoke volumes. There was attraction, yes, but also fear, curiosity, and hope all wrapped up in her eyes. It all hit me on a basic level.

Doug and Berto strolled over to them, both giving hugs with no hesitation on their end. When they went to hug my mystery gal, the interaction seemed clumsy and stiff. A few minutes later the guys went on their way, making the rounds while Colt stayed at the bar. The awkward greeting made me wonder.

I inched closer to the small group. No real clue how she'd perceive me or if I'd be welcome as the new guy. She clutched a glass of water in her hand, listening while her friend gestured something to Colt. A bemused expression settled on his face. Suddenly a burst of laughter escaped her. Her husky laugh left a warm tingle in the pit of my stomach. *You could use some of that in your life, Tapiro.*

She shook her head while their animated conversation continued, a smile resting on her perfect full lips.

I wondered about her age. She looked damned young right then. I racked my brain for any information Colt revealed about his girlfriend. *She'd been working overseas.* Still, I might've misunderstood because for all I knew she was in a study abroad program.

Dammit! I wish I had more information. I hoped she was in her early twenties or close to my twenty-six years.

As I got closer, I noticed how her purple dress clung to her ample curves. She wore black leggings and a pair of heeled ankle boots. I guessed she was just over five feet with their help. Either way I'd tower over her. I hoped she liked tall guys, even though most people considered me average at five ten. From here, I figured the top of her head barely reached my chin. She was a petite beauty.

*Sweet and sexy too.* And although I hadn't really gauged her sweetness, I hoped to. *Soon.*

I probably looked like a creeper if anyone gave me a second glance. A predator stalking its prey. Poised, alert, and looking for an opening.

I donned a neutral expression, like the one I wore onstage. When I played for a crowd it always fucked with my wiring, making me jumpier than usual. My energy—everything in me—focused on her. I wasn't even in her presence yet and she calmed me for some inexplicable reason.

My opening finally came when someone clapped Colt's back. He looked over his shoulder and saw me standing a few feet away.

Blood rushed through my veins, pushing that muscle in my chest to its limits, as I headed over to them. *Showtime.*

He waved me over then turned back around to the bar, picking up his drink. I hoped he'd make it easy for me. Plus, I wanted to see him and his friend close and in color. She was a hard person to ignore, in her own right. No wonder a big guy like Colt wanted to keep her close. Her fiery hair, big doe eyes, and freckles drew men in and made them beg, most likely. He was in a helluva lot of trouble. Redheads were no joke.

I strolled up to the trio and patted Colt on his back. Nodding at both women, I waited for the introduction as my gaze settled on the mystery girl.

"Darcy. Wynter. This is Rafael Tapiro, our new bassist." *Wynter, I like it. The name fits her.*

"Hi. Please call me Rafe." I shook Darcy's hand then leaned in a step closer to grasp Wynter's next, holding her nervous gaze. "Nice to meet you both." She was even more beautiful up close. Her skin a rich, dark brown. Like her eyes. The entire package enthralled me.

"You too, Rafe. You were awesome tonight by the way." The compliment from her low, breathy voice surprised me. We stood frozen in an awkward moment following her comment. I didn't hide my reaction. The looks between us, like before, seemed unfiltered. She broke eye contact first.

After all the years playing, I still rejected genuine praise about my ability. So much negativity stuck around, never the positive vibes. "All of you guys were," she tacked on.

"Uh, thanks," I said.

By many peoples' standards I was an okay musician. And in all honesty, everyone except the bassist got attention, so it was great to hear her shy words. Not sure why it felt good coming from this person I just met. But I didn't let myself think on it too long.

Darcy grabbed my attention when we got quiet again. "How do you like playing with the guys?" Drawn out silences must not be her forte then. I wondered how that worked with Colt. Most days it seemed like the man took a vow of silence that only went away when he was onstage and performing.

"It's good. Been playing with different bands for several years now. Playing with these guys challenges me in a good way." *You were a temporary replacement for those other bands too.* The stray thought cut swiftly and added to my frequent insecurities. Not much was set in stone. Nick, the guy I replaced, was enough proof. Opportunities come and go all the time. I just needed to pay my dues. And let some of my ideas loose and see where they landed with the band.

*That's all I can really ask for.*

"Yeah, I can only imagine. Those goofballs are a handful by themselves," she gestured to Berto and Doug, who were talking to a gaggle of women, holding court. She chuckled then glanced over at Wynter. I caught a glint in her eye, mischief maybe. Her look definitely had my spidey senses tingling. "Before everyone from the club got here, we were talking about the slight change in the band's sound. Weren't we, Wyn?"

My mouth twitched slightly. *Colt's in for some trouble with this one, for sure.* The redhead dynamo was up to no good. The devilment in her eyes even more obvious now.

"Oh yeah?" I studied Wynter, interested in hearing what she might've noticed. A long minute passed without either of us saying anything. I prompted, "I'm guessing you've heard the band play before today. You've piqued my interest now. How was tonight different, Wynter?"

The group remained quiet. I watched as she sent a death glare Darcy's way, surprised her friend hadn't gone up in smoke from the look alone. The redhead shrugged her shoulder, nudging Wynter. "Rafe asked you a question, sweetie."

Big, brown eyes darted over to mine, looking away within seconds. She collected herself, taking a sip from the glass of water she still held and squeezing her eyelids shut. Perhaps choosing her words.

Her change in demeanor screamed *Danger, Will Robinson!* As if our sudden attention drowned her. Before I could switch the conversation, she finally spoke.

"Wyn." She must've read the confusion on my face because she clarified, "you can call me Wyn."

"Okay, sure. Wyn." I watched her, waiting for a response from my previous inquiry. I didn't rush her because I didn't have to.

"Oh, um yeah. I saw the guys play for the first time about a year ago." Her hesitant words drew the hairs up on my arms. There was something there, hidden in her low tone. Since we'd just met, I couldn't put my finger on what exactly, but something had me on edge. "Y'all were great tonight. I enjoyed the set," she tacked on with more confidence. Wynter pulled at her purple sleeve which betrayed her nervousness.

She continued.

"I only noticed slight changes in the sound. Your melody and bass were crisper, more resonant." Wyn paused. Her comments already blew me away. "Oh, and the harmony was much stronger on 'Day Mourning' too, at least from what I heard. But don't mind me." She flicked her free hand as if I should toss what she said away.

*Fat chance of that happening because I think I'm in love.*

"Well, damn. You have a great ear." An image of her, unassuming, in front of a microphone popped into my head. "Do you play? Sing maybe?" I asked. She'd probably rock any stage, I thought to myself.

"Me?" A cute, surprised snort escaped her. "Uh no, I took a couple music appreciation classes in school, is all." The giggle that followed was also fucking adorable. The last twenty seconds of our interaction went straight to my other head.

*Play it cool, Tapiro. The scared Bambi look has almost vanished. You don't want to do or say anything to put a halt to this conversation. Slow your roll.* A voice that sounded a lot like Zi echoed in my head.

Wyn had my undivided attention. Which had to be why neither of us realized Colt and Darcy had slithered away on us. We were in our own little world in this corner of the bar. I settled in, content to enjoy the hell out of myself while Wyn was none the wiser that her best friend had abandoned her. I knew as soon as she realized the score, she'd get skittish again.

It was more than an inkling. I just knew.

I needed to learn more about her. "So, what do you do for work, Wyn? Or are you still in school?"

"Not in school. I'm a virtual assistant." She smirked, taking another sip of water.

"Hmm, that sounds interesting." And it did. I also high-fived myself, happy to hear that she was older than she looked. "I didn't know people did that type of work."

"It keeps me busy," she said, shrugging her shoulders. "I handle day to day administrative work for a few small businesses. At least twice a year, I do temporary work for some larger businesses needing extra manpower."

"How does that work?" The surprise on her face let me know she wasn't in the habit of talking about herself much. Or maybe no one ever showed an interest in her job.

She must've been around self-involved idiots. I told myself not to be like them.

"I'm assigned many tasks which I handle by email or phone. I prepare some of my clients' sensitive and non-sensitive documents and make travel arrangements. Ya know, that sorta thing," Wyn finished.

"Sounds interesting. How does one become a virtual assistant, Wyn?"

"Uh, well, I was an English major and accounting minor in college. I've gotten a few more certifications since graduating so…" Gravitating toward her as she spoke, the space between us got smaller and smaller. Hard to curb the urge.

Wyn's shyness—her reticence—faded away as she talked about her work, her personality showing itself more and more. Damn, she intrigued me.

An inch or two closer and a soft, fruity scent drifted over me. It teased my nose. *Sweet*, which just confirmed my earlier thought.

Wyn intrigued me with little effort. As the caution in her eyes faded away, her subtle personality came out more and more. The sparkle that drew me in earlier returned, making her even more radiant.

She gestured as she continued talking which brought a smile to my face. The Italian American in me liking her more and more for that small feature of her personality. Even if she didn't intend to, she spoke to something in me. Called to a basic need inside me. *I need to know this woman.*

Like the saying went, her eyes were a window into her soul. So much fear overshadowed the spark I saw trying to break free from behind a wall. It was still there, buried deep, and I wanted to know why. I studied Wyn while she talked on. I wanted to see more of the spark—that damn fire—that would burn so bright if she let it.

While we spoke, the air became stifled around us. It looked like another mass of people came in behind us. With a quick glance over my shoulder, I counted at least twenty more people jostling for a position in the already cramped bar. Wyn stopped mid-sentence and her expression froze. Right before my eyes she shrunk into herself, and I had no clue what to do.

I touched a shoulder, trying to get her attention. "Sweetheart, you okay?" The endearment rolled off my tongue. Wyn's swift change concerned me. I saw the walls closing in around her and I had no fucking idea what to do.

Wyn startled when I cupped her chin. She took a deep breath before she seemed to force her gaze to meet mine again. I dropped my hand, studying her as the fog cleared from her eyes and already missing the feel of her soft skin. But that reaction sucker-punched me in the gut.

*Has someone put their hands on her?* Because God help the bastard if I found him.

I knew right then I'd do everything in my power to take care of her. She didn't know it yet, but she was already mine.

I just needed a chance to show her.

# Chapter Five
*Wyn*

*What the hell did I get myself into?* I knew tonight would be a disaster. And it had zero to do with Rafe.

I wasn't whole anymore.

Case in point, I chattered on like a crazy person with no cares in the world. Rafe seemed engaged in our conversation. He'd asked his last question a while ago, yet I kept talking. It was hard to stop my word vomit.

When me and Darcy got to The Spot, there was hardly anyone here. No, that observation wasn't exactly true. A few spaces at the long bar top and at some of the booths had people at them. Regulars I guessed. As soon as the guys from Country Blue walked in, the subtle atmosphere of the place changed. And with a huge crowd from the Cradle not far behind them, the instant change was pretty amazing. A dramatic shift. It became an interesting mix of skinny jeans and black vests versus belt buckles and cowboy boots.

I'd swear the air in the room sparked with new energy at their arrival.

Colt approached us in seconds, grabbing and keeping Darcy's attention. She didn't hide how excited she was to see him. *Unfiltered.* And that was how the newness should feel. That's what I assumed, at least. I knew her fears because we'd been best friends for a long time. I also realized how much she cared about him. Her excitement was contagious, so I was distracted and unprepared when Doug and Berto stopped by to say hello. Then Colt invited his new bandmate over and here we were, minutes later, still talking.

It surprised me. When I saw him onstage earlier, I was so sure he'd pay me no mind. *And just because he's talking to you now, doesn't mean he's interested in more, Wyn. You should know better.* And I did.

There was a pecking order in bands. Maybe he wanted to get on Colt's good side by chatting up his girl's best friend. The new guy blues. He probably had it.

I was out of my depth as my so-called best friend pretended to sneak away with Colt while Rafe asked more questions about me. Yeah, I'd noticed, and planned on telling the traitor about herself when we got home. This was so far from the last thing I wanted or expected tonight.

As soon as we walked into the Cradle I knew. My plans for a couple drinks with my best friend went straight out the door. I was now alone and floundering with Rafe at the corner of the bar. The nervousness and disbelief kept me talking. I couldn't control it.

The hipster bar filled up as the volume increased. More bodies crammed into the building. The space between us became smaller and smaller as the crowd doubled in size.

A strong hand pushed my back, forcing me aside. The unexpected shove jarred me. I was back in the hotel room with him. The memories climbed over my walls. They grabbed me and held on tight.

The rough skin of Rafe's fingertips registered on my chin as he lifted my face upwards. My body warmed from the touch. I blinked my eyes open and read the concern on his face. His lips moved, but I couldn't decipher their meaning. His words sounded like they were spoken underwater. I was so out of it.

Frozen in place, he dropped his hand away. Once the fog cleared, I saw the question in his gaze that he stopped himself from asking. I was thankful.

My eyes darted around quickly, taking in the dim surroundings. *I'm at a bar with Darcy and the guys.* He wasn't here, I reminded myself. *He's not here.*

I wiped sweaty palms on the bottom of the sweater dress. Glad the material was thick and dark. All I needed was noticeable wet spots on my clothes. *I should just leave before I embarrass myself even more.*

"It's gotten stuffy in here, hasn't it? Wanna head outside for some fresh air, Wyn?"

Rafe's suggestion meant I probably looked more wrecked than I thought. Nodding, I took any excuse to get out of the cramped bar. I should've told him I preferred time alone, but the hand at the small of my back was strong and reassuring. It settled me like a warm blanket. *What the hell was going on with me?*

Suddenly, hulking bodies blocked our path to the front entrance. A trio of guys crowded around Rafe as they clapped him on the back and asked questions. He appeared stunned by their ambush.

All of the testosterone became too much for me, so instead of just standing off to his side, I slipped past the small group of men. In desperate need of the fresh air he mentioned only a minute ago.

Before I grabbed the doorknob, a rough hand caught my wrist. Its hold was loose. Still, it stopped me in my place. I jerked around; my body still strung tight from before. Then, I saw Rafe at my side.

"Let me get the door for you, Wyn." The deep words floated to my ears, his offer almost a whisper. Like I did him a favor. I nodded my assent. Maybe he wanted to escape as much as I did.

We made it outside without further interruption. Although I wasn't too cold, the cool night air rushed through my one layer of clothing. It was good out here. Safe. I found some warmth in the chill and from the guy standing next to me.

I breathed in, peeking up at Rafe. He blew out his own breath, relaxing against the bar's double pane window. *What was it about this guy?* I knew to stay away from him yet here I was anyway. We were now in our own little world, standing away from the smokers and others just loitering outside. I didn't know what to make of any of this.

When Rafe first approached us at the bar, I knew immediately he'd never hurt me. On closer inspection, he didn't seem like much of a bad boy. Even though he looked the part with his clothes and long dark hair.

He was almost too attractive. A few women had to wipe the corners of their mouths as he walked by earlier. I checked my own, making sure I wasn't drooling.

I wondered again what he was doing out here with me. There had to be more than a few open and flirty women in the bar and from the club vying for his attention. I noted several of them with bewildered looks as we walked out.

Rafe wasted whatever this was on me. I didn't understand it. Or maybe I assumed circumstances that weren't true. He could just be one of those guys who hated the fray.

I was so different from the people at the club and now at this bar. An outlier. *That must be the appeal; it had to be.*

His intense gaze trained on me, neither of us uttering a word since coming outside. He studied me as if there was a question on his mind. I didn't know of what though. Not knowing scared me most.

"H-how long have you been playing, Rafe?" I stuttered the question. His eyes found mine across the small distance. My heart went from zero to hundred in point one seconds.

*This rock star Casanova spells danger.*

"Uh," he drew the sound out for a long time, scratching his chiseled jaw. "I'm pretty sure it's been almost fifteen years. Yeah, just shy, I think."

Instead of wringing my hands like my jitters urged me to, I folded them and leaned against the window, mimicking his stance.

"Wow. Cool."

"Yeah. Yeah, it was. I lucked into it actually. It was the first week of sixth grade and I stayed late because of something stupid I did. Anyway, there was a door open at the end of the hallway and I heard a racket. Calling it music was an overstatement. Just banging and tooting. So, I went to investigate." He chuckled at the memory.

His voice drew me in word by word. It had me tangled up in his cute childhood story. It might've just been him too.

"The music teacher was trying to corral sixth and seventh graders in this crowded room. Mr. Sheppard. He found me almost falling in through the doorway. He shoved a guitar in my clumsy hands and that was that."

"I haven't really had to look back. I don't know where I'd be without music," he finished, shrugging a shoulder.

Rafe loved playing and being a part of a band. I saw it in his eyes.

Then, the ground dropped right from under me. I was in an alternate universe, the only explanation that made a lick of sense.

"Wyn, I wondered if you'd like to go out sometime. With me." A surprised snicker almost left my mouth from his stilted delivery, but I stopped it in time. If I wasn't so terrified by the question itself, it might have, especially since he sounded almost as nervous as me. *But that can't be true, right?*

"What a great idea, Rafe!" A pale, freckled arm came around my shoulder, wrapping me in a half hug. Trapped in this unexpected development, Darcy's excited reply startled me. *When the hell did she come out here?* She was way too chipper for someone digging her best friend's grave. Albeit unknowingly but still.

The shoveling continued while I stood there frozen. "How about the four of us hang out one night this week? You don't have a gig on Wednesday, do you?" Darcy turned around, twisting my upper body along with the quick motion, and throwing her question out to Colt. He nodded, looking down at her with a smirk on his handsome face.

Before this whole situation got too far out of hand, I tried shutting it down. "No, um, I don't think—" Darcy cut me off mid-sentence.

"Awesome. Wednesday it is! I can suggest one or two places we can go. Unless you have a place, Wyn?"

Numb, I shook my head.

"That's okay," she said. "I'm sure we'll find a good place." She nibbled her lips, glancing over her shoulder again at Colt. I swore the man hid his mirth behind a fake cough.

"Oh, how about Rusty's?" On a roll now, Darcy kept decimating me. "They have good food and pool tables in the back. It'll be so much fun, right?!"

None of us interrupted her one-track mind. My best friend was a bundle of wild energy tonight.

"So, it's settled. We'll meet you two at Rusty's on Wednesday at seven."

I'd never seen Darcy this hyper before except with her fish. Her spastic behavior concerned me more than my own pending demise.

"Uh, yeah sure. Wednesday's fine, Darcy." Colt seemed a little tense himself suddenly. I didn't know him well, but something was off. Or transference on my part. Random concepts from Psychology 101 came in handy at the most inopportune times, I realized.

Mind in the clouds, we walked back to Cru several minutes later while Dar kept up a mostly one-sided conversation, further solidifying my feelings of doom about our double date with the guys.

*I'll kill her. With my bare hands. And oh, so slowly.*

With a smile, I imagined how tranquil a jail cell would be as we started up the car and pulled out of the downtown parking lot.

# Chapter Six
*Wyn*

Murderous thoughts flooded my mind. I watched enough crime shows and figured I knew how to get away with the perfect one. *Make it look like an accident.* My plan was murky for exactly how I'd do it or when, but ideas brewed. The intended victim: my so-called best friend.

Darcy bulldozed her way into setting the four of us up on a double date last weekend. I hardly believed how swiftly she threw me under the bus. And right in the path of a guy I told myself to stay far, far away from. Just thinking about it made me furious.

The blame didn't lie on her alone, though. This alternate universe of the past couple days fell right in the middle of a nightmarish year, weighing down my overburdened shoulders. I was almost paralyzed with fear.

My first instincts were to stay my butt home instead of going along with her crazy plan. *But noooo.* I was a fool. And now the joke was on me.

I berated myself every day since the fiasco. The last few days spent faking the funk, pretending excitement about the double date I walked right into with Colt and Darcy and me and freaking Rafe Tapiro. A man who, by all accounts, should terrify me.

Now, Wednesday barreled down on me.

*Could I make it through tonight?* I imagined how awkward it'd be. Impossible. The ever-present voice in my head screaming *no no no.*

The one time I opened myself up a teensy bit to a guy, there were consequences. Devastating ones. Ones that haunted me still. I had to get out of tonight.

Although I brushed her attempts of talking about the date off, memories of my brief time with Rafe pulled at me. Never too far from the surface. The slightest thing reminded me of him. Seeing someone play guitar on TV brought to mind the fleeting, soft touch of his calloused fingers on my chin. The way he led me outside after I got shoved and froze up like a spaz at the bar. I remembered every second with him, vividly.

The end of that night knocked me on my ass, especially Rafe asking me out. If I didn't know any better, I'd swear Darcy set it all up. Set *me* up. That had to be my paranoia talking, right?

From Darcy's vantage point, he was one *smitten* guy. I laughed when she first used the word. I didn't see that from him. *Who am I kidding?* I hadn't wanted to see any kind of interest from him. Not with how I was now.

And there were more important things to think about besides my brokenness, like getting out of this date.

"Hey, Dar," I called, taking a deep, shaky breath and fidgeting outside her half-closed bedroom door. If she laid eyes on me right now, she'd see right through the façade. I wanted to keep the door between us for as long as possible. Yes, I hid from my best friend. And it made my heart hurt.

Armed with my sick voice, I pressed on. Calling myself all kinds of names. "I'm not feeling too great. Maybe we postpone tonight and do it some other time." I added an almost phlegmy cough for good measure.

Everyone had their go-to *I just want to stay the hell home for whatever reason* story, and I had this one loaded up for the occasion.

I wasn't ready for this date, admitting it to myself for the hundredth time. Didn't know if I'd ever be, but I couldn't confide in Darcy about why.

She hadn't said a word yet. I touched my fingertip to the door, pushing it open the rest of the way. Darcy turned from her small laptop desk and immediately called me on my bullshit. "Hun, don't play games with me. You're fine." She turned right back around. "Don't let the nerves get to you," she called over her shoulder.

I hated that she knew me so damn well.

"But…" I knew Darcy heard the quiet protest.

"Plus, it sounds like you've been a hermit since I left all those months ago."

Her comment hit the mark more than I wanted it to.

I wasn't much of a social butterfly to begin with, neither of us were, but I was always comfortable enough in my own skin. Way back when. Before my trust in people—in myself—got buried deep under this huge mountain of fear.

"I've just been focused on work, is all. Building up my skills and client base." Even I didn't believe the weak excuse coming out of my mouth. It was pathetic.

Darcy fell just short of whining when she pleaded, "Don't flake on tonight, Wyn. Come out. Try to have fun." She swiveled her chair around again, reasoning with me. "We have an hour before we have to get ready. All you have to do is try to have fun. Rafe's a total fox and seems like a sweet guy. Colt had nothing but good things to say about him."

The words slammed into me. *That's what everyone said last time.* "If you don't like him, I won't force it again. Even when I wanna see Blue perform, I won't ask you to come with," she promised. A cherry on top in her book.

She was the only person I'd run into a fire with or for. "Okay, Dar. I'll go even though I make no promises about having fun," I forced a smile. *This isn't like last time with the small quarters and forced intimacy of the hotel room.* It'd all be okay, I told myself. The unspoken lie fell unceremoniously to the floor. It was the only way I'd force myself out of our apartment in two hours.

That hour snuck up on me. Now, I peered in my closet for an outfit. Thoughts of a different night a year ago fresh on my mind. I remembered everything like it was yesterday.

A good night that quickly turned sour.

*The Colton Strong Band had just finished up on stage. They were amazing. Best of the night, I thought. With the last act coming on, we decided it was a good time to move to the bar. Let all the die-hard fans wrestle for the front of the stage.*

*Both of us really liked all the acts who played so far, especially the last band. Their music was a country-rock fusion, with some bluesy undertones. The lead singer pouring out gritty but soulful vocals, which lent itself to the sound they were going for.*

*Each act took several minutes to set up, so we had a moment to relax before rejoining the fray. I didn't care what Darcy ordered for me as I rested my back against the bar, noticing the lead singer heading our way. Fuck me. His stride was long and purposeful. A dark, intense gaze trained on my best friend.*

*"Holy shit, Dar. Colton Strong's headed this way!" Did she forget to tell me she knew him? No, she wouldn't forget to mention information like that. That look on his face, though. It was damned determined.*

*Darcy had his full attention.*

*"Hmm?" Distracted, she muttered over her shoulder, but didn't turn around. She vied for the bartender's attention as the crowd at the bar grew larger. The urgency of my words didn't break through her current, laser sharp focus for our fruity drinks.*

*One of Colton's bandmates, the bassist, strolled behind him, talking to a few people who stopped him along the way. I followed his progress even though I didn't mean to.*

*All the guys were hot. Colton with his intensity. I heard a story behind every note and lyric he sang. The lead guitarist seemed goofy, and I shook my head just thinking of the barbs he threw at the singer as he took time to speak to the crowd. The drummer playing up the showboat act and doing stick tricks every chance he got.*

*Last, the bassist. I classified him as a pretty boy. He was a little beefy, with dark features and a square face. I bet he did his fair share of breaking hearts. The sardonic smirk he wore seemed ever-present on stage and off.*

*This was all speculation, of course. Made from brief observations as I watched them perform. I had met none of them yet. Something told me I only had a few seconds before that changed. Colton maneuvered right through the small crowd at the bar. He acknowledged me with a nod, stepping up to Darcy and tapping her shoulder. The action finally drawing my best friend's attention away from her task.*

*I'd learn moments later the bassist's name was Nick Ferrara. And that he had no problem taking anything he wanted.*

"Hey. Are you ready?" Darcy stood just inside my room, putting earrings on. "Oh good, you're almost done. We need to leave in five minutes if we want to get to Rusty's on time," she stressed. Dar hated being late and no matter what she did, it was unavoidable. I shook my head. We had to get there early, but not for the reasons she suspected. I added more pep in my step.

"Just need to put on my boots, Dar. I'll be ready to go in a sec." I finished putting on a long-sleeved, asymmetrical sweater for maximum comfort and coverage. Paired it with my favorite black skinny jeans. It was stylish enough for Darcy not to complain about me looking frumpy and I still felt comfortable.

My face was free of makeup since I rarely bothered with the stuff on a good day. I hadn't cared enough to put on anything more than mascara since last year.

One more deep breath before I left my room. Not ready at all, my heart beat a harsh drum line in my chest.

"Breathe, Wyn." I looked up at Darcy still in my doorway. "You look great. I look great. Let's go have fun with two smoking hot guys!"

My lips pulled in a genuine smile. "You look amazing, Dar. Colt's a super lucky guy. You deserve the best. You know that, right?" We'd both had a rough go of it. My shitstorm was just more recent in a long line of *craptastic-ness*. Darcy's life was far from idyllic. I thought that was one of the reasons we bonded so quickly. Kindred spirits of sorts.

She whisked a loose strand of hair behind her ear. "You do too, Wyn." I turned away, picking up my wristlet from the corner of the comforter. I didn't believe that anymore.

We left the apartment. I double checked that the door locked behind us as Darcy walked downstairs to the parking spot where Cru waited for us.

*Here goes nothing.*

Cru jerked to a stop as I put her in park under a streetlamp next to Rusty's. From the looks of the empty parking lot, all seemed quiet inside.

"Wyn, this has got to stop." *Oh, thank God.* Was Darcy thinking twice about this date? A case of jitters now that we were here?

I had every mind to just back out and head home. No convincing necessary on my part. She huffed then started, "Ya know, Cru is seriously on her last legs. Or wheels, I should say."

My head snapped in her direction. *She's referring to my damn car?* The light from outside cast a shadow on the dash. She wore a shaky smile. I was *not* laughing. So far from amused it wasn't even funny.

I forced my door open because it stuck sometimes and stood up. "She still does what she needs to do which is get us places," I bitched back, waiting for a *just barely* retort from Darcy. It never came.

A peek over my shoulder showed my harsh tone hit its mark. I felt horrible for directing my anger and fear at her. Now I was more frustrated at myself than anything else.

"I'm sorry, Dar. You know how sensitive I am about Cru. Let's go inside. I know you're excited to see Colt."

"I'm sorry too." Darcy's phone pinged. She read the text with a slight smile on her lips as we entered Rusty's Tavern and I knew Colt put the dreamy look on her face.

I just hoped we beat them here.

Rusty's was part-bar, part-grill that sat on a lot at the edge of city limits. They served the usual bar food and from what I remembered, they always had great eats. They had a good selection of beers on tap too.

Too bad I already decided not to drink tonight. I needed all my faculties intact for the impending disaster of this date. Not one of my senses dulled. Plus, with the way my stomach fluttered, I probably wouldn't be able to keep food down, let alone booze.

We walked in, the familiar sights and sounds soothing me. It'd been awhile, but I remembered the chill atmosphere. A rock ballad played from the mounted digital jukebox a few feet from the bar.

The place was slow for a weeknight. My eyes swept across the interior. I didn't immediately see the guys and released a deep sigh. Since we were the first to arrive, I had more time to collect myself. The weight on my shoulders felt several pounds lighter now.

As options went for a double date, this was a good choice. A nice mix of booth and normal seating options spread out between the bar counter and the windows. The layout was expansive. There were small, round tables, and booths providing the illusion of privacy.

A secluded back area featured an even more chill atmosphere, pool tables and dartboards. It finally all made sense to me. The real reason behind Darcy's choice in venue.

*Pool.* She planned to hustle the guys tonight. I had no doubt. At least I'd get some laughs out of one part of the evening.

If I had my way, I'd avoid the whole *couples play against each other* situation altogether. That'd be my luck. Rafe at my side while we played. And with that image, thoughts of the dark-haired bass player popped into my head. Goosebumps traveled up my arm as though the ghost of his touch still lingered from days ago. *What the hell is wrong with me?*

If the mere thought of him reduced me to a tingling mess, then I was in deep shit.

"Oh, I got a text from Colt. He and Rafe are running a few minutes late. They should be here in five minutes." A deep breath got lodged in my throat. My brain short-circuited like a robot falling into a body of water. I was out of time.

My mind screamed at me to find a way out of this mess. But there was no trap door. No viable escape routes. Plus, leaving Darcy here, having to face the guys alone wasn't remotely an option. Not that they were dangerous or anything but still, I couldn't desert my best friend.

Unaware of my inner turmoil, I watched as Darcy continued scoping out a good table for the four of us.

Instead of just standing here, freaking out while she busied herself with her own excitement and thoughts of Colt, I turned to her.

"Hey." A shiver raced down my spine. "Dar, I need to run to the bathroom real quick, okay?" I made my way to the restrooms by rote, not waiting for her distracted response.

Without thought, I came up to an alarmed emergency exit just steps from the women's bathroom, not fully aware of my actions until I met the coolness of the push bar on my palms. So close to escape and the relative safety the outside offered.

Fear overwhelmed me. Grabbed hold and clamped down. Getting the best of me. Panicked and uncertain, I knew I could never ditch Darcy. She'd had enough people abandon her.

*Why was this so fucking difficult then? The real prospect of this date with Rafe?*

I sucked in a shaky breath then exhaled, squeezing my eyes shut. Nothing changed. The stress didn't miraculously leave my body. No relief from the pressure. Pushing through was my only option.

My feet shuffled over to the right, bringing me the last few steps to the door of the women's restroom. My intended destination. The two-stall bathroom was quiet. At least I'd have my freak-out in relative peace.

*A hand slithered down my stomach. His palm wedged inside the band of my stretchy skinny jeans without undoing my button. Fingers rubbing over my underwear before they pushed against me, his touch harsher there than expected. I was new to this. Nick must've noticed because he lifted his upper body slightly, returning to my breasts. His lips found my tender flesh, continuing to rub between my legs.*

*The motion was fast and rough. I was uncomfortable, not aroused like all the books and movies told me I should be by now.*

*I didn't really know what to do. Not wanting to seem selfish, I searched out his erection and jerked him off, hoping a mutual rub satisfied him. It took a few minutes of up and down strokes before he spilled early ejaculate. Taking that as a good sign, I followed my instincts. Then he kissed me and I began to feel excited.*

*He moved my hand away just a few moments later, pushing it to my side. Returning to touch me, his movements became hindered by my tight jeans.*

*He popped the button before I realized his intentions. I told him no. I wasn't ready. This wasn't what I wanted. "I won't put it in," he whispered over and over. My breath caught in my throat as his crown rubbed against my sex.*

*"Stop, Nick. I don't want this," I cried. My mouth felt like a desert. "Stop! No," I croaked. Terrified now, my mouth had gone dry several minutes ago. This must be what swallowing cotton is like, I remembered thinking.*

*"Fucking tease." He threw the words at me like an insult. My tongue stuck to the roof of my mouth. This had gone too far. I should've stopped him before now. My refusal hit a wall, like he wasn't even listening to my protests.*

Before tears fell, a knock sounded. The loud creak of the bathroom door jerked me back to the present, startling me. Darcy.

"Wyn, you doing okay in here?" The click-clack of her thick heels echoed off the tiled walls as she slipped into the small, confined space, closing the door behind her.

The linoleum floor had several scuff marks and sticky spots, I noticed. Much like the sound of her heels, the concerned question bounced off the walls. She waited for my response, the slight crease on her forehead obvious in the bright, fluorescent lighting.

She hadn't noticed my headshake, but I imagined her gaze on my back. I wasn't standing in front of the mirror. It was intentional. I had to calm the hell down before she saw my face. Before the guys got here.

The memories continued tormenting me even in my waking hours. I had thought of them as nightmares, and yet I was so fucking wrong. Now, they pulled me back all the time. Trying to escape them was futile. The memory of him lingered like a tough stain. I couldn't get rid of it, no matter how hard I tried.

"Wyn, you went pale there for a second, which is something I never thought I'd say." The worry evident in her voice and on her face. "I've never seen you look like that. It's freaking me out. You sure you're okay?"

I snorted from the pale comment. With my dark complexion really going pale was a hard thing to imagine. I still hadn't looked in the mirror, though. The thought terrified me. That I embodied the fear. Out there and visible. At least my waking nightmare came to an abrupt halt with Darcy's arrival.

"Uh, yeah. Just give me a second, Dar." Finally, I caught sight of myself in the small mirror above the sink. Although there was no sign of tears, my blown pupils could give me away. I pumped the soap dispenser a few times, shoving my hands under the faucet. The cold water shocked my system. My nerves quieted down with the act of washing my hands. I grabbed paper towels from the dispenser and sighed, turning to Darcy. "I'm ready." The words more for me than her.

"Good. Colt and Rafe are here. They got us a booth," she declared, giddiness coming off her in waves. I might've found her excitement contagious if I wasn't so filled with trepidation. But I wouldn't ruin this date for her, I promised myself.

She had every reason for some reticence. More than anyone else, I understood her fear of letting people in, especially a guy like Colt. A musician, for Christ's sake. A man whose career required travel all the time. Still, she hadn't let any of that get in the way of her excitement tonight.

I had to try. Not just for her sake, but for mine too.

"All the pool tables in the back are free right now. Maybe we can play a game after eating," Darcy offered excitedly. She almost bounced on the tips of her toes. I wanted to giggle at her eagerness but didn't have it in me. Instead, I mustered up enough sass to show her I was alright.

"You don't have to lie, Dar. I know the real reason you picked this place." One reddish blonde eyebrow lifted with fake innocence. "You just want to kick Colt's ass at pool. Your secret's safe with me," I promised her. "I'm sure he's a smart man. I bet he'll figure out your pool shark ways soon enough."

Darcy had the nerve to act insulted. "Nuh uh. So not true." She didn't clarify which of my statements she disagreed with, although her smirk gave her away. *The guys better be ready to get their asses kicked.*

I chuckled. "Yeah, okay." We left the restroom. Darcy paused in the hallway before reaching the main area.

"You sure you're okay, Wyn?" She turned, her eyes searching my face. I made the process difficult for her, going back into myself, not showing my emotions. She'd never understand. She'd be pissed at me too. Even I knew I punished myself. There was no reason to go through this all on my own. Without her.

I softened my expression, meeting her concerned gaze. "I'm good, Dar. Nervous though." She'd understand. Relate to it.

"Don't be, hun. Rafe likes you. That gorgeous guy wouldn't let you out of his sight the other night." Her words were meant to reassure but only made me more anxious.

*Whatever you say, Dar.* I wasn't the least bit convinced. And I didn't trust his attention one iota. Not in the romantic sense, at least. I had little to offer a guy like him. He saw me act like a spaz the other night. Probably wanted to see the total spastic, chatterbox again. Just icing on the worst cake ever.

This was a pity date. I was here for Darcy and that was the end of it.

"Let's go. Mustn't keep the guys waiting," I smiled, pushing her ahead of me. All the extra seconds to put myself back together mattered.

I caught my first glimpse of him since last weekend. He sat at a corner booth on the other side of the restaurant area with his back to us. His dark hair loose, the ends settled just past his shoulders. I really liked his long hair, my fingers itching to pass through his thick strands just one time. The impulse was unexpected.

My eyes found Colt next. He faced our direction but hadn't noticed us yet. I wondered what they talked about. I knew on some level we were a possible topic of conversation. Us or band business. I hoped for the latter.

I was nervous enough.

Rusty's had filled up since my desperate sprint to the bathroom all those minutes ago.

We were a few feet away from the guys when Darcy grabbed my hand and squeezed. I clutched the lifeline then let go. This date night was a milestone for both of us, for very different reasons, and it was an important fact to remember.

Colt's gaze flicked to us then. A heated look immediately raked over Darcy before glancing at me. Assessing. When we finally arrived at the table, they both stood up and to the side, making room for me and Darcy to scoot in. I sniffed, my nose brushing past Rafe. A big mistake. *So good.* I didn't really know if it was his natural scent or the soap he used. Woodsy and sweet. Cedar came to mind. I enjoyed his scent. A lot.

I murmured a quiet *thank you,* taking the seat and pressing myself against the wall. More than necessary, I knew.

"Hi, Wyn. It's great to see you again." His husky timbre traveled down my spine. *Did his voice drip sex like this last week?*

Jasper green eyes captivated me. I didn't know what to think with them trained on me like that. They captured mine and mesmerized me.

"You too," I purred, not recognizing my own voice for a second. *What the hell?* Something must've been in my throat. I cleared it then held his stare.

Every part of me knew this man was dangerous. Not in a sinister way. *No.* Yet I knew deep in my bones when he showed his interest in someone, he'd want all of that person. He'd want to know a woman's deepest, darkest secrets. Sharing his in return. I saw it all right there in his eyes.

His sharp, green-black gaze might see what I hid. Truths I wished stayed buried deep. Pushed away and forgotten for good.

Rafe could get under my skin if I let him.

*Shit, who am I kidding?*

He was already there.

And I was *so* screwed.

# Chapter Seven
*Rafe*

Strung tight. Wyn had me so fucking flipped and twisted I didn't know which way was up. Her? She sat pressed against the wall and booth like she wanted to disappear, just pass right through to the outside.

Wyn intrigued the hell out of me, but the not-so-subtle fear from her confused me. Made me angry, damn near wanting to pound my chest and protect her from bad guys and demons.

And they existed. I believed that with everything in me because we all had demons. With her reticence, her standoffish posture so intense, she seemed to be locked in a room with her own.

The tension rolling off her was palpable, right there at the surface, unsettling me. I wanted to rip someone's head off because if observation taught me anything, the concerned looks from Darcy and Colt made me think this wasn't her usual behavior.

I couldn't quite reconcile the tiny spark I saw during our too-brief conversation all those days ago with the look of dismay on her face now. She sat quietly next to me, wound up so damn tight. I wanted to see it from her again. That spark—her smile—had teased me in my dreams the last few nights.

Several emotions pulled in opposite directions, a battle waging inside me. I wanted to know Wyn. A force in me also wanted to slay her demons. For any of it to happen, I needed to gain her trust. Something leading me to believe that we'd be good together.

Upright and alert, I relaxed my body, slouching against the high-back of the booth and turned my neck toward her. *I'm not a threat*, I communicated with my new posture.

We'd had an easy rapport until some dumbass shoved against her at the bar. Then, we were back in this precarious position where she seemed jumpy and uncertain of me. Back at square one.

"So, how was the rest of your weekend?"

"Good. I prepped for work while Darcy ran errands." She shrugged nonchalantly. I guessed that was all she'd share, even though I wanted to hear more from her.

Colt piped in. "You weren't causing trouble, were you?"

"Maybe a little," Darcy answered him, wearing an impish smirk. Maybe these two would lead the way for us, conversation-wise.

Darcy chattered on about some fundraiser she was helping put on at the downtown aquarium. I listened with half an ear; my attention drawn to Wyn.

Some force drove me towards her. It couldn't be helped. A slide here, innocent brush there. My body, all of me, craved closeness. The promise I made the other night to slow my roll was shot straight to hell when I got my first look at her earlier. She paired tight jeans with a long-sleeve sweater, ending unevenly at the bottom and settling against her thighs. A dark jacket finished her outfit, looking overly warm. She had this innocent sexy aura going on. Despite her aloof body language or because of it, Wyn drew me in more.

With our food and first round of drinks long gone, we made our way to the back area for some pool.

Colt racked up the balls for our second game. The first was a battle of the sexes and, *surprise surprise*, the women kicked our asses. Actually, Wyn couldn't play worth a damn. Her attempts were cute as hell, though.

I knew Darcy was trouble. It never even occurred to me she'd be a pool shark, playing all meek for the first few shots and then *bam!* She ended up clearing the table, holding it down for them both.

This next round was couple against couple. *Much more to my liking.* I'd have more reason to sidle up to Wyn for the duration of the game. See if I could make her comfortable around me. I hoped Colt and Darcy would go easy on us.

Regardless, I'd count this next little while as a win in my book.

Low on quarters, I headed to the bar for change. The back area was separate from the other parts of the tavern. We were in our own little corner, no other groups coming to the back for the second pool table, so the noise level in the main area shocked my eardrums.

The atmosphere seemed drastically different from when we first arrived. The quiet hum in the main bar was gone. A cacophony of laughter, hushed conversations, and some playful roughhousing occurred while I strolled up to the bartender.

It appeared more people found their way here for a midweek break with drinks and friends. I didn't blame them for choosing Rusty's. It was new to me, but the bar was super chill. I may have to change up my spots. Good food, a laid-back atmosphere, and cheap pool. What else could you ask for in a hangout?

It had its obvious benefits. I quickly noticed the low-key atmosphere provided low stakes for all of us. Conversation flowed over the quick meals we had at the booth and it continued over pool. There was some ribbing all during the first game, although none of us were good shit talkers. The vibe was fun. And I hadn't done the whole double date thing in a while. I was having a good time so far.

I just needed to lighten the mood. Talk to Wyn on my own. Maybe, we could learn more about one another like we started last week after the show. Even if our well-meaning friends interrupted us.

The dining area was twice as busy, more people seated at tables and posted at the bar since we finished dinner about an hour ago. Whoever picked the time had a good idea of when it got busier. I hadn't lived here long and didn't know what all the city had to offer yet. My nightlife pretty much included the venues we played at... and that was it.

The lone bartender rested against the back bar near the cash register, surveying the busy areas.

After noticing me, he strolled over to my corner of the bar. "Hey, man. Can I get quarters?" I placed three dollars on the dark wood surface and watched him turn back to the register.

"How's your night been?" I asked when he placed the handful of quarters on the counter. I took another look around the lively crowd.

"Tonight's been slow. It's not quite the weekend, ya know? Thursdays, Fridays and Saturdays can get rowdy." His tone let me know he preferred those nights. Probably for the tips alone.

"A DJ comes in every second and fourth Saturday of the month. It's a fun and crazy time, man."

"Good to know." An image slammed into me of Wyn swaying in my arms to a slow, sexy song. An irresistible thought. A fantasy I wanted to make a reality. "I might suggest coming out for one of those nights to my friends. Speaking of…" I gestured behind me. No more stalling. "Thanks, man." I tapped my knuckles against the bar counter.

Like a siren's call, Wyn summoned me back to her side.

*And it's exactly where I want to be.*

Leisurely strolling to the backroom gave me another opportunity to take in our small group with my approach. Especially Wyn. She stood off to the side holding the pool cue with both hands, clutching the long stick between tight fists. The tip shifted back and forth at the bottom of her chin. I wondered if a small chalky imprint marred her dark complexion. I'd appreciate any reason to touch her, even if it was to wipe away an inconsequential smudge.

As I walked back into the space, I noticed her black boots. The short heels brought her to just under my chin. Still sexy as hell, they beckoned my attention to her compact legs and thick thighs.

Wyn removed her jacket, putting it with Darcy's on the counter along the wall by the pool stick stand. Most of her covered, the v-cut of the sweater called attention to her neck. The small peek of skin made me wish she revealed more of herself. Seemed like she even hid behind her clothes.

Rapid anger flowed through my veins unchecked. The difference between rushing her and not being a fucking impatient idiot was an obvious fine line.

Before Wyn caught my hungry stare, I turned my attention to Colt and Darcy. Like me, Colt seemed reserved tonight, not that he was the most outgoing guy ever. I just assumed with him and Darcy being an item for almost a year now that I'd sense more intimacy between them. I wanted to ask him about it, but something told me to keep my mouth shut.

My eyelid twitched, imagining the shiner he'd have no problem giving me. I'd probably deserve it too. Colt kept aspects of his life close to his chest and probably for good reason. I should keep my questions about their relationship to my damn self anyhow.

*Maybe I can ask him more about Wyn on the drive home.* Warning bells didn't immediately go off, so I set my mind on the idea. Confident in that move. At least it wasn't one I'd get a black eye for.

The stack of quarters made a resounding clack on the corner of the pool table. My barely touched Yuengling and Colt's half empty jack and coke sat next to the girls' ginger ale and fruity cocktail.

"Great. We're already set up. Since I don't want the game to end in five seconds..." I sent Darcy a pointed look, a clear message I observed her pool shark tendencies. "Maybe Wyn can break this time," I offered, extending my hand across her front to grab my sweating bottle. The motion made me brush up against her arm.

Not touching her wasn't an option.

Before returning to my full height, I lingered near the top of her head. The tip of her ear peeking out between her braids stopped me. "What do you say, Wyn? You game to break?" I whispered. My words were innocent enough, yet the tone struck me as indecent. Downright lewd.

She jerked her head to the right, one hand slipping from the tight grip she had on the cue stick, jarring her position and moving away from me.

"Um, yeah," she muttered to no one in particular. Wyn tried downplaying the dramatic reaction by pulling herself upright. My questions caught her off guard. I was more interested in knowing why. Was it simply what I said or how I said it?

Seduction crossed my mind. *This game of pool is getting interesting.*

"Uh... sure." She shuffled over to the pool table. The nervous energy around Wyn grew. It bruised my ego that she felt spooked. She walked on eggshells still, and I knew it wasn't just about me.

I preferred her flustered, though. Next to me. Because of me. But never frightened. I imagined her blush although I couldn't see it. Wyn brushed some of her braids to one side of her face, hiding from me as she moved past.

The sexy sway of her hips had me spellbound. Her fluid movement across the space enthralled and captivated me. Like everything I discovered about her, it grabbed all my attention. As my eyes traveled up her body, I caught the uncertain look on Wyn's face.

*Is she nervous about taking the first shot of the game?*

I walked up to her, taking position right behind her. Not even giving a second thought to my actions.

"You got this Wyn. Let's kick their butts." My smack talk hit its mark when a slow smirk curled her lips. She tossed a glance over her shoulder, and I saw the look on her face and the shake of her head. She thought I was being silly.

I'd take that particular look from her over fear any day of the week. One point for teasing.

"Never gonna happen, Tapiro," gruffly reached my ears. Colt threw a serious, challenging look from across the room, on the other side of the table where he stood near Darcy. He acknowledged my intent with a nod, and I returned one of my own. He was onboard.

"We will squash you like little bugs, my friend. You are no match for us." My brained stuttered for the longest time. Colt used a freakishly weird and simultaneously hilarious accent, reminding me of a certain Austrian bodybuilder turned actor turned governor turned actor again. The accent was so unexpected that all our gazes whipped over to him then each other. We locked eyes on him again in equal levels of astonishment and amusement.

Although the silence felt like an eternity, it only took one of us to laugh before we all followed long seconds later, Colt included.

"You two are beyond ridiculous," Darcy said between chuckles.

Wyn giggled, a short breathy noise. Her body shook as she bent down to line up the opening shot. The delighted sound from her was music to my fucking ears.

The quiet, sullen spell of the night broke, freeing us to breathe easier and enjoy ourselves. The back and forth banter eased some of the elevated stress of the evening. It was the first time tonight we all really laughed together. It felt damn good.

Wyn took a deep breath, settling down her mirth. The position of the cue stick, the tip sitting between her thumb, held little to no control on her end. She also stood too far from her play. There wouldn't be enough balance or leverage to put power behind her shot.

I let her do it her way. This time. Next shot though, I'd show her a few moves. Purely a selfish reason on my part to get my hands on her. Everything in me looked forward to it. She geared up for the shot, striking the white ball just off-center, breaking the table. *Just barely*. There was really no power behind her strike. Wyn's disappointment and embarrassment ripe in the air, I could almost smell it.

"You did good, Wyn." I called, pushing off the counter from my lean. Colt went next, so Wyn backed up from the table, coming to stand near my spot.

"Yeah, thanks." My *atta girl* didn't comfort her in the least. She gave me a slight smile, anyway.

Pool was not Wyn's game, yet she tried her best. I respected her for it too. With my track record, most women I dated in the past were princesses. They wouldn't have made it this far in a game of pool. Shit, a few of them would've asked me to take them home by now. Or worse, flirted with another guy right in front of me.

Yeah, I had sucky taste in women. At least until now.

The sound of Colt putting a striped ball into a side pocket brought me out of my revelry. I watched him miss his second shot.

"Guess we're solids," I murmured to Wyn.

During my turn, the red solid slid smoothly in a corner pocket. Before figuring out my next move, I noticed Darcy whispering to Colt on their side of the table. It was more conspiratorial than lovey-dovey. I wondered about it but put my attention back on the table. Drawing out my shot, I pulled the cue back and hit the white ball in the center, propelling it across the green felt of the table.

It missed its mark. Worse, the table now lay in Darcy's capable hands, if she took any of the shots my play accidentally lined up for her. I knew she would.

*Well damn.*

"Good job, Rafe." It was the first time her husky voice uttered my name. And damn, it sounded good on her lips. Without realizing, I stopped right in front of her. It was instinctual, wanting to be this close. Wyn peeked up at me with those doe eyes and asked, "what?"

I spoke the truth because she deserved nothing less.

"I like the way you say my name, Wyn." My words hit their mark. Although I'd been a piss-poor student except in music, I became a quick study in Wyn's expressions. Several darted across her face, all in a matter of seconds. Shock, joy, alarm. Her face settled on disbelief.

I saw it all there in her big, dark brown eyes, telling me everything I needed to know. She'd learn soon enough. *I mean what I say, especially when I have something or someone important in my sights.*

She continued processing as I grabbed my warm beer and took a swig. I turned back to our game as Darcy missed her first shot. *What the fuck?* The table had been hers for the taking. Every play, every angle was in her favor.

The answer slammed into me. She missed on purpose.

Darcy shrugged her shoulder at Colt then turned our way. "Wyn," she called. "It's your turn, hun." Long moments passed before the announcement filtered through to Wyn. I tapped her shoulder. She came out of the fog, looking across at her friend, nodding mechanically.

This game just got a whole helluva lot more interesting.

# Chapter Eight
*Wyn*

*What the hell?*

"Yeah, okay." I walked the short distance back to the pool table, shaking myself out of the stupor Rafe's comment put me in.

I knew this man was dangerous. A few words from him and they struck me dumb. Most of all, I wanted to know what game he played at. Because there had to be something I wasn't getting.

Although my self-esteem was down a deep, dark well nowadays, I knew I wasn't a troll. I was a few pounds heavier than I wanted to be, and yet I loved my curves. Even still, Rafe was out of my damn league on a good day. And I learned a hard lesson the last time. Even thinking about letting him in nicked the frayed pieces inside me. And comments like the one he just made had me wanting things I couldn't possibly consider now.

Rafe and these last couple days confused me, filling my brain with screwy ideas. Wishful thinking. I had lost my ever-loving mind going along with this farce of a date. And it had nothing to do with Rafe. Well, mostly.

By the time I got to the table and bent down to aim, the conversation in my head only complicated the situation. I probably took too long standing there, because suddenly there was a presence at my back. I knew immediately it was Rafe.

I fidgeted with the stick, the wayward thoughts plaguing me stopped in their tracks. His warm presence remained. A subtle uneasiness prickled my skin, raising the hairs on my neck.

I sort of froze, sensing his stare on me.

"Can I show you some quick tricks, Wyn?"

Even though I expected something, his words startled me, making me jump out of my skin. The cue stick dropped from my loose grip and bounced on the edge of the wood. I caught it, fumbling in my hand before it toppled to the floor.

"Good catch." He coughed. A look crossed his face before he put on a self-deprecating grin. "Sorry about that, sweetheart. I just want to help you with your form." Sincerity laced his tone, but I wondered at his actions. Crowding my personal space like this, tossing endearments out there. He unnerved me. And I didn't want him to.

In my position, the hem of my long sweater rode up my thighs. My jeans covered me, but I still felt somewhat cornered with him at my back. We were in public with friends. I was relatively safe, yet this whole episode stressed me out.

I pushed myself up, hating that I questioned everything now.

"May I?" Rafe asked. He felt closer somehow, and I shivered. *I really am losing it.*

"Here." One hand brushed my left side. "Bend at the waist and line up your shot." His warm breath skated across my right ear, urging me to comply. My mind struggled with how much I wanted to follow his instructions; how easy it was. He moved with me as I bent down, finding myself back in the vulnerable position I started in.

On autopilot, I had access to the controls, but so did he. And he damn well took the gear.

Even the hint of his nearness lingered on my skin even though he hadn't touched me. Not really. None of this made any sense.

"However you hold the cue, you want it to be secure and comfortable for you." I huffed. He must've heard the frustrated sound because he continued. "First, Wyn, you've got to pick your shot. It's best to do it when you're standing upright and can see the entire table." My name on his lips moved over me like a caress.

*What the hell is wrong with me?*

I said nothing. I couldn't utter a single word. Watchful and detached, his hands came into my periphery. They landed gently on mine. Instead of freaking me out, his touch dampened the frenetic noise surrounding me. The tension in my body dissipated in waves.

Rafe's impromptu lesson continued. "This game is all about lines and angles." The notes of his deep voice tingled down my spine. "Now, rest the cue in position." I returned the cue between my pointer finger and thumb.

"That grip good enough for you?" It wasn't, so I shook my head.

"No," left my mouth. I didn't know if he saw the motion, so I asked, "How do I make it secure then?" I bit my bottom lip in frustration.

I wasn't the best pool player and it showed. I had no business playing this game. Darcy was the pool shark, not me. My best friend never missed a shot.

That simple fact stopped me cold. The last few minutes hadn't even registered with all the thoughts rolling around in my head. It shouldn't be my turn because Darcy could've—should've easily— cleared the table. Why hadn't she cleared the damn table?

The neurons in my brains pinged, sensing a trap. The whole damn night read like a setup, and I was on the wrong end.

"Take a deep breath, sweetheart. I want you to try some positions for me, okay?" Rafe's whiskey-coated voice paused the anger simmering in my bloodstream. I shook my head in agreement again. I knew if I said anything, Darcy would see right through me.

Rafe maneuvered my fingers in a few positions, one where the cue rested against the flesh of my hand, in between the thumb and index. He wrapped my index finger around the top part of the cue and moved the stick back and forth like he'd done after showing me the other positions.

"Whichever one is the most comfortable and gives you the most control of the cue. That's the one you use, Wyn." He then lifted away from me and stepped back, his comforting warmth going along with him. I hadn't realized the feeling of being crowded left me a long time ago. His closeness, his voice, and unexpected lesson had a soothing effect over me the last few minutes. After he moved away, an emptiness assailed me. *What else is new?*

I'd felt empty for almost a year now. Got used to the hollowness a while ago. Even though Rafe's gentle presence was growing on me, it wouldn't change our circumstances. I didn't mind him being around. Much. But it wouldn't work.

All the negativity brought my anger back. Frustration pooled in my feet and pushed up through my veins, fueling the tempest inside me. I didn't want to be like this anymore. Closed off and afraid all the time.

My eyes registered the green felt of the pool table. I pushed up, taking another look at my options. I didn't know how much time passed since Rafe left my side, but I couldn't bring myself to look at anyone. Target in sight, I bent down again, chose the last technique he showed me and struck as hard as possible.

"Ohmygod, Wyn! What a great shot." Darcy's piercing praise hit me as I stood up.

"Huh?" I looked around the table. It all looked pretty much the same since before I took my turn. A few of the balls kept spinning, slowing down but yeah, nothing went in from what I saw.

"Do you notice the difference between this shot and your others?"

"Hmm." I did. I was certain the power behind this particular shot came from some of the emotions I exorcised from my body just now, which wasn't information to share with the group. It'd make me sound crazier than I already felt. "Yeah, I did. Still haven't made a shot that's actually gone in though."

"It comes with practice and time. You have a grip that works for you now." He nodded like he answered his own question.

Slightly defeated but less tense, I walked over to our jackets and grabbed my drink, taking a long sip. My tongue dried up like cotton, parched all of a sudden. Rafe joined me, standing close and drinking his beer. He picked at the label on his bottle. The game continued, Colt grabbing his stick from where he placed it against a wall. Like Darcy, he missed his next shot, glancing off a stripe and disturbing the other balls on the table.

*Hmm. Interesting.*

Rafe was up next. My eyes followed him as he strolled over to the table, the cue in his right hand swinging back and forth. He analyzed his options, pacing the short end, taking it all in. Only five feet away, I watched his long-legged body and damn near salivated. Doing what I didn't dare do when he was up close and looking my fill.

Tonight, he wore dark wash jeans. Like the night we met, he coupled it with a black button-down over a plain gray T-shirt. The ensemble brought out the deep olive tan of his skin, the green of his eyes. His black hair lay fastened in a tight ponytail against his collars. I dropped my eyes to hide my stare and noticed his dark suede boots.

From top to bottom, this man was perfection. It made me wonder about him. Why me? Why the deep whiskey voice, sweet endearments and all this attention? Aimed at me. Wasted on me.

I didn't get it. *And I don't deserve it.*

*But this must be what actual lust is,* I thought. The ghost of his touch on all the places where we connected, still lingered. I couldn't shake the emotions he brought to the forefront. Again, the thought of losing my marbles over this came to mind. I had no business tracking him around the room like I did. There was a hunger, an intriguing question inside I hadn't found the answer to yet. It scared me more than anything.

"You're up next, Wyn." Colt called from the other side of the table. Darcy stood to his left, waiting.

Again? Our last game went quick but not this damn fast. Seemed like I just went a minute or two ago. I had little clue about what was happening, yet everyone was low-key about it. As if they orchestrated it all. A well-planned romp.

However this conspiracy got started, I seemed to be the only one getting played.

# Chapter Nine
*Rafe*

Wyn shrugged her shoulders. I walked past and noticed immediately something was off with her. She appeared upset. Even angry. At all of us, most likely.

The jig was up. I couldn't speak for Colt or Darcy, only knowing the motives behind my own actions. My reasons seemed selfish and borderline salacious, and I wasn't ashamed to admit it. I wanted Wyn. Wanted to get to know her.

Her innocent beauty slayed me over and over. I had a hard time ignoring the way her curves fit against my front earlier. A damn struggle for sure. I ached to return to her side, get up close again, show Wyn more pool tricks and just be near her. I stopped myself. Decided not to overstep again. From her current expression, it'd probably be unwelcomed anyway.

So, I waited.

I watched as Wyn considered the remaining plays on the table. She didn't lack in choices. As her partner, I wanted her to enjoy the game. Shit, on this date she probably felt forced into. Darcy and Colt's exploits were harmless enough even if my subtle seduction tactics weren't so innocent. I'd win her over, eventually. I had to.

Because damn, Wyn intrigued me. I couldn't curb my caveman instincts with her. Nor did I want to. The realization would've knocked me for a loop if I wasn't already aware of my fate. She had me all tied up, with little idea of the roller coaster she put me on.

My attention zeroed in on her. I knew exactly when she chose her target: the four cue ball off-center. She had this determined expression on her face, a hard set to her eyes, an arched brow. Fuck, she was hot with that fierce look. I wondered if she'd ever turn the look on me. I wished for it.

*Back to the game, Tapiro.* Her choice wasn't a bad one, not in the least. Wyn had the instincts for this game although she lacked confidence.

The cue ball sat inches away from the right corner pocket. I couldn't help myself, walking up behind her to whisper in her ear, "just breathe through the shot".

"Easier said than done," she retorted. Her choice was good but difficult. Wyn took her time lining up the shot. Her pointer hooked around the cue stick which pressed against her middle finger. Her other digits spread wide, holding firm against the table. A closed-hand bridge.

*Atta girl! Secure your grip then shoot.* The tension mounted as we all watched her. All the pressure must've been too much for her because her shot went wild. She struck the cue ball at a hard, downward angle causing it to fly off the green felt. Wyn missed every single ball, overshooting the table. It would've been comical if abject horror hadn't settled across her round face, eyes wide with shock. The cue ball finally crashed against one of the tall chairs at the back of the room with a loud crack.

"Oops. My bad, y'all. I totally meant for the ball to go flying." She looked at us with slight shame in her eyes. I imagined she blushed furiously, the skin of her cheeks blazing hot to the touch. "The cue stick didn't slip. Not at all." She recovered from the embarrassment quickly with a dose of snark.

I liked that about her. Liked her more than I probably should.

The term *Mulligan* rushed out my mouth unbidden. "Let Wyn have a do-over since the table wasn't disturbed." Before the others agreed, I retrieved the flying cue ball from the floor and brought it back to the table. She resettled it near the top of the table, centering it before returning to a bent position. Without warning and little preparation, she struck the cue ball. Dead center.

The purple four ball shot straight into the corner pocket.

*Where the fuck did that come from?* Mind blown.

Wyn's shot was damn near perfect. Crisp. No fanfare. With an accurate precision none of us expected. I sure as hell didn't.

Darcy squealed from the other side of the table, practically skipping to Wyn. She crushed her in a hug, saying something in her ear, making her laugh out loud. I attempted some lighthearted teasing, wanting to hear her happy sound for myself.

"I got myself a pool shark too, huh?"

The shot must've surprised her as well. I watched the expressions flutter across her face, chuckling under my breath. Her shocked grin said so much right now. The open smile curving her lips brought one out on mine. *Damn, she's beautiful.* Especially when she was happy. It radiated from her. I liked seeing that unfiltered look.

The smile slipped and a stern look took its place. "Alright, you two can stop going easy on us now. I've had enough 'practicing' to last me a lifetime." She sashayed the few steps toward my spot, "And you, stop missing shots for my benefit. Alright?"

"Yes, ma'am!" I snapped to attention, saluting her. Wyn shook her head at my antics and returned to the counter that held our drinks and her belongings.

"Do we need another round?" My voice carried across the room for Colt and Darcy's benefit. A chorus of "waters" and "ginger ale, please" answered my question, so I went to do their bidding.

The night was coming to a close. I promised myself, as they finished this last game or two, I would get some much-needed one-on-one time with my date.

I returned in two minutes flat. The main restaurant and bar areas remained busy with the late dinner crowd. The loud crack of cue balls met my ears when I returned to the backroom. *Guess Colt and Darcy decided to play another game.* Great! Now was my chance.

The cold glasses balanced in my hands, I made eye contact with Colt and Darcy. I placed two glasses on the counter closest to the pool table where they stood. "Thanks, man," he muttered. Colt jerked his head in Wyn's direction at the counter. I got the message. Loud and clear. His attention stayed riveted to Darcy.

"Here ya go, Wyn." I passed her the ginger ale, my hand skimming hers as she grabbed the cold soda. I hadn't touched her in ages. At least that was what it felt like. More than a few minutes for sure, so I was hard up.

*And this is getting fucking ridiculous.*

"Oh." Pulling out a stool under the counter, I sat down next to her. I noted the not-so-subtle competition happening between our friends just a few feet away from us. "Thanks, Rafe." Wyn's soft words snapped my attention back to her.

"I still can't believe the last shot you made. It was incredible." If my dad or older brother saw me now, they'd throw all types of insults my way. I gave zero shits right now. I wanted to learn more about this woman sitting next to me. As much as she wanted to share. "So, how's your week been, Wyn?"

Her eyes lit up in amusement when Darcy cheered. I watched as she danced a little shimmy around Colt, my eyes returning to Wyn.

"Things are good so far. Spring always brings steady work my way. Keeps me busy." I listened as she described some of the work she's been doing. "What's going on with you?"

"Well, the band just got a slot on a music festival lineup next weekend. It came up sorta last minute but should be great exposure for us." It was the first thought to come to mind when she turned the tables on me. As I spoke, a lock of hair escaped from my band and fell in my face. I pulled it back behind my ear in frustration. I just hoped she hadn't noticed the slight panic in my voice.

The music festival gig fell into our laps the other day. Some festival organizer had an old demo of Colt's band from a year ago. He mentioned it surfacing on the top of his pile, so he stopped by our show last week. And loved it so much he thought of us when someone backed out of his festival.

Two great factors came out of that show: laying eyes on Wyn and this new gig. *Fortune's sure as shit favoring us right now.* It was also scary as hell. Nothing ever went this well for me before. I didn't want to fuck any of this up for the band. Or myself.

Opportunities like this came up with the other bands I'd played with. And yet, this shit felt new. Different. This feeling like I finally belonged somewhere, not just holding the fort down for someone else to take my place. Like I was on the right path with Country Blue. I wasn't just some temporary stand-in musician; I was part of the band. And this festival slot next week was an enormous deal for us.

"That's fantastic, Rafe. I'm so happy for you. You guys, I mean." The most sincere and beatific smile graced her face, the genuine excitement for us right there in her voice. Pure and happy. "So cool. You'll have to tell me how it all..." Wyn's mouth snapped shut, her lips smashing together in a worried line.

A smile teased my lips, enjoying how her enthusiasm shined through. So different from the cold welcome I got earlier tonight. I'd take Wyn any way I could get her. This side of her was my favorite, though, revving me up like no other.

Not missing a beat, I continued our conversation as if she finished the rushed statement. "Most definitely, Wyn. I'll tell you all about it." *You can bet your sexy ass on it.*

Just like the opening it was, I spun my body around to face her. We both, more or less, leaned against the counter. My mouth opened to ask my burning question, but Colt's woman hurried over in a flash of red hair, interrupting us.

*Darcy with her impeccable damn timing.* I grabbed my glass of water and made my way over to Colt who was putting the pool stuff away. I pitched in.

Just as I grew some *cojones*, as Berto would say, to ask Wyn for her number, the best friend cockblocked me. I'd kick my own ass if I could reach it. Like a total doofus, I neglected to ask her last week. The ladies left so quickly after this double date planning happened on the sidewalk that I hadn't thought about it until it was too late. Plus, the cards were already in my favor with this date and all. I thought I was a patient guy before, but it seemed to wane thin lately. This time around, the heavenly beings looking down on me wanted me to put in some work.

"Hey, you two." Darcy called from her place next to Wyn. "I, uh, think we're ready to head out. I'm stopping by the ladies' room first." She already walked away, her words breaking through the musings about my overall lameness.

"Hold up, Dar. I'll go with you." Wyn hopped off the stool, catching up to Darcy after grabbing her jacket and clutch from the counter. Obviously alive and well with our ladies, the innate need for women to travel to the bathroom together was definitely not a myth.

About a minute later, Colt and I left the backroom. Our dates would probably take their time in there, gossiping and exchanging notes. Speaking only good things, I hoped. The noise from the main part of the tavern met us as we strolled to the front. Rusty's brimmed with way more energy now. The bar hopping, busy with twice as many people since the last time I came for our waters. We paused at the end of the hallway, not too far from the ladies' room.

I wondered about the dance nights the bartender mentioned. Immediately picturing me and Wyn coming back, holding her close in my arms all night. The imagery had me buzzing. One of our dates must include dancing, I thought.

*I'd make damn sure of it now.*

My body hummed from our too-brief conversation just a few

minutes ago. Wyn had me thinking and planning so much that I vibrated with it. I realized we all needed to make an early night, the clock ticking closer and closer to ten. Yet, I wanted to stop time somehow. Grab more moments near Wyn. Talking. Laughing. Just being with her. I craved it after only a short time in her presence.

The band planned to meet early tomorrow to hash out our setlist for the upcoming festival slot. An eleven in the morning practice. Any band member worth his salt would reject the idea of waking up before dinner, let alone lunchtime. Still, this gig was a huge deal even if none of us voiced it. *Big for all of us.* And we took it seriously.

We talked about random shit as we waited for them. They finally emerged moments later, and I noticed the slight smile resting on Wyn's plump lips. I took it as a good sign.

We exchanged few words while exiting Rusty's. The limited parking lot was now quite full with twice as many cars since our earlier arrival. I heard the *clack-clack* of Wyn unearthing keys from her clutch. My time was up. The women led the way to the clunkiest and most outrageous junker I'd seen in a while. But *who am I to judge someone's ride?* Colt had to come get my ass because my gas tank was empty with a big fat E.

I shoved my hands in my pockets, trying to stop myself from touching her. Instead I opened my mouth, not caring about our friends hearing. "So, uh, Wyn. Can I call you sometime?" The quirk at the corner of Colt's mouth let me know he heard the awkward segue. I wondered how the bastard fared tonight. Once we moved to the pool tables, our attention went straight to our beautiful dates and not on keeping tally for who did what. I couldn't be bothered anyway; tonight wasn't a competition.

I heard snippets of conversation on their end. Suffice it to say, Darcy was the more chattier of the two. Wasn't hard to believe since Colt was such a quiet fucker.

"I should've asked for your number on Friday but I'm asking now," I pushed on. It bugged the hell out of me when I didn't have a way to keep in contact with Wyn leading up to this date. The last few days had been a struggle in patience. I almost asked Colt to get her number for me from Darcy about a dozen times. I'd had to check myself in the meantime.

I took my phone out quickly, just in case she tried rejecting my small request. With two pair of eyes on our tense exchange, it was awkward for both of us. I unlocked the screen and Wyn quickly shot off the ten digits, my fingers flying over the phone's keypad.

"Great, Wyn. Thanks." I pocketed the device, patting my pants to make sure it didn't disappear on me. Wyn's back rested against the driver's side door. She nodded her head and turned away, about to descend into the car. The moment dragged on in slow motion. I knew it was just my overactive mind exaggerating the stressful situation. At the last second, I had a bright idea for a bold move.

I bent down, pressing a kiss against her soft cheek. Because of her angle and my abrupt decision, my lips glanced too close to her ear. I whispered a soft "Good night, Wyn," committing to memory my last hint of the fragrance she wore. I remembered it from the other night. A subtle, sweet fragrance that stayed with me long after she'd gone. Delicious.

"Oh, um, good night, Rafe." The goodbye left her lips on a stuttered breath, her grip on the car door going limp. The clenched fists in my pockets went slack. I crossed over to grab the door and opened it for her. She got in almost on autopilot with a mumbled "Thank you." Always so polite, *my Wyn*.

I closed the door once she was all the way inside. Colt finished his goodbye with Darcy, closing her door and tapping the roof. Wyn turned the ignition and the car sputtered before starting. Darcy waved as they backed out of the spot, making a right turn out of the parking lot exit. Colt and I stood off to the side, an unspoken need to watch them drive off.

"Alright, Casanova." Colt slapped my back, jolting me out of my complete distraction. "Time to get our asses home. Our band meeting is damn early."

"Yeah, but you set the time, genius."

His smug grin told me it was intentional. Probably to keep us all sharp. I didn't blame him. Even more so, I appreciated it.

I knew the fifteen-minute ride back to my place would be quiet. The silence suited me fine. The feeling of being *settled* crept over me again. Teasing the recesses of my mind.

The experiences and decisions leading me to this moment, with this band and to the woman who just drove away, it was all starting to make sense. I took the phone out of my pocket and flipped the sleek object from side to side, tapping my thigh.

Heading *home* sounded damn good right now.

# Chapter Ten
## *Wyn*

Ugh. I struggled to find a comfortable position on my full-size foam mattress. The act was proving damn impossible tonight.

My bed had called to me about an hour ago. I had every intention of going to sleep quickly. Now, it just wasn't happening fast enough.

The bad dreams seemed to be on a hiatus the last couple nights, only cropping up once since Darcy's homecoming. More than a few welcomed distractions kept my attention, from hanging out with Darcy to work picking up. And then the unexpected happened, namely Rafe. I didn't know how to feel about him yet. Couldn't wrap my head around it all.

It was great having Darcy home even though I knew she wouldn't stick around for too long. Her work took her around the world for weeks or months at a time now, but I savored our days together. She was like the sister I never knew I wanted.

My mind turned to work. Mountains of digital files waited for me tomorrow, and I had just a few days to wade through it all as deadlines loomed. One business manager needed specific edits to an annual report completed by midweek, and I hadn't even started. My long task list raced through my head now, giving me a slight reprieve from all other worries.

I was just kidding myself. I hadn't had a good night's sleep since last year. And now something... no, someone was proving even more dangerous to my psyche. *Rafe.*

His name whispered on the edge of my thoughts like an

unexpected caress. His warm breath ghosting across my neck lingered from last week. Even the memory of him leaning over me, directing my body at the pool table the other night teased me. His soft touches and suggestive words continued to drift through my mind, at warp speed, only slowing down for a few seconds. Obsessing over one detail before something else he did or said came to mind. It all kept me awake, driving me mad.

No wonder my brain refused to settle enough to sleep. The man messed with my already unsteady equilibrium and threw me off.

Sunday night and I obsessed over a guy I met. Didn't even know if I really liked him. I couldn't, *could I?*

He texted me a few times since the double date, but we hadn't talked on the phone. Saying he'd call was just another broken promise. It kept good company with all the other broken pieces of my existence.

I had to be real with myself. Rafe was just being nice. Nothing more, nothing less. Worrying about his intentions got me nowhere. *Literally.*

Maybe having him star in my dreams wouldn't hurt too badly. Shoot, I'd even live with a couple cameos. With all the thoughts running through my mind, he was pretty much front and center for most of them.

I wondered if anyone else noticed how his voice got deeper, huskier when he spoke my name. It was probably just my imagination... like the song said.

I rolled over, fluffing my top pillow one more time. I probably heard and saw what I wanted anyway. What I didn't even deserve. Because I sure as hell wasn't ready for whatever it was he wanted from me.

Zilch could happen between us, I was sure. Despite the fact that he seemed like a great guy, I couldn't think about that right now. The date at Rusty's had gone okay, but how would I act when we were alone? I couldn't rely on group situations or very public places all the time.

God forbid I freaked out if he touched me in more suggestive or aggressive ways.

Speaking of aggressive, *what if* Rafe ended up being like *him?* Taking what I hadn't willingly offered while I screamed no in my head, over and over again.

Giving him a chance, he could surprise me. In a good way. I just had to fight against visions of pain, fear, and disappointment. Those feelings lived in me now, festering inside, making me second-guess my choices time and time again.

It was a risk I wasn't willing to take. Not for anyone. Rafe and I included. Now or ever again. It just hurt too damn much.

I was warped.

My hand felt around for the cup of water I left on my nightstand. *Eureka!* I brought the rim of the glass to my lips, taking a long sip before placing it back behind my alarm clock. My bladder would probably force my hand in a few hours, but I needed the drink. The racing thoughts had me parched, like I'd run a two-minute mile. Funny thing was I hadn't been out of the apartment all day.

My jaw extended on the biggest yawn as my head hit the pillow again. My eyes finally drifted closed when I heard the soft rumbling of my cell phone vibrating where it lay charging. The rumble stopped right before the obnoxiously loud ringtone broke the silence of the too-quiet room.

Darcy went to bed hours ago. Most likely out cold and sleeping in the room across the hall.

In my hurry to catch the call before it went to voicemail, I almost toppled off the side of my bed, catching my fall with my right hand.

"Oh shit," left my mouth as I went down, wincing at the sharp pain shooting up my forearm and vibrating in my elbow. Just before the fourth and final ring, I slid my finger across the screen and answered.

This better be good because an ER visit could be in my future because of it.

"Wyn? Hello?" Busy untangling myself from the layers of the sheet and comforter wrapped around my legs and torso, the deep voice of my late-night caller stopped me cold.

*Rafe?*

Maybe I actually fell all the way off the bed, hit my head on the way down because I was, for sure, in la-la land.

"Um, sweetheart. You there?" I heard rustling on his end of the line. "Shit, is this a bad time?"

"Yeah, I'm here." Breathless and raspy, the sound of my voice startled me.

His call startled me even more. As if my earlier thoughts summoned him somehow.

I wiggled my upper body back on the bed and sat upright on the pillows. *Ugh, so embarrassing.* I told myself it could've been way worse. "Almost took a nosedive off my bed."

And there it was, the way worse.

The words left my mouth without a filter. Why didn't I just let the call go to voicemail like any other sane person would after eleven o'clock at night?

My brain-to-mouth connections were borderline appalling when we were face-to-face. Now, it seemed like hanging upside down for a few seconds totally cut my wiring altogether. I blamed the owner of that damn whiskey-steeped voice on the other end of the call. In-person or on the phone, it mattered not.

A rich, deep chuckle came through loud and clear. It sounded like he moved around, getting more comfortable wherever he was. "Um, uh, yeah. Hi, Rafe." I cleared my throat, my words still forgotten. *My life sucks so hard right now.* "Wassup?"

"Not much, sweetheart. We haven't talked except for the text messages, and I wanted to hear your voice before calling it a night."

*Ohmygod, ohmygod, ohmygod. This can't be real, right?*

"Oh well. Um... okay." Well damn, how was I supposed to respond to him and his titillating comments? "Why do you do that?" The mouth diarrhea never ended.

"Do what, Wyn?" His voice, with the same damn sexy timbre, sent a tremor through me, settling in the pit of my stomach.

*This guy is dangerous,* I mused for the hundredth time in the last week.

"You call me babe or sweetheart an awful lot." The endearments warmed me down to the bone. They also scared the bejesus out of me. How right it all felt even though I didn't know him from a hole in the wall.

Rafe made me want to stop hiding. Face the nightmares haunting me. Last year. All of it. And I needed to stay far away from him because I wasn't ready. Not for any of it.

*What does this bona fide rock star Adonis really want from a girl like me anyway?* Besides the obvious.

"It feels right." The breath caught in my chest. He stated a fact. No hesitation. It was all there in his tone and those direct words.

*Straight talk, no bullshit chaser.* My uncle, my father's brother, liked to say. Rafe's simple explanation reminded me of his go-to phrase.

How could it be this easy for him to tip my world off its axis these last few days?

I kept telling myself I shouldn't trust whatever this was. He had all the right words since the beginning. *So did most guys who wanted something.*

He had to catch my shortened breath over the pregnant pause; our cell reception was quite clear.

I heard more rustling on his end and wondered where he was. Did he share an apartment with other people?

His call and the clarity in his voice told me he was wide awake. I was now too. For no reason at all, him being a night owl didn't surprise me. Most musicians were more alert at this late hour because the lifestyle pretty much called for it.

"I had a great time on our date the other night." He filled the silence with the directness I was coming to expect from him.

"Me too, Rafe." I couldn't lie to him or myself. I'd had fun, even with the night starting off rough and awkward. *All because of me.*

While we had dinner, Darcy chattered on more than usual, most likely trying to quell the awkwardness of the group. Then, the silences all but dissipated with each game of pool. I even talked more with Rafe after the built-up tension broke.

It was way better than all my lowest expectations put together.

My worries crept back in when we said our goodbyes at Cru, where he surprised the hell out of me. The soft press of his lips against my cheek. Perfectly subtle and most likely an accident. He stepped back and then we left, not making a big production of it. I couldn't have asked for a better ending. It still knocked me off my feet, especially after none of us knew how *to be* around each other at the start of the date.

"God. I wish I could see you right now. Be near you." I didn't know what to say. Before I stupidly replied with *thanks* or another inept response, he rushed out, "But just talking to you now is brightening my fucking day."

That gave me the perfect excuse to ignore the first part of his bold and intimate statement. I didn't even want to grapple with it. "Did something happen?"

"I talked to my best friend earlier today. And I swear as soon as something puts me in a good mood, someone comes out of the woodwork to fuck it up." The seconds ticked by as I heard his breathing on the line, no other sound coming through.

"Wanna talk about it, Rafe?" I wanted to hear his deep voice a while longer. It was crazy and dangerous how he calmed and rattled me all at the same time.

Wide awake and interested, I settled back into the pillows and waited.

The topic sounded serious. Like he needed to get whatever it was off his chest.

"You don't have to tell me if you don't want to. It's none of my business anyway." But I wondered what was on his mind even if it wasn't really my place. Sharing like this was a two-way street, and I wasn't in any way, shape or form ready to reciprocate with my own deep, personal information.

I'd only shared small facts with him thus far, so why did I expect him to confide in me? I was a big, old hypocrite.

A grunt and the sound of more rustling came over the line.

"I had other ideas for how this conversation was gonna go. I didn't intend to spend this entire time dumping my personal shit on you, Wyn."

"You can if you want," I rushed out. "Talk to me, I mean. About whatever's on your mind." Ugh. *Way to fumble around and put pressure on him to talk to you.* I still couldn't stop myself.

"On several occasions people have told me I'm a darn good listener." Rafe chuckled. I rolled my eyes. He didn't need to know all I've done this last year was lend an ear to everyone else's problems, not reciprocating with anyone. Not even Darcy. All listening and no talking; it's any wonder my ears weren't bleeding.

Whatever got me out of my own messed up headspace now and then was good, I told myself.

"So," he started. I pulled the comforter up some more, settling in and suppressing a yawn. "I got a call from my dad right after I ended my conversation with Zion." Must be the best friend he mentioned a few minutes ago. I didn't interrupt him for clarification. It seemed like he needed to get this off his chest. "He wanted to know if I'd talked to my brother lately."

"Oh, you have a brother. That's really cool." I'm an only child and always wondered what it would've been like having an older or younger sibling. Sister or brother, it hadn't really mattered when I was younger. Now I had Darcy. She was more like a sister, so I didn't feel like I missed out anymore.

"Yeah, Alanzo… Lanni, he was awesome when I was younger. I idolized him actually…" Rafe remembered with a slight trace of fondness. "But people change."

"Oh, you don't have a good relationship with your family then?" I waited for his response. Now that he started, I didn't want him to stop talking. Getting to know him was risky. Something I tried my damnedest to avoid. Then he called. Even though I acted like a spaz each time we were together, I felt good about reading his moods whether he was in front of me or not.

*His brief silence speaks volumes.*

"When I was seven years old, my old man got demoted from a detective down to a beat cop. I never really learned why it all happened although I have a few guesses now. Truthfully, I've always been afraid to ask." The change in his position brought on more drinking, Rafe continued, which led to his father *smacking around* his mom, Rafe, and his brother. His story wasn't over though, I knew there was even more *bad* to his childhood.

"My brother began emulating my father, taking his frustration out on me. What's fucked up is that my father egged him on. It gave them material to bond over, I guess. Then my father stopped using my brother as a punching bag and they both focused their hate on me."

*Oh God, poor Rafe.* I ached for the boy he was and knew in my heart he wasn't sharing this with me because he wanted my pity. He didn't need any asinine platitudes from me, so I kept quiet.

"As I got older, I just escaped to Zion and Chloe's house when it got to be too much. Which was pretty fucking often once I got taller and filled out some."

I hadn't moved in quite a while and my lower back felt tight. I turned over, curving my back to stretch it. The sound of changing positions must have drawn his attention because I heard him shifting around a bit too.

"So, I've been speaking way more than I wanted to. I called to hear your voice." He really knew how to shock the hell out of me with the sweetest statements. *What am I supposed to do when he says stuff like that?* "How are you doing, Wyn?"

"Oh, uh, I'm good. It's been great having Darcy home again." Although I didn't want to bore him with my work stuff, he'd asked, and it'd been on my mind. "Since it's the end of the fiscal year, my clients have quite the workload these next few weeks. It's overwhelming at times, but I enjoy having project-based work. It fits meh—aahhhhh." The yawn came out of nowhere as I finished my thought.

"Shit, babe. That's the second yawn I've heard from you since we started talking. I'll stop being a selfish bastard and let you get some sleep."

"Oh God, I'm so sorry." I was so embarrassed. The more I talked to him, the more I liked him. *What the hell am I going to do?* "But it's definitely past my bedtime."

"I'll call you again soon. Sweet dreams, Wyn."

"You too." He really had the huskiest voice I've ever heard. It surrounded me like a warm blanket, even better than the one I was under right now. "Okay. Good night, Rafe."

"Bye, sweetheart." My phone beeped twice as the call ended. A smile settled on my lips as I placed mine back on the nightstand. I set my alarm to wake me up at seven—exactly six and a half hours from now.

*He did it again.* The endearment, with his sweet tone, lulled me. I already felt myself drifting and knew Rafe would be at the forefront of my dreams.

I couldn't ask for more.

# Chapter Eleven
*Rafe*

*Dammit, that was not how I wanted my conversation with Wyn to go the other night.*

The same thought popped in and out of my head the last couple of days. On repeat.

I hadn't intended to call her late either. My thoughts strayed right to her after the disastrous exchange with my father. And right after I spoke to my boy Zion too.

All of it put me in a sour fucking mood.

And Wyn was my salvation.

The next minute, my phone was back in hand, and I was pressing the touch screen and dialing her number. Her being asleep hadn't even crossed my mind until she picked up, her winded voice coming over the line.

*I'm an inconsiderate ass sometimes*, I thought. It didn't stop me from wanting to hear her voice though.

Wyn's rushed words and nervous chatter dragged me from the proverbial cliff. *Damn. This shy woman gets to me.* I knew it wasn't an act either. And her soft voice sure did something to me.

Baring a piece of my soul the other night was not a part of the plan. It was hard not to, though. If only I could get her to share more of herself with me.

*There will be more time for that*, I promised myself.

Compared to any other woman I'd been interested in, Wyn seemed different. I wanted to get to know her better.

In the music business, you learned pretty damn quick how to see through bullshit. If not, people took great pleasure in chewing you up and spitting you out. She wasn't the type; I could tell right off the bat.

I caught sight of her in the club the first time, knowing there was something different, maybe even pure, about her. Wyn's shyness wasn't her only alluring feature. Not by a long shot. She hid past hurts, I didn't know from what for sure, but her brilliance still shined through at certain times. I needed more of that in my life. Whatever scared her, she didn't let it stop her or break her spirit. I respected her for it even if the story behind it remained a mystery.

Darcy had obviously dragged her to our concert two weeks back, and she'd made the most of it. Discomfort and other emotions radiated from her.

Wyn was different from other girls I've dated, for the simple fact that she hadn't thrown a tantrum when she didn't get her way. Getting to know her better was rising to the top of my priority list, and I hoped she'd meet me halfway. Gave me a chance.

A hand slapped me on the back of my shoulder, jarring me and knocking those musings straight out of my head. "What the—" I turned to see which of the guys came up behind me.

"Mano, what the hell's up your ass and making you deaf? I been calling you for five minutes." Berto's other hand waved over to the full van parked at the curb. "We're almost finished here." Doug stood just inside the wide-open back doors trying to shove some of our smaller equipment and chords into the non-existent space.

"Dude, give it up already!" Forgotten, Berto turned around and yelled at Doug. The front door of the studio opened then. Colt walked out, taking in the scene. The guys and I were there picking up the rest of our equipment and trying to pile our instruments, overnight bags, and contingency items into the little ass van Doug secured for this trip. We'd be lucky if the four of us even fit in the damn van after filling it to the max.

By my watch, we'd be late if we didn't hit the highway soon. The festival grounds were more than a six-hour drive away. Traffic would be a bitch too. The organizers told us to get to the grounds by eight o'clock tonight to sign in and make sure we had everything we needed. They scheduled our slot for tomorrow mid-afternoon on the small stage. We expected a big crowd even though it was a Friday slot, the first day of the festival. Thousands of music lovers attended every year. I heard people camped out as early as midweek.

The crowds at these multi-day events were hella crazy and could make or break Country Blue and any other hopefuls getting on a stage these next couple of days.

"If you fuckers weren't such slackers then we'd be done already," Doug yelled from the van.

Emotions obviously ran high, differing levels of anxiety plaguing all of us. It would make the long ride tense and testy. *I'm nervous. It didn't matter how easy it is for some of us to hide, we were all feeling it.*

Before getting on the highway, we stopped at a gas station and convenience store to fill the tank and grab snacks for the road. Colt pumped the gas while Berto and Doug were on snack and drink duty. I stayed outside propped against the van, not really in the mood to raid the shelves of junk food the guys were sure to bring back.

The trip, the slot at the festival, and Wyn, the lot of it made me fucking antsy. My current circumstances felt too new and unreal. Precarious. But I craved it all the same.

"Something on your mind, Tapiro?" I glanced to my right and Colt stood at the back of the van eyeing me.

"Nah, man, just thinking about random stuff." I didn't bring up Wyn. It wouldn't be the best idea, especially since I saw Doug and Berto already heading to the cash register with their hull of junk food. "You know how it is," I added.

He nodded as if he knew exactly what filled my mind. He just might. I had little doubt a certain perky redhead occupied his thoughts like a dark-skinned beauty with the sexiest voice consumed mine.

I heard a loud click. Colt tapped the hood of the van, turning around to put the pump back. Still stuck in my own head, I heard the fellas come out of the store, catching the tail-end of one of Berto's animated and borderline pornographic escapades.

"You need to be careful, man. One of these girls is gonna wisen up to all your philandering ways, cabrón, and string you up by the balls," Doug imparted like the big brother he tried to be to us. "I, for one, want first row seats to that show."

"Bullshit. You just want a look at my balls, mano." I knew he itched to make a vulgar gesture, but his hands were full. *Small favors*, I thought to myself.

Berto laughed as Doug knocked him against the van's passenger side door. Luckily no snacks were lost in their brief horseplay.

"Again, I just don't understand the appeal," I muttered.

"What can I say? The ladies love me." The words left their mouths at almost the same time. They looked at each other and roared with laughter. Good thing I've been with them a few months now or else I'd be dreading this long ass car ride. Even though they acted like little kids most of the time, they really were more like family. It was all harmless fun to them. They got serious when it counted. *Like brothers should act.*

I shook off the depressing thought and climbed in the back after Berto.

I planned to fiddle with a song idea or two stuck in my head. Talking to both Zion and Wyn the other night brought on the urge to write and finish one of my songs. It'd been difficult in past weeks even though pen and paper were never too far away.

*Time to work out some stuff rattling around in my mind.*

"What you working on, bro?" Doug turned around in the front passenger seat to look back at me, munching on chips he'd just shoved into his mouth. Colt's eyes focused on the road and Berto leaned against his window dozing. *Lucky sonofabitch.* I always had a hard time sleeping in moving vehicles, my brain wouldn't rest.

"A song's been rattling around in my head for a while. Hoping to tease it out."

"Well, keep writing, Rafe. I can't wait to hear what other good shit you got in that noggin of yours." He shifted to the front again, his attention back on his bag of chips and the highway.

I forced out a laugh which sounded awkward even to my own ears. It was just my luck they came across my notes the other day and saw what I'd been working on. Now, their comments about my writing almost felt like a daily occurrence when, in reality, it was hardly the case. I was being overdramatic, but a long history of negatives seemed to overshadow the positives.

We drove for a few minutes before getting on the highway heading north, our lead singer agreed to drive the first jaunt of our road trip. I offered to drive on the way back tomorrow night since I'd be ramped up after our turn on stage.

Looking down at the notations in my book, I got to work figuring out the lyrics and music rolling around in my noggin.

Adrenaline rushed through every part of my body. It fueled me. Felt fucking fantastic. We rocked the shit out of our set.

With my shirt, I wiped the sticky sweat clinging to my face and neck. *I should bring a towel on stage with me*, I mulled over. The idea held some appeal. My hair felt wet and glued to my skin even though I opted to have it out of the way, tied at my nape.

We were all drenched, pouring our hearts and souls out on the small outdoor stage. The slight wind did little to cool us.

Again, I considered cutting off a few inches, but liked having some length to my hair. Another thing about me my father would hate. *I don't know how I raised a goddamn pansy like you. You don't even play that fucking instrument to get laid, ya dumb shit!*

My father spat out much of the same anytime he saw me playing my bass around the house, booze wafting from his every pore. Even now, the stench of it permeated my nostrils like he was right next to me.

Dear old dad was a real class act for sure.

Tugging the band from my hair, I ran my fingers through it. Doug and Berto were a few feet ahead of me bouncing on their toes; they had so much energy left over. I couldn't blame them. Colt was not far behind me, taking his time like he did after every set.

I was still in awe. We never played together like that before, exploding with electricity and fire with each song. So far, there were only a few moments where I felt out of place with the guys. This had been different.

Our synergy was off the charts. The notes of our last song still vibrated through my veins. I wanted to share what I was feeling with my best friends, with Wyn. None of them were here right now, and I couldn't really contact any of them. Fear kept the need at bay.

The guys stopped just before the entrance to the talent VIP section, talking to someone up front. Before our set, we took a five-cent tour around the festival grounds. I hadn't really been paying attention, too wrapped up in my own head. I should take another lap around, maybe spend down this extra energy coursing through my body.

I'd seen some people from my studio musician days earlier, only counting a few of them as friends. I told one or two of them I'd try to catch them before the band got back on the road. This downtime seemed like the perfect opportunity. I'd search the VIP area or the festival grounds for however long and clear my head.

With my mind set, I walked up behind the guys and got a good look at who they talked to. Nick Ferrara, the ex-bassist for Country Blue and Colt's best friend, stood at the entrance to the roped off area with a beer in his hand and a shit-eating grin on his face.

*I'm not in the mood to deal with this prick.*

The guy's presence instantly grated on my heightened nerves. I didn't know why. Well, that was a damn lie.

I disliked the guy from jump because I knew a bully when I saw one. The chance to tell Wyn all I wanted to hadn't come around. Like how I accepted what happened to me a long time ago.

My childhood sucked, no question. It made me into the man I saw in the mirror every day, healed bruises and all.

But I hated bullies with everything in me. And assholes. Still hadn't decided if he was one or both. Either way, I'd interacted with Nick once before while working at a studio and the very brief encounter got under my skin.

That incident was enough for me.

Before I could excuse myself, Colt brushed past, knocking my shoulder, glad to see his friend. Shit, I couldn't just back away and disappear now. "Hey, Nick," he called.

"Colt, my man. Good to see you." They slapped palms and pounded one another on the back in a bro hug. I tried hiding most of my disdain for their brother, friend, and ex-bandmate. Some of Nick's beer sloshed out of the red cup and onto my leather boots and the grass below our feet. I stepped back, but he hadn't even registered his party foul.

*Right, asshole then.*

Colt mentioned hoping to see Nick's band perform on the grandstand stage. He had a few more hours to wait since Devil's Tea had a later slot; it was why we agreed to stick around for most of the day.

Since we had talent badges, we saw and heard some of the other performances from the separated area, leaving the craziness of the crowds to everyone else. I now craved an escape to those crowds.

"I caught a few minutes of your set earlier. Quite a few changes you guys are making. It's definitely a different sound for you, Colt. What brought it on?" Nick asked the guys, not even acknowledging my presence in the cluster we formed.

With a shrug he replied, "Well, ya know. We're trying some new stuff for a change." This guy annoyed the hell out of me. A huff-cough slipped from me, and Doug smacked me on the back.

Colt turned, bringing me into the fold and gesturing between the two of us. "Nick. Rafe. You two met?"

I was just about to remind him of our brief meeting at R&J Sound Recordings not too long ago when he leaned forward. "Nah, man. Ralph, was it?" he asked while pretending to shake my hand. Before letting go, he squeezed hard enough to get his point across. Guessed I was two for two. He was most definitely an asshole and a bully.

Why was I even surprised? Nowadays, I could pretty much peg someone from a mile away. I was thankful for all of my experiences up to date because they honed my bullshit meter. *It was time to be the bigger man and walk away*, I decided.

"So, hey. I'm gonna walk around the grounds for a bit. Hear some acts, see the sights." *Get away from this fucker.* "I'll catch you guys later. Meet back here by seven, yeah?" Berto looked down at his watch and then nodded. I thought I heard a "sounds good bro," but I'd already moved away from the group.

"Douchebag prick," I growled between clenched teeth. When I called Wyn the other night I'd been in a sour fucking mood. And just hearing her voice lifted me up. *I shouldn't make it a habit of calling her only when I'm pissed, even if I want to hear her voice all the time.*

I walked away from the VIP area, no destination in mind.

The chaos of the large crowds and loud music distracted me from my temporary ire.

Guys like Nick made me want to put my fist in someone's face. But the violent impulse wouldn't fix a damn thing. I was far removed from my father or brother who defaulted to violence for shits and giggles. *I learned early on that there are better ways to handle people like him.* He wanted to get to me. And so, I walked away.

I could've shown my strength, egged him on. I took his place and already made some changes, *for the better*, in such a short time with the band. At the end of the day, it wasn't worth it. He wasn't worth it.

I had a good deal going on with my new bandmates and didn't plan on fucking it up by getting into a pissing contest with their longtime buddy. I was smarter than that.

The strong aroma of marijuana assailed me as I passed by a cluster of kids at the very back of a large crowd. *Was I ever that fucking fearless and stupid?*

I walked on, wondering about the next performer as the crowd gathered in front of another small stage, waiting under the hot sun.

I saw a friend up ahead struggling with some heavy equipment. "Erik! Hey, need some help?" A little manual labor would do me some good right now.

"Rafe? Hey man! I won't say no." At my approach, he put down the large bundle of cords and amp he carried and shook my hand. "Long time, no see. How's it going?"

"I can't complain. Just got off-stage with the band I'm playing with and decided to take a walk around the grounds," I told him. Wiping my brow, I picked up the amp and got to work.

"Good deal, good deal. I got one more trip to make. You have time to catch up after?" Erik moonlighted as a roadie for his brother's band when they toured. In his own right, he was a kick-ass studio tech. The man knew his shit, and I counted him as a friend.

"Sounds good, man. Lead the way." This walk was turning out to be just what I needed.

The perfect distraction.

# Chapter Twelve
*Wyn*

Almost a week since our conversation and there'd been radio silence the last few days from Rafe. It was Tuesday evening and all my attention was on him.

And it really sucked. His surprise late-night phone call last week threw me for a loop. Then nothing. Probably because of me. Now, here I was second-guessing myself.

Whatever was happening seemed to have fizzled out due to my inept conversation skills. Maybe he didn't want the hassle of dealing with a girl with my issues.

*He's just busy, Wynter. Ever cross your mind?* My conscience questioned me.

Nope, I told myself. My mind headed straight for Kooky Town on a one-way ticket. I had no hope of bringing myself back to the world of sane people. Add in the fact that I became more neurotic as the days dragged on with zero contact from him. But why was I even surprised? *I worry about everything.* What he said or didn't say.

All of this just proved how much I liked Rafe.

*Wait, say what now?* I stopped in the middle of the hallway, on my way to the kitchen.

I couldn't like this guy that much. We hardly knew each other! One deep breath in, then out. Rinse and repeat.

On one end, I was dealing with circumstances beyond my control. On the other, I tried locking away heavy stuff for so long the ugliness of it continued to manifest in my dreams.

I should count it as a plus I hadn't heard from Rafe, needing a break from us circling around one another. A pause to stop fretting over his intentions towards me. A break from worrying, from looking over my shoulder all the damn time.

*From pretending to be okay.*

I'd been obsessing over every aspect of our interactions, the face-to-face and wireless alike. None of it good for me. The guy shook loose all the restless fears while wrangling my runaway hopes. He made me want things I couldn't have.

I had no business pining for him, wishing he thought about me enough to call or text. *Hopeless.* I was ridiculously hopeless and beyond frustrated with myself.

*Bang!* The loud crash came from the kitchen, jolting me right out of the pointless musing. I rushed to the living room and heard another round of clatter. A pained "oh frick" soon followed. Darcy looked down; her eyes glued to the tiled floor out of my view.

"What's with all the noise in here?" I peeked over the breakfast counter which separated the kitchen from the living room and my makeshift office space in the far corner. Darcy's head jerked up, wide green eyes meeting mine with what could only be morbid embarrassment. A flash of pain crossed her face when I was about to laugh.

*Oh shit.* She must've hurt herself.

"Dar? You okay?" I walked in the kitchen; my voice laced with worry. Darcy had always been clumsy, usually laughing off stuff like this. But at second glance, she looked ready to bawl her eyes out.

"Go sit down while I take care of this," I ordered, already heading to the pantry where we kept most of the cleaning supplies. The shards of one of our cheap plates lay scattered on the floor. "And for God's sake, watch your step please." She walked gingerly around the small kitchen area even though she wore thick socks.

"Wyn, I have something to tell you, okay?" Darcy asked in the softest voice ever, as she limped to the couch. I crouched down and started sweeping up the debris of the broken plate. The dejected tone in her voice worried me more than I wanted to admit.

"What's up?" I shouted from my position near the cabinets under the sink. I rushed through sweeping up the floor, wondering what she had to say.

Small and large shards littered the dustpan. The mess had me wishing for energy to give the entire kitchen floor a good cleaning.

The whole apartment, to be honest. Susie homemaker I was not, but I hadn't been myself lately and everything around me seemed to suffer.

After finishing, I rummaged around the kitchen and put an ice pack together, passing it over to Darcy then plopping down on the armchair of the couch.

Ready to listen, I waited for her to speak.

"An aquarium in California called me yesterday. They want me to work for them on a—" Darcy started tentatively.

Before she could finish, a loud whoop left my lips. I was so excited for her. Even though she just got home, I knew she looked forward to the next opportunity to work with her sea babies.

"That's great—" My excitement died a quick death as a pained expression crossed her face. I didn't think the look was only due to her foot. The shadows in her eyes told me something altogether different.

Darcy was always ecstatic about the next project or learning opportunity. She talked about doing this work for as long as we'd known each other. This wasn't like her at all.

*What am I missing here?*

"Dar, what's going on? Help me understand why you're not jumping for joy right now." I thought for a moment and got a little peeved. "And why am I just hearing about this job offer when you got the call yesterday?"

It made no sense feeling hurt because of this, right? We usually told each other everything. Now, she was keeping secrets.

*Pot meet kettle.*

But this wasn't about me. Not this time. Darcy needed her best friend right now. I turned off all the selfish thoughts running through my head and was there for my friend.

She propped her tender foot on a throw pillow I placed on the coffee table. I circled the piece of furniture and sat down on the other side of the couch.

I asked again, "What's going on?"

The floodgates opened. Darcy poured out her heart for what felt like hours, and I only caught half of what she said.

The gist was a former professor/mentor recommended her for this opportunity in California, and it sounded major, even to a clueless person like me. One part of the project included the chance to operate on a sea turtle with a cracked shell.

Holy hell, but the opportunity sounded life changing. Like a job my best friend wouldn't dream of passing up. She rushed on, "Then there's Colt. And gosh, Wyn, I really like him and think he likes me too. Like beyond friends, ya know. I don't think it's a good time to leave again. We're really just getting to know each other face to face. And I don't want to leave you again either. I was away for almost a year this last trip."

Darcy finished with a sad pout, burrowing into the sofa cushions.

"Wait. What about Colt now?" I must've misheard her. I could take care of myself although it didn't seem like it lately. *But Colt?* He was a much safer topic.

Was she seriously thinking about choosing a guy over her career? He seemed like a good guy, but how much did she really know about him? And did he know anything about Darcy's past? Her hopes or fears?

"What do you think I should do?" She asked earnestly. I didn't know what to say to her. Darcy loved her work beyond anything. Or so I thought. However, I also knew how much Colt had already come to mean to her.

A long moment passed. I tried finding the right words. Words to help guide my best friend and not cause her more stress in the process.

"Dar, I know we haven't talked much since you've been back, and I'm sorry." This year's had its ups and downs for both of us and for very different reasons.

"Wyn, that's not—" She interrupted my overdue apology.

"No, listen." I continued. "I haven't been around for you like I should be. I'm a sucky friend, I know it. I'm keeping it one hundred and I'll do better. But I need you to answer me honestly right now." Sitting up straight, she jerked her head in acknowledgement. "Do you want to take on this new project in California?" I saw her figuratively crawl into herself again before she gave me another nod.

I hummed. "Then you should. If Colt's the right guy, he won't disappear on you." The tears she held at bay the last few minutes finally fell, trailing down her freckled face. Her usually rosy cheeks were drained of color. I had verbalized her biggest fear, and it made me feel like a huge bitch. It needed saying, though. There was no time to sugarcoat, not with this.

"People do leave. They disappear. Forget about me. Always, Wyn. I-I-I don't want that to happen this time."

I couldn't lie and say it wasn't a possibility. You never really knew what was in someone's heart, what they were capable of.

I didn't know Colt. He seemed like a good enough guy. Soon, his music and band would take him far and wide. *It's just a matter of time.* Their fan base grew this past year, if their concert was anything to go by.

Was Darcy planning to put her career on hold for a would-be relationship? I didn't think she wanted that for herself. I turned to look at her, hunkered down on the couch. We needed BFF time. It was long overdue.

"Talk to me, Dar." Her indecision worried me more than I could say. She's been the steady rock in this dynamic duo for so long. It was about time I returned the favor. My best friend needed me. We needed each other.

Mild exhaustion weighed me down. My heart and mind were equal parts fulfilled and frustrated. The talk with Darcy was tougher than expected.

So much revealed, however not nearly enough. No resolutions or major decisions made. We talked for hours, both of us getting stuff off our chests. I neglected to bombard her with the one crucial incident plaguing my own spirit these past ten months. It hurt not to tell her. It just wasn't the right time. She had enough of her own worries to deal with.

All my crap would've cracked her. Broken something in both of us even more. That night had meant something different to her. She told me how safe and secure she felt wrapped in Colt's arms. He expected only what she offered him. How they were just able to be with each other with no strings.

A slither of hope blossomed in her since meeting Colt. The current limbo she found herself in notwithstanding. My secret would just darken an already precarious spot. I couldn't do it. Not now.

In a weird way, I was happy she got hurt in the kitchen earlier. I never wished harm on my best friend, but our conversation obviously needed to happen. We both had stuff bottled up and at the cusp of spilling over.

We hadn't really talked in a while. Shared our hopes and dreams, the new and not-so-new. Our fears and insecurities. Our family drama came up whenever heavy shit weighed on us. A whole other heap of baggage both of us needed to wade through. The same but different.

Colt and Rafe claimed most of our conversation. Neither of us knew what the hell to do. This was all new territory. Even though our teenage years were behind us, neither me nor Darcy got the dating bug in high school. She focused on her studies, and I was too quiet and flew way under the radar to catch anyone's interest.

Both men confused and intrigued us, even without it being their intention. Darcy had one leg up on me because she'd at least maintained a friendship, by way of chats and emails, with Colt. But it sounded like she'd only learned a little about the man through their exchanges. Imagining an iceberg, I thought about how only the tip showed while there was still so much underneath the surface of the water.

Like me, her first real date was the double date last week, so they were just starting out too. Darcy and I were in the same boat, figuratively speaking, and it sucked big time.

We ended up ordering from our favorite Chinese restaurant, eating dinner on the couch while we talked. A good option since I hated the idea of cooking right now, and she couldn't stand on her left ankle for longer than a few minutes.

I told Darcy she needed to do what was right for her. Her relationship with Colt might work or it might not. Neither of us could predict the future. But she couldn't give up on a passion that drove her for most of her life.

She decided to give the California offer a few more days of thought, having the foresight to tell the director of the aquarium she'd give them an answer by Monday. Darcy had several days to make up her mind.

I wanted her to take the job. Since I've known her, she dreamed about this career. She needed to continue pursuing those dreams. What if she came to resent him or the other way around because the other's career goals took a backseat? Colt's music career held precedence for him, from my understanding. She had to do what made her happy and hopefully, at some point, they'd somehow meet in the middle. *And if it's meant to be...*

My issues hadn't quickly resolved themselves either. And I knew they wouldn't.

We hugged for a long time after the talk. I finally got up to put away our leftovers. Darcy stayed on the couch for a while longer, keeping her foot elevated. We both needed to clear our heads. She turned on the TV and settled on a popular sitcom from the nineties.

I closed the door to my room and sat on the edge of my bed, falling back on the mattress, my socked feet remaining on the carpeted floor. My heart jackhammered in my chest, unable to settle down. *What the hell did I just do?*

On the way to my room, I sent off a brief text to Rafe asking how he was. The act was so out of character for me. But I missed him and wanted to reach out.

The room became too quiet as my growing anxiety suddenly battled for dominance. I didn't do spontaneous well, apparently. I hit the button on my clock radio, forcing myself out of bed. R&B currently played on one of my favorite stations. On Tuesday nights, they played slow jams. I moved to the crooner's melodic voice while I got ready for bed.

I couldn't worry about it now. I went to my dresser as the DJ introduced the next song. His deep voice mentioned someone named Brenda missing her boyfriend who served overseas. Swaying to the early nineties' girl group singing about men being gone too long, I grabbed my favorite sweatpants and paired them with a camisole.

Finished in the bathroom, I walked back to my room and tied a silk scarf around my head. I'd almost missed the ringtone of my phone as the radio played on low. I looked over at the clock and couldn't figure out who'd call at this hour. *Oh crap!* I shivered, reminded of my text to Rafe only half an hour ago.

Taking a deep, shaky breath, I swiped the screen's icon before the call went to voicemail. "Hello?"

# Chapter Thirteen
*Rafe*

Like our first call, rustling came over the line before Wyn's breathy greeting. Music to my ears. *And is that actual music playing in the background too?*

Her text message a few minutes ago surprised the hell out of me. I'd planned on contacting her again this week, but with spending my days back in the studio as a tech, I forgot how wiped out it left me. Why the hell had I said yes to Erik in the first place?

When her name popped up on my phone screen nothing could stop me from calling her. She initiated contact this time which I figured worked in my favor.

*Don't get too excited, Tapiro. Let's see how receptive she is first.*

True to form, as soon as her low, sultry voice came over the line I was a goner. It got me every time.

I calmed my two heads down while struggling to find words. "Hey, Wyn. How are you?"

"I'm okay, Rafe. What about you?" I wondered what she listened to, hoping my ears caught a melody or familiar lyrics. She turned the volume down so low it was near impossible to hear. I always said the music a person listened to at home said a lot about them. I wanted to get to know her on that level and every other.

"I'm good. The last couple of days have been busy. I ran into a friend at the festival we played this weekend. He put me to work in the recording studio as a technician for a few days." I tried hiding the fatigue from my voice.

"Sounds really cool. Do you do studio tech work often then?" She hesitated. Her question revved me up and got the blood racing through my veins.

"From time to time nowadays." I hadn't done it since joining Blue, deciding to focus more on my music. Not just helping others mix theirs. The paycheck from the two fourteen-hour shifts during the last forty-eight hours wouldn't hurt though. "It's been really good hanging out with my friend, Erik, again too. We went through the same program together."

The random run-in with him had been a good surprise. The sneaky bastard had no problem roping me into a minimum of two days of labor. But I had desperately needed the distraction. Now, I was damned tired.

"Hmm," the low sound teased my ears during a quiet moment. I jumped right into my reason for calling.

"I had a great time the other night, Wyn," I said. Mr. Suave I was not, dead tired from those two shifts and band practice. It wasn't my best line ever. I hoped she focused on my earnestness.

"Me too, Rafe." Those words and my name leaving her lips felt like heaven on earth while I paced my studio apartment. Even though the night started off awkward, the four of us eventually found our stride around each other. It only took some silliness and a few games of pool.

"I'd like to repeat it." A rough whisper escaped when I was actually going for more of the boy-next-door vibe. Her quiet affirmation, though, had me feeling like goddamn Superman taking flight with his main squeeze.

"Oh, another double date? I'll talk with Dar about it, and she can mention it to Colt." Surprise and a hint of wariness laced her rushed reply. At least it hadn't been an automatic *no*. I wasn't opposed to another double date, per se, but I wanted to cut out the middlemen altogether.

This time around, I was after some alone time with Wyn.

Of course she misunderstood me. *Well, why wouldn't she? A pansy like you can't do anything right. Even the simple act of asking her out on a fucking date.* The voice in my head sounded eerily like my father, and I didn't need his hypermasculinity bullshit messing with me right now. *Get it together, Tapiro.* I hyped myself up, getting back on track. Time to be more direct.

"No, that's not what I meant. I'd like to take you out... just the two of us this time."

Learning more about Wyn was my primary objective. We didn't need our friends there to run interference. They were safety nets. And if I had any chance, I needed to do this on my own.

I wasn't usually a selfish, presumptuous bastard. I just wanted her all to myself.

Tumbleweeds blew across the invisible line connecting us as she got quiet. Too quiet. I could almost hear the spikes in her breathing. My asking-a-girl-out-on-a-date skills needed some brushing up because I seemed to be failing at it. I felt way out of my depth with this girl. The too-long hesitation and real possibility of Wyn's rejection weighed heavy on my shoulders through the extended silence.

With one last ditch effort, my brain decided it would have diarrhea of the mouth. "I know it's late notice, but would you like to go out with me this Thursday? I've been meaning to ask you out again. The last few days have been hectic since I was helping my friend." *Shut up, Tapiro. You're blowing this!* "If this Thursday doesn't work then maybe we can try this weekend."

I zipped my mouth shut and forced myself to wait her out.

"O-okay," she murmured. The single stuttered word was unmistakable and so fucking good to hear.

"Yeah?" My body relaxed, releasing the tension holding it hostage. I let out a relieved sigh, a mix of disbelief and awe settling around me. Wyn surprised me often, keeping me on my toes without even knowing it.

"Yes, I'd like that." *Fucking-A that's the best sentence I've heard all day.* "And Friday would be better for me. Does that work for you?"

*Hell yes!* "Yeah, of course. Our next gig is on Saturday, so Friday works great." Colt set practice for Friday and Saturday afternoon so I wouldn't have to worry about it too much.

Again, her reticence cautioned me to slow my roll on this one. And I would try my damnedest to let her take the reins, so to speak. I wanted her to feel comfortable around me. "Okay, it's a date then. Send me your address when you get a chance. I'll pick you up on Friday at seven."

"Okay. I'm gonna get ready for bed now. I guess I'll see you soon."

"Sweet dreams, Wyn." I ended the call after her whispered *good night, Rafe.* My week was definitely looking up.

Now, all this energy racing through my body needed an outlet. I walked to the other corner of my apartment, sat down at my desk and tried focusing this pent-up energy on my songs.

The midnight oil would burn tonight.

*Dammit!* We were ending practice later than I anticipated. The hours slipped by me with little notice of the time. We'd hit another stride and kept churning out the tunes. Doug's rumbling stomach at a quiet point between songs got our attention. I had the good sense to drive my truck to rehearsal today. Usually I hitched a ride with Colt since I lived between him and downtown.

It was already after six as I finished packing up my equipment. The guys were taking their sweet ass time when I didn't have that luxury.

"Yo, Sonic. You're in quite the hurry." Leave it to one of them to razz me right now. "What's the rush? Hot date?"

"Actually, yeah." I snapped my bass in the battered case I've had for years and hoisted all my stuff. "Later," I called over my shoulder.

As I made my way to the exit, smooching noises reached my ears. I paid them little mind. With all the shit in my arms turning the knob was damn near impossible, so I paused to ask for help. Colt already headed my way. Realizing my predicament, the guy decided not to act like a child and instead helped a friend out.

Home in record time, I practically tossed my shit to the floor and headed straight for the shower. It must've been one of the quickest scrubdowns in history because I was out of there in under three minutes.

Grabbing a pair of jeans hanging off my ladder bookcase, I gave them a sniff to make sure it was all copacetic. I snatched up my favorite tee from the corner of my bed and searched around for a decent button down to go over it. Leather jacket in hand, I headed out the door.

I shot a text over to Wyn, letting her know I was a little behind schedule. While I raced across town, no telltale notification lit up my phone. I ran a red light *or two* getting over to her apartment complex, keeping the minor transgressions to myself, figuring Wyn for a goody two shoes. *An idiot I am not.*

I took the stairs to her second-floor apartment two at a time and headed for her door. Waiting after three knocks, I tried composing myself by catching my breath.

Her complex was in a nice neighborhood, a twenty-minute drive from the heart of downtown. Before long, I heard some shuffling inside the apartment and the deadbolt unlocking. The door crept open. Once I got my first head-to-toe look at her in the entryway, she left me speechless just like all the other times.

*Shit! I'm in more trouble than I realized.* Wyn looked fucking amazing standing there. The backdrop of warm lighting from inside the apartment surrounded her in this ethereal and innocent glow.

I refused to rush this part, taking her in from boots to braids and then back again. The burgundy color of her dress complimented the rich, dark tone of her skin. She wore black tights although the dress hit her knees. The black boots accentuated her plentiful curves, finishing her sexy but sweet outfit to perfection. Wyn wore her braids half up, half down. I studied her pretty, round face for a long moment and noticed she'd put on a hint of makeup. Whatever she did suited her just fine.

*I'm a lucky S.O.B. tonight.*

"Hi." She jiggled the set of keys she held in her right hand, then fiddled with her open clutch in the other. She was nervous. From my lustful gaze or something else… I didn't know. I forced my one-track mind on important matters, like sweeping this girl off her feet tonight.

Picking my jaw up from the floor, I closed my mouth and returned her greeting. "Hey. You look great," the compliment coming quickly because it needed saying. All the time if I could help it. "Are you ready to go?"

I would've liked to see the inside of her place, but time was an issue due to my unexpected lateness. Reservations were for seven thirty and the restaurant I chose was about a fifteen-minute drive from Wyn's place. There was no reason to push my luck anymore.

"Thank you. You too. Look great, I mean," she said with a shy smile. "Yes, I'm ready." I moved back as she stepped out. Wyn hadn't yelled back into the apartment, so I assumed Darcy was elsewhere tonight. Colt hadn't mentioned any plans with her, but I did leave practice like the hounds of hell were snapping at my heels.

Wyn closed the door and locked it. She dropped her keys in the clutch and looked up at me. *Okay. Right. Time to wow her with your date-making plans, Tapiro.* I gave myself a mini pep talk, barely resisting the urge to rub my clammy hands together.

The car ride was quiet yet not too uncomfortable. She still seemed unsure of me. I hoped tonight banished some of her shyness. I had the radio tuned to a classic rock station and caught Wyn's knees twitching and bouncing.

*Similar taste in music, check.*

We arrived at the restaurant in record time, finding and squeezing my truck into the last spot in their small parking lot. I moved fast enough around the rear to get Wyn's door. She thanked me as I helped her down, and we walked the few steps to the restaurant. The steady click-clack of her shoes acted as our soundtrack.

The hostess sat us down immediately since we were right on time for our reservation. Our table was near one of the windows framed by dark curtains, parallel to the sidewalk. The dim lighting lent to the dining area's overall intimate ambiance. Although most of the tables had patrons, there was the illusion of being in our own private nook.

Wyn played with the inside of her plump bottom lip as she reviewed the menu. Damn, this girl tempted me like no other. I considered breaking the promise I made to myself a few weeks ago about taking this slow and steady. Wyn's cute mannerisms made it damned difficult though.

The eatery I selected for tonight was a small, family-owned Italian restaurant. The waitress came back around to take our order and left with the menus. I decided for an easy start to the conversation.

"Are you originally from this area, Wyn?" I took a sip of water to show I wasn't in any real hurry for an answer.

A server promptly delivered our glasses of wine and a basket of assorted bread to our table. She placed the white napkin on her lap then looked up at me with the slightest smile teasing her lips.

"I moved around a lot growing up." Wyn shrugged her shoulders with the vague comment. "I lived a couple hours from here for half my life, since middle school. That's where I met Darcy." I opened my mouth to pose a follow-up question when she asked, "Are you from here?"

"No, I grew up in Chicago. Most of my family still lives there. Zi and his parents." I needed to make more of an effort to get back there to visit. There was really no other reason to make the trip except to see the Wallaces.

"I've been to Chicago a few times. I like the big city vibe since I lived in New York for a short time when I was younger. There's always so much going on. Non-stop it seems like." I watched some of her nervousness dissipate as she talked. It was good to see her like this. "Do you have plans to go back soon?"

Her question brought me back to my previous thought. "I need to but not yet." I ran my fingers once through my hair. "Before I joined, the band played a few gigs in the city, and I think Colt is looking for opportunities to go back." *We'll see.* Although I had no intention of visiting the house I grew up in, I still had family in Chicago who cared about me. I had to remember that.

"Oh, cool." Before I could tease more personal information out of her, she continued. "So, how was the festival last weekend? Did your set go well?" I didn't mind Wyn's questions. If it set her at ease to control the flow of conversation, then I was game for it.

Our food arrived, the server carefully setting hot dishes in front of us. I placed the cloth napkin in my lap and tried replying to Wyn before taking a bite of my penne alla vodka with chicken. I signaled to let her know it was fine to start on her seafood alfredo. We both paired a glass of wine with our dishes. She ordered white while I decided on a red.

"Yeah. Me and the fellas played well. I think the crowd enjoyed themselves." *We just keep getting better.* I didn't voice the statement out loud, scared to jinx the band and how well we've been getting along.

"I've kinda always wanted to go to one of those festivals, ya know. But, in all honesty, I prefer hearing music in the smaller venues the best," she added in a quiet tone.

"Yeah, there's nothing like a small crowd. It makes the exchange more intimate. But I won't knock the opportunity to play in front of hundreds or thousands of people either." I chuckled. "The festival was great. The crowd had a bunch of energy and our set went really well, actually." The impression that my life finally headed in a good direction popped into my head again. The corner of my mouth twitched. It felt good.

We already covered most of the usual *get to know you* questions during our first meeting and phone conversations. I wasn't really a *chat on the phone* type of guy usually, but Wyn was different. Our conversations continued to surprise and unsettle me, especially with how comfortable they've been from the start.

I'd hoped we could recreate a similar ease during this date. *The night isn't over. Patience, Tapiro.*

"Mm…" The forkful of pasta froze midway to my mouth

because the sexiest sounds were coming from the other side of the table. From Wyn's lips. And I concluded right then that this dinner would be the sweetest and most hellish experience of my life.

My unabashed leering went unchecked as she whispered a decadent *yum* under her breath next. A pained groan rumbled from deep in my chest. She was killing me and didn't even fucking know it.

I prayed for some restraint before I jumped over the table and ravished her. *Spooked her, more likely.* A woman tucking into her food and actually enjoying it was a damn sexy sight. It was a long moment before I took my eyes off her and focused on my own plate. Every noise out of her mouth had my two heads working in overdrive. Wyn had me all heated up and revving to go. I needed to slow down and get us talking again.

"Did you enjoy your meals, miss, sir?" The server asked a half hour later as she came around to collect our silverware and empty plates. "Would you like to see the dessert menu?"

Wyn sipped the last of her wine. I settled back in my chair and looked to her for a response. She wiped her lips with the cloth napkin and shook her head. "No, thank you. I'm full." She giggled at the innocent admission.

"I'll be right back with your check," she nodded and walked away.

"It's still early. Would you mind if we drive around for a while before I take you home?" I hoped my question sounded harmless enough. I wanted more time to get to know her. Her brisk nod told me she didn't want our date to end either. Our server returned, placing the check holder on the table. I retrieved my wallet and waved off Wyn's attempt to split.

I asked her out and *a gentleman always pays when it's his idea!* The words in my nonna's accented voice whispered in my ear like she was sitting next to me.

I exited the restaurant with no real destination in mind. But after sitting behind the wheel again, I knew exactly where I wanted to take her.

To my favorite spot just outside of town.

We got on I-69 and drove for a few miles before taking the nearest exit to our destination. Once we hit the rural road, I flicked on the truck's high beams. There was no one else on the two-lane road at this hour. A few minutes into the drive we stopped as flashing red lights alerted us to an oncoming train.

I knew we'd sit here for several minutes, so I turned to Wyn. Not wanting to waste this prime opportunity. "How was your week?"

"Oh, um, it was okay. Work's been busy, but that's due to the time of year." She fidgeted with the clutch on her lap. I stopped the nervous tick with a hand on her left arm, wanting to calm her jitters. She stared at my hand for a few seconds before focusing her eyes back on the road. "Oh, the train's passed."

I zoned in on her, the noise of the evening cargo train becoming a distant memory. As the railroad level crossing lifted, I took my foot off the brakes and continued down the road.

We drove for another mile while I watched for the turnoff onto a well-hidden access road. The road led us to what looked like a maintained open field. I drove the truck a few hundred feet then swung it around. Turning off the ignition, I hopped out and walked over to Wyn's side. She jumped down on her own before I could reach her and looked around.

The stars were vibrant and beautiful, twinkling in the night sky just for us.

"This isn't the part where you kill me, is it?" she quipped.

I chuckled, shaking my head. She had this quiet humor about her that I liked. It came out more with every interaction.

"Not at all, sweetheart. I wanna show you something." My hand found hers across the short distance. Her slim, dainty fingers caressed then laced with mine.

Despite her joke, what she didn't know was that I'd take care of her. Any way I could. *If only she let me in.*

I led us a few steps forward in the near dark, only the stars and the moon's shadow illuminating the way. One more step and she'd see what I wanted to show her.

Funnily enough, it never crossed my mind to drive any of the other girls I dated up here since finding this spot. Too special for me to bring just any girl. But I knew Wyn wasn't just anybody.

"Oh wow," she gasped, astonishment clear in her voice. The view was amazing here. We were on the top of a small hill overlooking the creek below. This was one of my favorite places. I came up here sometimes to think, play, relax and write.

Once we got in the truck after dinner, I knew I wanted to share this place with Wyn.

"It's beautiful," she added.

"Yeah, I love it here." I spoke into the beautiful night. "The view,

the quiet. It centers me when I need the time to just relax... think."
Usually I came in the daytime. Brought one of my guitars and played.
If I sat around long enough, the scenery would inspire me for hours.
During my visits, I often heard the laughter and happiness of the
families and groups of friends down by the creek. Sometimes I'd
even find myself jealous at the scenes below, wishing I had what
those couples or families had.

Not now.

This time with Wyn was all about possibilities.

I studied her expressions as she looked down at the creek and
surrounding areas. Wonder shone on her face. It was a beautiful
sight, seeing her this open.

"Thanks for bringing me here, Rafe. It's breathtaking."

*So are you.*

"Glad you like it. Let's go back to the truck. I'll put down the
tailgate and we can sit for a while. Sound good?"

"Yeah, sure." We walked back the few feet to my truck, the glow
from the moon lighting our way. Once I helped her onto the bed, I
hopped up after her. My palms itched from holding her at the waist
for those few moments. Impulsively grabbing her left hand, I
brought it over to rest on my leg.

The moon provided just enough light for us to see each other.
"Tell me more about yourself, Wyn."

"Hmm." Her gaze settled on our entwined fingers; her eyes rose
to mine seconds after my question. "I don't know if there's any more
to tell. I'm pretty boring, actually."

"That's hard to believe."

"Oh, it's true," she nodded. Wyn worked from home, yes, but
that just made her more interesting to me. "What about you? Besides
playing with Country Blue now, what do you like to do?"

"I'm a stereotypical musician, I guess. I play constantly, even
when I'm not set with a band. Sometimes I get hours helping friends
at various studios." I hesitated to tell her about my songwriting, not
yet at least.

"Oh, cool. You have an associate degree?"

"Yeah." School had always been such a headache and a means to
an end. I got the feeling that Wyn was a bookworm, so I kept my
horrible student days to myself.

"Nice. I have my associate's too. I worked for a few offices
before going out on my own as a virtual assistant." She impressed

me even more.

"When did you decide to pursue music full time?"

"I've always known I wanted to be a musician. Ever since my music teacher handed me that guitar in middle school, I was hooked. Me and some friends even put a band together in high school. Zion was our manager since he couldn't play an instrument worth a damn." I shook my head at the memories. "We didn't last long due to creative differences." Wyn chuckled along with me.

"But yeah, these last couple of years I've spent all hours of the day working to fine-tune other people's music. I wanted to be a part of something I could make my own."

"I get that."

Wyn wore her hair in a loose ponytail that continued unraveling throughout the evening. I watched as one slim braid finally escaped and landed on her cheek. I grabbed it between my forefinger and thumb, slipping it behind her ear. She gasped as my fingers lingered on her cheek, turning her curious eyes to my face where her focus remained for a long stretch of time.

A cool breeze blew past and she shivered, a noticeable chill in the air now.

I shrugged off my jacket and draped it around her shoulders. I felt like an ass for not doing it sooner. Wyn wasn't wearing a jacket to combat the cooling weather. "You ready to go home?"

"Sure." She inched her ample bottom closer to the edge of the flatbed, and I helped her off, taking any excuse to put my hands on her. "Thank you again for bringing me here, Rafe."

*My pleasure.* I nodded and walked her around to the passenger side.

We carried on the laid-back conversation during the twenty-minute drive back to her apartment complex. In my head, I pumped my fist in the air and danced a little jig. She was opening up.

Wyn seemed more comfortable with me as we continued to talk and share things about ourselves. Even our silences were companionable, no longer tinged with awkwardness and anxiety.

I parked the truck in an open visitor spot, intending to walk Wyn to her door. Without words, we found our hands floating towards each other.

An intangible attraction.

We'd made it to her front door too fast; I wanted to stop time and stay in this moment a little while longer. Wyn opened her clutch to retrieve her keys. I stood there awkward as hell, wanting to kiss her again so damn bad, yet fighting my instincts. Fucking this up was not an option. I didn't want us to lose this forward progress. *The potential for even more.*

When she turned back around to say goodnight, I watched a curious expression cross her face. Like she'd just made an important decision.

Next thing I knew she was two steps closer, her hands finding their way to my shoulders, the grooves of her keys grinding into the thin layers on my left side. I didn't care. What mattered was Wyn's furtive approach.

She tiptoed to me, aiming her chin up and in my direction. I bent down to meet her halfway as she moved the last inch to place her ultra-soft lips on mine.

Her mouth opened on a slight gasp. Sparks jumped between us this close together. I took the small invitation. There was the taste of the Italian food and wine we had earlier, but also a hint of caramel. I liked it. The flavor described how I saw Wyn in a nutshell. Soft and sweet.

I didn't pretend to know what I did to deserve this, but *'Please, God. Keep it coming.'* My hands found their way to her waist, planning to hold on for as long as she'd let me.

I hadn't expected quite this ending to the night, but I for damn sure wouldn't squander the opportunity to drink from Wyn's lips. I was all in when it came to her.

# Chapter Fourteen
*Wyn*

It was hard to explain what came over me as I inched closer to Rafe. The brazen urge lasted only a heartbeat, my lips pressing so softly against his firm ones. The need to kiss him on my terms was at the forefront of my mind, and I didn't want to take it back. Then he took control. And I hung on for the ride.

His hands moved to my hips. My heart skipped several beats. *Gah, this man put ideas in my head. Things I didn't think I'd want to experience anymore.* I needed to get a grip.

I eased back on my heels, regretting the retreating motion because I was leaving the comfort of his arms. His lips followed mine for a second before moving back and letting go.

"Um…" I stalled, trying to get my brain functioning again. Our kiss was practically chaste, I tried telling myself. Just an innocent, prolonged press of lips.

*With a little tongue action!* My inner voice taunted me. The lack of oxygen in my lungs and the tingling sensation on my lips called me a liar too.

"That was… unexpected." He seemed to have the same breathing problem as me. "And phenomenal." He added a moment later.

My lips twitched. *How does he do it?* I wondered how he knew the right words to say. Words that wouldn't cause a total freak-out, like the ones that seemed to seize my entire body at the drop of a hat nowadays.

I'd been nervous the whole night, but in a good way. There was a comfort level with him I hadn't felt before with anyone else. Although we didn't get to talk much over dinner, I found myself enjoying the food and his company. Before he picked me up earlier, I told myself to keep an open mind and heart. The pep talk seemed to work its magic on me, making me feel almost normal again.

It'd been easier to talk with him face to face tonight. More natural. I still had a long way to go, yet I was optimistic. Rafe made me want to get back to the person I used to be. And his steadfast interest made it easy to hope.

The unexpected romance of the evening surprised me. I didn't know what to think, just going along for the ride. And Rafe driving us to the hill overlooking that magnificent scene was the cherry on top of a wonderful date.

*Just breathtaking.*

The cool night air zipped through the thick layer of my dress, a cold reminder that we stood outside. We watched each other, unspoken emotions passing between us. I took another step back. "Rafe, did you want to come in for a while?"

I was a habitual night owl during the weekend, and it hadn't yet turned eleven. And if I was being honest with myself, I didn't want our date to end yet.

It was easy to talk to Rafe. I wanted to learn more about him. Plus, Darcy was out of town and I buzzed with so much unspent energy.

A shocked look crossed his face. "Yeah, sure. Great." He overemphasized the T and I almost giggled. Maybe I imagined his look, it disappeared so quickly. Rafe wasn't the only one surprised by the offer. "Lead the way," he said. I turned the knob since I'd unlocked the door just before our kiss.

We stepped over the threshold into the apartment.

*My sanctuary.*

The short entryway led us straight into the living room. My favorite space in the entire apartment. It wasn't because my office nook in the corner sat opposite the kitchen area. No, the large open space was my spot because it included both mine and Darcy's design touches, different as could be.

When we first moved in together Darcy nicknamed me *Mismatched.* I had a nerdy fondness for unique and tacky furniture and got a kick out of the name back then. *I was actually darn proud of it.*

Looking around, I tried seeing the room through Rafe's eyes. Still thinking the pieces I chose added a smidge of character to the large space.

What Darcy described as a fugly loveseat sat perpendicular to her large couch. I found the two-seater at a secondhand store for a steal three years ago and immediately fell in love with its funky patchwork. It looked like a rainbow and a quilt had a baby and their baby threw up all over the loveseat.

It was a beautiful mess.

An oversized carpet took up a third of the floor, another one of my great finds at a local thrift shop. Darcy tried taking over decorating after she saw what I was bringing in. Now, she stopped bothering since she traveled so much. A game I started over two years ago was to bring home small and interesting finds and wait until Darcy noticed them.

My most recent and favorite addition was a lamp stand in the shape of a howling wolf. The handmade item sat on the end table between the couch and loveseat. I found it right before Darcy left for Scotland. I related to the yearning, the desolate loneliness I saw in the animal's small but detailed features.

*It still spoke to me.*

I dropped my clutch on the breakfast counter and turned to Rafe. "Can I get you a drink?" I planned on making myself a cup of tea.

"A glass of water would be great, Wyn." Rafe continued looking around while I walked into the kitchen. "Where's Darcy tonight?"

"She's out of town this weekend."

What I didn't say was that my friend flew to California last minute to tour the facilities of a possibly new project. I kept the information to myself, almost positive she hadn't share it with Colt.

It was just me and Rafe alone in the apartment.

*Why the thought didn't cause one of my instant panic attacks was beyond me.*

"I see you have a sweet tooth," he said. I peeked over the counter as he nodded at the bowl on my desk filled with candy.

"Yeah, I can't resist caramels." I craved them while I worked. *Who am I kidding? All hours of the day, really.* "Take one if you want," I offered. Hearing his snicker, I ignored it and focused on my reason for coming into the kitchen in the first place.

I put the kettle on and got two cups down from the cupboard.

*What the hell am I doing?* These last few minutes finally hit me like a freight train. A man I hardly knew stood in my apartment waiting on me. I wondered if I was of sound mind when the invitation had left my mouth.

I wasn't ready for this and yet here I was. Here *we* were.

*What the hell am I doing?*

No answer magically came to mind after repeating the question.

The kettle whistled which meant I'd stood in the kitchen looking into space for the past three minutes. *Ugh, I'm losing it.* I tossed a tea bag in my mug, pouring the hot water. Opening the fridge, I finally retrieved the water pitcher and poured some in a glass for Rafe.

*Calm down. Breathe, Wyn.*

I walked back into the living room, claiming a corner on the couch and sitting down carefully. The absolute last thing I wanted to do was spill my tea. Mishaps like that were never fun or flirty.

*There won't be any flirting!* That's why I stayed clear of my beloved tacky loveseat. I didn't know how to flirt. It was an art form I never learned about in school.

Rafe took a seat on the other end of the couch and picked up his glass from the coffee table where I'd placed it. Some of my wariness returned even though he hadn't given me any reason to be on guard.

*He can still surprise you. Hurt you. You don't know what he's capable of.* The thoughts warned me to remain cautious; however, I finally realized the paranoia was taking over my life. This was no way to live. That bastard won if I continued torturing myself.

We sat on the couch, neither of us saying a word. I wanted to make the most out of this situation… inviting him into my home. It was time to relax and get to know Rafe better. Besides what I learned at dinner tonight.

I blew on my tea, taking a sip. "Tell me about your life back in Chicago. You said your best friend still lives there?" I pulled my leg up under me and got more comfortable. Rafe turned his body toward me and stretched his arm over the back of the couch.

I asked questions when I was out of my depth like this. It was another sign I was getting back to my normal self. *The inquisitive mind should never be idle,* my grandfather liked to say.

"Well. Honestly, if I talk about Zion, I can't not talk about his little sister, Chloe. Even though me and Zi hated her tagging along when we were kids. We could never shake her." It sounded like brother and sister were a packaged deal. "I have some pretty great childhood memories, all things considered. All due to Zi and his family." He chuckled then quieted. His expression turned sad and I wondered if he thought about the abuse he'd endured at the hands of his father and brother. I still got angry for young Rafe. No child deserved abuse like that. Ever.

"The last year has been hell for the Wallaces." Rafe shifted, seeming uncomfortable with the conversation, he reached for his water glass and took a healthy sip. "Zion had a bad accident around the holidays last year and it left him in a wheelchair. Chloe blames herself."

My mug sat in the dip of my chunky thighs, still warm, and practically forgotten. "Oh, God. Is he, like, okay? I-I'm sorry to hear about Zion but..." I hesitated, not wanting to upset him further. "I don't get it. Why does Chloe blame herself for his accident?"

"Chloe was always a good kid. She's a few years younger than us, so we kept a close eye on her. As we all got older, Zi and I became super overprotective I guess." He shrugged.

"People thought twice before messing with her and it's the way we liked it." I imagined Rafe being great in his role of protective older brother. "Of course, she wasn't happy about us 'always getting in her business,'" Rafe said with air quotes. "She rebelled a lot. Got into some trouble. It amazed us just how much trouble she found. Yet everyone said it was just a phase. Then, one day she was back to her old self again. No explanation. No fuss."

"All too soon, we were back at the drawing board. She became closed off. Scared way too easily. Whenever we got her out of the house, she was always looking over her shoulder." Cold shivers raced up my back. His story had my full attention.

"Chloe withdrew from her family, from me." Rafe sighed. "I couldn't understand what was going on with her. She wouldn't talk to any of us. Not even her brother." The tension was all there in Rafe's body, his voice. He had even more memories haunting him. More recent, just like me. "Me and Zi were playing ball in his driveway one day when she found us. I remember Chloe shaking uncontrollably, tears streaming down her face. It's when she told us what was happening to her."

Rafe recalled how afraid Chloe looked standing in front of them. Shaken to her core. She told them she was being watched. Someone out there was stalking her, and she had no idea who they were or what they wanted.

I had a difficult time imagining myself in her situation with all my equilibrium taken away—my safety called into question—by an unknown. It was bad enough I let fear—these nightmares—hold me back from the normal *me*. I couldn't fathom the hell Chloe continued to go through, shaking my head at the thought. And her brother getting hurt at the end. I clutched my chest while he continued.

"Oh, God. That's horrible. I'm so sorry, Rafe." My words were useless and small, even to my own ears. Before I realized the action, my hand landed on his bent knee closest to me. It was instinctual.

"Yeah. Zi's accident was her last straw. Chloe had already decided to leave town as soon as Zi woke up from his last surgery before Christmas. She left a note at the house." *Why'd she feel like her only option was to run away, leave her family?* "She didn't want anyone else hurt because of her. The sonofabitch in the other car got away; cops still have no leads. She's positive it was the guy stalking her." He ran fingers through his hair, a sign of his obvious frustration. "Chloe calls me every few weeks to check in and I relay the message to Zi and their parents. But we don't know where she is, and she wants to keep it that way."

Rafe still worried about his friends—his true siblings even though they weren't related by blood. It was all there in his face. They were his second family and they were hurting. Some bonds were thicker than blood I knew.

Rafe's hand found mine and laced our fingers together. My heart jumped with the touch, even though I still grappled with his story.

"Thanks for listening, Wyn. I haven't been able to talk about this with anyone." He squeezed my hand.

Oh. "Of course." What did it mean that he's only shared this with me? *I'm nobody important to him.* He just needed a space to vent, I assured myself.

*I did mention I was a good listener while we talked on the phone.* That was it. He just needed a sympathetic ear.

Whatever this was couldn't mean more, *right?*

Our gazes clashed.

His green eyes flashed fire at me as a deafening silence descended on us in the large living room. My hand remained on his knee, his hand grasping mine. We were both mesmerized and held captive by traumatic emotional baggage. And maybe each other.

"Uh." He cleared his throat. "Your bathroom?" Rafe's question broke the heated moment.

I pointed him to the second door down the hall and on the right. Once he closed the door behind him, I sprinted quickly to the kitchen. I plopped our cups down in the sink, deciding to clean them in the morning if I hadn't just broken them. Then I headed straight for my bedroom to catch my breath.

I remembered stopping dead center in the room.

*Why did I come in here again?*

I stood there frozen, staring into space. The reason for escaping to my room now forgotten.

If someone asked me how we came to be lying on my bed, his face just mere inches from mine—*sharing breaths*—my answer would be unintelligible. I didn't know how we'd gone so far this fast. But it was where I found myself with Rafe...

It all happened after he found me frozen like a statue in the middle of my bedroom.

# Chapter Fifteen
*Wyn*

"Hey, thought you disappeared on me." Hearing the unexpected voice in my room startled me. *Rafe.*

His statement had an undertone of concern. Unasked questions. My mind couldn't wrap around either right now. I quickly walked over to my bed and flicked on the lamp there, facing him.

"I, um... I came in here for something but then forgot what it was." I shrugged.

*Awkward much, Wyn?* I felt like a complete dork confessing that to him. *Ugh, spastic Wyn at your service, Rafe. I should curtsy just to complete this ridiculous one-woman show I have going.*

"Yeah, happens to me too. Sucks big time." Rafe strolled through my open door, glancing around the room. I wondered what he saw, what he learned about me just from seeing my bedroom.

Right now, this space appeared more cluttered than my office area in the living room. It was clean enough, though. The neat freak in me only appeared in my professional endeavors.

A framed collage hung over my dresser, which Rafe studied now. Mostly a collection of snapshots of me and Darcy through the years. A few pictures of my family were up there too.

"Your father was in the military?"

"Yes." I walked over to where Rafe stood. "He was stationed in North Carolina for most of his career. He died serving overseas." I touched the only photo I had of him where he wore his uniform. I dropped my hand when Rafe cupped and squeezed my shoulders.

"I'm so sorry, Wyn."

"Thanks. That was over fifteen years ago now." I didn't want to talk about this anymore. It brought up tough memories about my mom. How she just couldn't deal. How I ended up on the doorstep of my mom's parents two years after his death. *Thank God* for them. They kept this particular picture of him from when my parents were getting married.

At some point, Rafe grabbed my hand and held it as we took the few steps back to my bed. His thumb stroked my skin in a calming, gentle motion I appreciated as he sat down. I followed him, tilting my head to gaze at him from under my lashes. My lips parted in surprise; his watchful gaze hid very little. No one had ever looked at me with such intensity before. Not without warning bells going off in my head like a five-alarm fire. This was different.

*It's all Rafe.*

"I really want to kiss you again, Wyn. Can I?" His voice dipped low, those arresting green orbs studying my every twitch for a response. How could I say *no* to him? I gave him the only answer I could, a slight nod, no words forming in my dry throat.

Our hands sat connected between us, but it wasn't enough contact. He lifted his other hand to my cheek, caressing it. I gasped from his feather light touch. My eyes closed unbidden. I was nervous, not scared. Not yet, anyway. I just concentrated on breathing and waited for his next move.

The cool air in the bedroom circulated around me, the act of waiting so much more intense with my eyes shut. The slightest sensation magnified, expecting his lips to touch mine at any second. Rafe's hand cupped my jaw, a finger tickled the underside of my ear. And then nothing. As if the moment froze. I couldn't handle the blind quiet any longer, so I opened my eyes. And I knew right away that's what he waited for.

My heart sped up, craving his kiss more than my next breath. Rafe's smooth handling secured me, made me feel safe with him.

This point in time seemed to spiral in slow motion. His movements seemed languid, yet tactile, prolonging—dragging me down—this sensual rabbit hole with him. His eyes held mine as he moved forward ever so slightly. Rafe released the hand still holding mine and brought it up to brush against my other cheek, holding my face with both hands.

*What's he waiting for?*

Before I built up the nerve to ask out loud, he brushed our noses together. Teasing me. Playful and sensual all at once.

His lips barely whispered against mine. I was already at his mercy. My eyelids fell to half-mast as his tongue pressed and teased against my lips, requesting entry. I granted it without question.

Rafe was slow and measured, his tongue delving into my mouth, melting me. With twists and swirls, he took me on a rollercoaster ride of decadent wonder. He tasted and devoured me. I couldn't help but like it and wanted more. I'd kissed only a couple times before, but never like this. He took his time and savored me. It seemed so wanton and unbelievable.

*Under all my fear and doubt, he's been making me feel like this for a while now*, I admitted. I felt cherished.

I wasn't passive, amazingly, just taking what he gave with no participation on my end. The brazenness from an hour ago returned, surging into me. My hands found their way around his torso. Drawing myself toward him and holding tight. I pulled my head away to nibble on his full bottom lip. Not believing how playful I was being with him, but he brought it out.

A deep rumble came from Rafe. Suddenly, he pulled me into his chest and took my mouth with so much hunger I could do nothing less than respond with my own.

He eased me backwards, our mouths still connected while the memory foam mattress cushioned me with its softness. One of Rafe's hands spanned my mid-back.

*Oh wow.*

Heady and a bit dazed from his kisses, I floated from the sensations. When his full weight landed on me, I tensed. *This is Rafe. This is Rafe.* Those three words repeated in my mind. He must've registered the knee-jerk reaction because he stopped a moment later, slowly pulling himself back. It was good timing since we both panted, needing oxygen and a break.

He leaned down to peck my lips before shifting most of his weight off me. He wasn't exactly heavy, but we obviously needed to slow down since I'd already freaked out on him. It brought back memories of feeling trapped. Forced. Memories that didn't belong here with Rafe.

Seeing and touching him up close like this, I couldn't help but notice his swimmer's build. He wasn't bulky or muscle-bound, but long and lean with broad shoulders even visible underneath layers of shirts and the thin jacket he wore tonight. The cuffed look suited him too. His sleeves were rolled up, drawing my attention to his toned forearms.

*Good lordy, I'm noticing the man's dusky forearms now?*

My gaze followed a path down to his fingertips. I'd noticed the tattoo on his right wrist earlier and took a longer, uninhibited look. An infinity symbol. And it was hot on him. Not that I didn't expect him to have a tattoo, but it stood out against his tanned wrist.

Rafe ran fingers through his hair, giving him this sexy, tousled look. *Help me, Jesus.* I felt awkward complimenting him earlier when he came to pick me up. He was probably one of those guys who didn't have to work at looking so yummy. But he did look good. Almost too good.

Attempts at containing his long locks were cute, yet useless. Strands continued to fall in his face every few minutes and he swept them back again and again. I couldn't decide which style did it for me more, the messy hair-in-his-eyes look or pulled back. Either way he was sex incarnate.

Even though he'd moved away, Rafe's arm remained on me, his long fingers rubbing the side of my waist in languid circles. My skin tingled. I made the mistake of squirming from the teasing touch.

"Wyn, are you ticklish?" I quickly shook my head. Rafe probed further, "Not even a little?" His mouth twitched and eyes twinkled with mirth.

This situation spelled trouble with a capital T.

"Uh, n-no." Self-preservation kicked in as I stuttered. I knew what the look on his face meant.

*My demise.*

He moved toward me.

"Oh no. Nuh-uh." I shook my head even though it was too late. His fingertips were like ninjas, carrying out precise, sneak attacks against the curves of my belly, neck and under my arms. I couldn't help my giggles. Then the unthinkable happened.

I snorted.

And once I started, it was almost impossible to stop. Beyond mortified, there was nothing to be done until he stopped the tickle torture.

"Oh God. Rafe you have to—" I tried appealing to him between snorts. He finally took a break from tormenting me with those guitar-playing ninja fingers. I looked up at him, needing to catch my breath and ended up gasping instead.

Rafe's deep, green eyes pinned me in place. My heart hammered in my chest. Laughing definitely qualified as my work out for the next week, but it was more than that. His gaze held mine like a missile locked on its target. I couldn't believe he focused all the hunger in his eyes on *me*.

"I really love your smile, Wyn. And your laugh." Again, his sexy voice penetrated my foggy brain. Braids fell on my face from all my wiggling. He scooped most of them behind my ear with one calloused finger. "You should do both more often, sweetheart."

"Mm," humming my agreement. I used to be the girl who smiled at a new day, finding good in the world even after my father's passing and my mother leaving. Those days were few and far between now. *Rafe is right, though.*

It was time to get back to who I used to be. Before last year happened. A girl who took a chance or two. Someone who was cautious, but not overly so. The woman who finally learned how to be comfortable in her own skin.

He continued studying me. I could tell whatever we were doing here wasn't finished. Not for either of us. I readied myself for another deep, searching kiss. Craved it. Kissing Rafe wasn't a hardship on my part by any means. That unabashed desire in his eyes knocked me on my ass even though I was already lying down.

Rafe had the potential to unravel me.

He rested an elbow next to me, his warm breath trailed against my neck, shaking me to my core. He made me feel again. Want things. I didn't know which way was up anymore.

Something precious died all those months ago. Snatched away during that night. Now, I was broken inside. But with Rafe, I felt confusion and excitement and fear. From the inside out, I shook with all the emotions mixed up in my soul. These feelings remained just beneath the surface, lighting up everywhere he touched.

He leaned over me again, his head and silky, dark hair casting a shadow. In our own cocoon. And I was safe here. With him.

"Open for me, Wyn." His quiet urging jarred me from my contemplation. My lips parted. "Can't get enough of your taste," he murmured before kissing my lips.

Rafe reminded me of a man seeing a mirage. And my lips were the body of water he yearned for. With a playful flick of his tongue he drank from me, sipping from my lips and taking what he needed.

My heart galloped and slowing it down proved impossible. Rafe had me on a rollercoaster ride, reeling from every dip and valley. Inexperienced with kissing like everything else, the electricity vibrating from Rafe and building in me was all new. The horror of that night was pushed to the background by Rafe's soft touch. I shut the door on the darkness and brought my focus back to Rafe. To the here and now.

My hands clutched the sheets under me. Disconnected from what was happening, like I was not really in this moment and *dammit*, I wanted to be. I uncurled my fingers from the bedding, bringing them to his mid-back. At my touch, the muscles under my hand moved, like an electric shock strummed through him.

His hands left my body for mere seconds to whip off the long-sleeve shirt he wore over a T-shirt. He got right back to kissing me after tossing the garment over his shoulder.

Rafe had the hands of a musician, rough and calloused from playing his guitar. Yet they were tender when they returned to my face.

"Touch me, sweetheart." Rafe grabbed one of my hands from his back and slowly urged it down his body. *Oh God*. My breath caught in my throat as my fingers grazed his pecs, trailing down, down, down. I cataloged the indentations of his abs underneath and the muscles rippling from the barest touch of my fingers, my palm resting on top of his thin T-shirt. It hid a sinewy, muscled physique I was still coming to grips with.

He guided my hand just above the waist of his pants. I froze, expecting my anxiety to rear its ugly head. I didn't know what to think of this heightened moment between us and wasn't exactly sure how we'd gotten down this road so quickly.

*What if I give him this? Pleasured him with my hand, would it be enough, or would he want more?* Naïve thoughts ran through my mind, like making sure our clothes stayed on so nothing could happen.

*That plan didn't work out so well the last time, Wyn.* My inner voice decided to remind me of my previous naiveté.

"Wyn? Is this okay?" Rafe's hands ran from my forehead into my braids, skating through my hair feathered out on the mattress. The only noise in the quiet room was our combined pants and gulps.

Instead of answering his question, I stared into his hooded eyes, askingly. "Show me how," I whispered, then looked away before he caught the worry and doubt in my eyes. Was I ready for this again?

A more essential question was, *would he stop if I asked him to?*

In all honesty, I wanted to try this with him if only to test myself. See how far I could go on my terms. Could I do this with him tonight and be okay—as whole as possible in the morning? I needed to know for myself.

Unbuckling his slim leather belt, I reached down to undo the fastener of his pants and heard the sharp grinding hiss of the zipper. The sound made this situation all too real for me. *Just need to take a short break*, I told myself as my hands fisted both sides of his opened slacks.

Rafe unclenched one of my hands and guided it to the hardness in his boxer briefs. I wrapped my fingers around him, weighing his length in my loose grasp. Velvet-soft over hard steel. The texture of it fascinated me. I fumbled, trying to figure out what to do with the girth my fingers just barely wrapped around.

My eyes stayed lowered as I moved my hand, up and down, slowly stroking him. I watched what my hand did to him, hearing a slight change to his breathing. The stuttered breaths made my heart race even faster.

A pearl of white precum leaked from his tip. I wasn't sure what came over me then. Catching it with my thumb, I swirled it around his crown, coating him. Satisfied, I went back to dragging my hand along the length of his shaft, stroking him.

He stopped my hand a moment later, forcing me to seek out his eyes. Afraid of what I'd see in them, I turned away at the last second. *Test over! I couldn't do this. It was all wrong.* The zing of energy I felt seconds ago whooshed out with the thought of Rafe rejecting me. I withdrew my hand and shifted away from him.

Rafe's fingers crawled up my sides, following my curves. A hand landing on my shoulder with a squeeze pulled my attention back to him. He grabbed my chin and angled my face in his direction. His lips pressed against mine after a short beat passed between us. I tingled from the urgency of his touch while he nipped and sucked on my bottom lip, easing off after a few pulls. "God, babe. If you kept touching me like that, I was gonna blow."

*Oh! Why did my mind have to go straight to the worst-case scenario?*

"I wanna see you blow, Rafe." The bold statement left my mouth, shocking us both into silence. I watched his pupils dilate while he stared at me, processing the startling words.

Even before crawling into myself and becoming this withdrawn person I no longer recognized, I was never the flirty girl. I needed to try this small step for myself.

I liked Rafe. With his voice, so deep and warm, I wanted to try with him. Try stuff I thought was unlikely for a girl like me, well before last year even happened. I wasn't sure about the rest. If he wanted to get naked, I might freak the hell out and bring our activities to a grinding halt.

"You're fucking killing me, sweetheart." The strain in his voice got to me. I scooched around to face Rafe and reached for him again. He tried holding in his groans, not the least bit successful at it. He was close to the edge. Realizing that I was doing this to him made me feel all kinds of powerful and wanton.

His irises turned deep turquoise, taking on the color of a turbulent sea. His hot gaze encouraged my decision to continue, roaming over me like a long, sensual kiss.

So much *want* vibrated off him, the need for what we were doing all there in his gaze. I needed to apologize for teasing him, but before I could he said, "I wanna be inside you. Damn baby." Rafe dropped his head on my shoulder. I turned mine to the left, and his lips fell to the skin at my collarbone. Butterflies fluttered around my stomach from these feelings he evoked in me.

We couldn't go further than this. *I can't*, the words repeated in my head. Not with him or anyone else. I didn't think I could give him what he wanted right now *or ever,* but I could please him.

He continued kissing and nibbling my exposed skin. The heated attention distracted me only momentarily from my plans. I moved my hand between our bodies, slowly inching my way back to his erection, a trail of fine hairs teasing me along the way. My hand found his exposed staff easily, and I returned to my earlier mission.

"Fu-uck." Rafe grunted then nipped at the meaty part of my shoulder.

He dipped his hands low to touch the sides of my stomach, thrusting them behind my back and bringing our bodies closer. *This is not the same,* I chanted. We still lay on our sides. I thought I had solid control of the situation even though his touches scattered my brain.

His teeth nipped my skin again, and I shuddered. It was like he marked me, claimed me. My hand stalled from the image, hoping his suction left a mark on my dark skin. It was weird I wanted a memento from tonight as if this was it for us. I pushed the dark and lonely thought out of my head and came back to the moment at hand.

Licking my dry lips, I nudged Rafe's head with my chin. His hair felt good against my skin, *silky smooth*. I turned more to my side, causing a small hiccup in my stroking motion, and I brought my unoccupied hand up to run my fingers through his dark strands. I've wanted to do this for a while now.

"I want to see you lose control from just my hand on you," speaking to his previous comment. His usually vibrant green eyes, like lake water on a sunny day, were cloudy and murky, drilling into me as if he wanted unfettered access to my soul. I wasn't ready for him to see that part of me, the bleakness inside. He wouldn't like what lay beneath.

Maybe if I'd met him more than a year ago, I'd be more normal. Now, though? I didn't know if I'd ever be ready. I looked up and saw questions in his eyes. Before he voiced them, I pulled him in for another kiss. Confidence drummed through me as he seemed to grow even harder in my hand. It amazed me Rafe wanted me like this. It also scared me that he was bigger than the one and only experience I've had.

"God, you're gorgeous," he murmured. I didn't believe him. *How could I?* I knew he found me attractive as evidenced by his straining hardness pulsing against my soft belly. But I was almost positive another warm body could fit the bill too. I wasn't anybody special.

His movements halted suddenly. Rafe ducked his head in my neck again. He took a deep breath against my skin, retracing the folds and curves of my midsection, and scooping his hand around to the small of my back. He turned me so that my back was against his front.

The change in position jarred me. And so did his words. My hands on him became an afterthought.

"Enough about me, Wyn."

*What does that mean?*

Rafe pulled his pants back up a few inches, but I was sure he hadn't snapped himself closed. I turned my neck to look over at him. My confusion was evident because he smiled gently and said, "Want to take care of you now, baby." He pushed the thick strap of my dress aside, emphasizing his words with a kiss to the back of my shoulder.

My bare toes curled from his words, my heels pushing back

against his rough jeans. I'd been barefoot since we came through the front door, kicking my shoes off and tucking them in a corner.

Black tights and my burgundy dress were Rafe's only obstacles.

"If I tell you…" I squeezed my eyelids closed and huffed. I needed to get this out. My back against his damp front. In our new position, I now faced the wall opposite my window. My eyes strayed to the bedroom door standing ajar. It reminded me that we were all alone here. "If I ask you to stop, will you?"

"Of course." His words were quick, his tone surprised yet firm. He nudged his forehead against the back of my head. I felt more than heard his deep inhale and long exhale. He breathed into my hair, arms wrapped around me, palms resting on my stomach.

"Whatever you ask, I'll do. I'd never force or hurt you, Wyn. Ever." Rafe pulled me closer, wrapping me more into his arms. He bent his head down and returned to kissing and nuzzling my neck. I tilted my head to give him access to more skin, encouraging him.

*What am I doing?* I wanted so bad not to regret this decision in the morning, in the next few minutes even. I prayed he was honorable and that I could trust him with this. With my body. And my heart.

Rafe's hands grazed my midsection again, continuing past my stomach. I held my breath as his hands roamed to my thighs then reversed direction to squeeze the side of my butt.

The hem of my dress had ridden up with our earlier antics, settling midway up my thighs. Rafe had one hand under the dress, hesitating over the elastic band of my tights, tracing a finger above them. Our breathing was almost in sync, oddly calming me. In a moment, he brought both hands to either side of my waist and rolled the thin, stretchy material slowly down my shapely legs.

His warm, calloused hands were now on the bare skin of my legs, and I tensed. "Everything's gonna be okay, sweetheart." He hugged me close.

*Famous last words, those were.* But I wanted to trust them. Trust him.

One hand continued traveling up my leg at the top. The other snuck under the hem of my dress, nudging it up further, centimeter by centimeter. My skin tingled from the contact.

Rafe didn't seem interested in removing my dress entirely. My breathing slowed. Whatever he planned didn't require completely disrobing. The dress I wore tonight wasn't quite bodycon, yet it hugged my plentiful curves in flattering ways. I was glad Darcy helped me pick it out after we made plans earlier in the week.

All the while, Rafe continued kissing wherever he could, but I missed his lips on mine. One hand settled on my midsection again. The pleasure and trepidation he caused were two very distinct emotions zinging through every cell of my body. The sneaky hand made its way further up my inner thighs, skimming the material of my cotton underwear, pushing it to the side.

I was even more exposed to the cool air in my room. He traced my mound with his fingers, grazing my pubic hair and separating my folds. The gentle touch teased me. My head fell back, sinking down and pushing myself into his hand.

"Yeah, Wyn." Rafe's voice was dark and husky, full of emotions I couldn't decipher. Not now. My body felt too much, nerve endings shaking from all the sparks his light touches sent over my body.

Heat crawled up my skin. I was weightless and weighed down all at once.

A finger traced my walls as he opened me to more of his touch. I didn't know what to do or say, yet I *needed*. Once his hand was down there, my body craved something I couldn't put into words.

My toes curled as one finger swept across my uncovered nub. The direct touch extinguished the world around me except for Rafe, reigniting like a wave of fire.

Rafe flicked the nerve again and again. I quivered in his arms. It was a triple assault now: a hand stroking me between my legs, another caressing my breasts over my dress, and his hot breath tickling the back of my neck. I licked my lips, biting down to stop the mewling noises. I didn't even know I could make those sounds.

His touch was different, so soft but intense. He was taking the time to set me aflame, dismantling my walls and re-erecting them. Now, all I felt was pleasure and need in his arms.

A digit slowly entered me while a steady pressure from his thumb worked me still. *He's trying to kill me with all this pleasure, and I'm too powerless to stop him.*

My head dropped forward. Rafe strummed me like one of his instruments, playing a tune so seductive and intense and frightening. It entranced me. And just like the crescendo of a song, I'd explode into little, tiny pieces because of his fingertips. He stroked over my swollen bud again and chills flowed through my body. I was close but to what, I wasn't sure. A noise I'd never heard before left my throat and his lips scraped against my neck. I imagined him smiling at the noises he pulled from me.

"Please." I didn't know what I asked for, begged from him, but I hoped he did. "O-oh!" My mouth hung open. I grabbed his wrist and shuddered from the gentle yet confident movements of his digits. Rafe withdrew his long finger, only to tease me with it again by pushing it back in slowly. This time the stroke was sure, more intense but not rough. He claimed me in all ways but one.

"Let me see you. Let go. Come for me, sweetheart." My eyes popped open, head turning to look at him. Rafe took me in, seeing deep into my soul. The good, the bad. Every damned thing.

"I—". Rafe put pressure on the sensitive nerve again and my body froze, splintering into a million pieces. I quaked, every cell in my body going up in flames. Sensation after sensation wracked me from head to toe. *Shattered from the inside out. Wrecked.* I called his name on a guttural scream. My throat, my body, all of me stripped raw from how he claimed me. He unraveled me, and I couldn't stop it.

"So fucking beautiful." His continued attention and light strokes only extended my pleasure. My tears and silent sobs didn't register until I heard Rafe murmuring in my ear, shushing me. Shoulder, neck, cheek, he kissed them all, placing a soft caress behind my ear. His hand slowly moved up my body, touching all the parts of me he could, without letting me go. His care consoled me.

*Oh God, I'm so embarrassed.* I turned into him, ducking my head under his chin, hiding and opening the floodgates on his neck. The tears were beyond my control now. I couldn't stop crying and he let me get it out.

"It's okay, sweetheart. I have you. You're safe with me." I believed him. Questioning it right now seemed stupid and a waste of time. His soft, caring words were a balm for my too-fragile heart. I was easily breakable now, more than ever before.

"Let's get some rest. Okay?" I bobbed my head and turned around so that my back rested against his chest. His arms surrounded me. My bedside lamp remained on, neither of us moving to turn it off. I realized too late Rafe never came after turning his attention on me. Nestled deeper into his arms, I locked the thought away for safekeeping.

I closed my eyes, drifting off to sleep hoping no nightmare waited in the shadows. That I hadn't imagined Rafe's soft, gentle touches.

I didn't want tonight to be a dream.

I was safe in his arms.

For now, at least.

# Chapter Sixteen
*Rafe*

When I became a full-time musician, mornings were the bane of my existence. Late gigs meant sleeping in and waking up well after the sun rose. I liked that aspect of the life. A lot. But if every morning began like this one, I was fucking sold.

I woke up to Wyn in my arms a few minutes ago and haven't been able to quit watching her since. Taking in her every breath and soft murmur.

So goddamn pretty. Unfiltered and real like this.

I slept without shadows hanging over me for the first time in forever, her cradled in my arms.

I couldn't believe what went down last night. Wyn surprised me. From the first kiss to inviting me in, I never expected the night to go as far as it did. I didn't think she saw it coming either. Everything about it was unexpected, yet last night felt right. Kismet.

It was far from perfect. Those glimpses of Wyn's fear broke my fucking heart. I sensed her hesitation, felt this strong tension in her body a few times. She doubted herself and me on multiple occasions. I didn't like it one damn bit.

There was something more going on with her. In a too-quiet voice, she asked if I'd stop. I saw red at the implication of her words, taking deep breaths just to calm myself down before reassuring her.

I assumed some bad shit happened to her in the past and cues from last night made my guess more than likely. My anger rose just thinking about it. I wasn't a violent man, but if I ever found the bastard who hurt my girl, nothing would stop me from taking a pound of flesh.

Wyn's smile lit up whatever fucking room she was in. And she didn't do it enough for my liking. Whatever troubles caused her to close herself off were all there in stark detail last night. Although she began opening up to me, I saw hints of nervousness. But I witnessed her resolve too. She started to enjoy herself, smiling and laughing with me.

And God, the world needed that. *I* needed more of that.

Wyn shifted in my arms, the first signs of her waking up. I wasn't done taking my fill of her but figured she'd want some space after last night. My intuition spoke loud and clear. I tucked my face against her neck, expelling small puffs of air. Playing possum, I closed my eyes and feigned sleep.

She woke up a moment later, tensing slightly, reminding me of her reactions last night. I hugged her to my chest then relaxed my body, hoping Wyn thought it was an unconscious act. For me, it was pretty much an accurate response since I wanted to keep her in my arms for as long as possible.

I felt her eyes on me for several minutes. I tried keeping my breaths slow, even though my body reacted to her being awake and so close to me.

After another moment, Wyn shifted, wriggling out of my embrace. My time was up. I forced my body to relax more, letting her leave my arms. The sound of clothes rustling against the sheets reached my ears. As soon as she left the bed completely, I turned around and sprawled across the mattress.

I had a stubborn problem behind my unfastened pants. Morning wood which Wyn probably wasn't ready to see. I'd need to get a handle on my unwieldy equipment before seeking her out. A few more seconds passed before I heard the quiet snick of her bedroom door closing. *Time alone.* Apparently, both of us needed it.

Thinking back on last night again, I was satisfied overall with the events. I hadn't finished and it was my choice. I'd never been a selfish partner and I for damn sure wasn't becoming one with Wyn. Her pleasure was my main priority. Especially after the question she asked last night. I made the right decision to focus all my attention on her.

The glazed look in her eyes, the pleasure and confusion on her face while I teased her with my hands and fingers, I remembered every quick breath and soft hum. She felt damn good coming apart in my arms.

Thoughts like those would only take me down the road to another full-on erection I couldn't take care of, so I stopped them in their tracks, rolling over. I forced myself up from the comfy mattress. My thoughts went straight to Wyn. *Like they ever aren't on her these days, Tapiro.* I scoffed at myself because it was true. She was on my mind all the time now.

Was she freaking out in the other room? Or worse, did she regret what happened between us? I wanted to run out there to see if I screwed myself by rushing. Which I told myself not to do with this girl. My mind and body had conflicting ideas about what it all meant. But the events last night felt right. Like a building block.

I shouldn't jump to worst-case scenarios yet, I told myself.

My footsteps were quiet on the carpet, so I made as much noise as possible heading into the hallway. She'd probably appreciate knowing I was up and about. Taking a slight detour to the bathroom, my priorities were relieving myself then going to find Wyn and seeing about my fate this morning.

Good or bad, I'd deal.

It took longer than I'd hoped for my boner to recede enough to piss. I washed my hands and took a long look in the small round mirror above the vanity sink. The familiar features stared back at me. Tanned skin and sharp green eyes I inherited from my mother's side of the family. I looked exactly the same as I always did, but I felt different. A slight shift.

Playing with the band had a hand in my minor transformation. And to be honest, I couldn't really pinpoint how I changed, just that I had.

I was more like myself than ever before, and it all felt damn good. My decision to move here a year ago was a good one. No regrets. Especially since meeting Wyn.

*Enough with the introspection, Tapiro.*

It was time to see what waited for me in the living room. To see about Wyn.

I strolled down the hallway and stood quietly at the entrance to the living room, pausing to watch her. *More like devour her measured movements around the space.*

She walked from the kitchen over to the bright loveseat with a mug of tea. Unaware of her captivated audience of one.

I reached up and took hold of the entry frame, stretching my back. Although I had ample opportunity while I'd been alone in her bed, this was a good time as any. As I let go, I heard Wyn's gasp. It was tempting to keep holding on so that she could look her fill, but I had other plans this morning.

"Morning, Wyn. How are you?" I bounced on the balls of my feet before settling, walking into the room.

"Good. Thank you." She glanced down at the mug cradled in her hand. Wyn teased the rim with an index finger. "Good morning to you too. I haven't had a sound sleep in… I can't remember how long," she shook her head, sharing the tidbit freely. I really liked her innocent honesty. Our gazes met and held as she took a long sip from her mug.

I wondered what went through her mind now. The mug and her hesitant expression hid her thoughts well.

"I hope I didn't wake you. I'm an early riser, even on the weekends."

"No worries, sweetheart. I was about ready to get up anyway."

"Did you maybe want some breakfast? I could make us something." She made a move to rise until my hand went up, stopping her.

"Yeah. There's no need for you to cook, though." She put her mug down on the coffee table and unfolded her legs. "I'll put on my shirt and shoes. We can go to a diner or someplace." She rose from the psychedelic two-seater next to the couch as I asked her, "Do you have a favorite breakfast spot, Wyn?"

She'd stayed away from the loveseat last night, I realized. An image of us cuddling on it popped into my head regardless. *Another time.* If I had my way.

She hadn't kicked me out as soon as I walked in the room, so I assumed we were okay.

Wyn appeared to be a consummate tea drinker. I, on the other hand, needed my first cup of the dark brew. Stat. Shit, if I wasn't such a pussy when it came to needles, I'd strap myself to an intravenous drip all the damn time. Just for coffee.

I went back to get my button-down shirt from the bedroom. She walked to the kitchen then followed behind me moments later. It lay half on the floor, half draped off one corner of the bed. Putting it on, I watched as she pulled open her dresser to rummage around.

"I'll wait for you in the living room."

"Okay," she nodded, peeking over at me through her lashes as I closed the bedroom door.

Last night had been fucking amazing. Unexpected, sure but Wyn and I connected on a deeper level. Both sharing parts of ourselves many people hadn't seen. At least that was true for me.

Now in jeans and a T-shirt, she wore her braids up in a ponytail, looking downright scrumptious in the no-frills outfit. And she had no idea the effect she was having on me right now.

Wyn opted to drive, so we took her car to the diner. I didn't have to meet up with the band for another few hours, so I left my truck in the visitor parking spot at her apartment complex. When she told me the nickname for her car, I stifled a laugh. Although Cru appeared to be on her last legs, it was obvious Wyn did what she could to keep her running.

Another reason I liked this woman.

Being in the passenger seat this time around allowed me time to think. My thoughts immediately strayed to last night again. The whole night knocked me on my ass.

Wyn's reticence. Her hesitant demeanor in bed angered me even now, especially since I was more certain than ever someone hurt my girl.

And then she came apart in my arms. In more ways than one. I held her tighter as she cried, so afraid of the wrong fucking words coming out. I told her she was safe in my arms. And I planned to do everything in my power to make sure that statement remained true.

She fell asleep in my embrace while I stayed awake just holding her, listening to her deep breaths and low murmurs as she slept. During the night, she'd turned around and melted into my chest, a soft sigh falling from her lips.

Wyn belonged in my arms.

I wanted to do right by her. Wanted her to put her trust in me.

We parked in one of the downtown public lots and strolled toward Paula's, she shared. Downtown was busy for a Saturday morning, but to be honest, I was never up this early. For good reason.

"This is it." I looked up to see a small marquee with Paula's Diner in the center. I held the door for Wyn. Someone behind the counter immediately greeted us. The strong smell of bacon, maple syrup and hint of days old grease assaulted me.

"I've never been here before. What do you recommend, Wyn?"

I asked as the young hostess led us to a booth in the back corner of the diner. Most tables had occupants which immediately told me the food was good. Plus, I trusted Wyn's tastes. And I really wanted to hear her soft, raspy voice since she'd gone quiet on the drive here.

"You definitely need to look at the menu. I get the same order most of the time: the hotcakes with eggs, bacon, and toast." She looked pensive for another moment as we took our seats across from one another. "Their milkshakes are really good too." I picked up the menu and immediately approved of their all-day breakfast items.

"This is my kind of place." My mouth watered just perusing all my choices. Wyn softly chuckled at my comment. *Music to my ears.*

I was pondering other ways to hear the mildly happy sound when a nice, older lady came around to take our order. True to her word, Wyn ordered the pancakes meal. I went for the hungry man option which was the same order as Wyn plus two sausage links and hash browns. I joked with our server, Lucy, asking for an IV bag for my coffee and received a hearty chuckle. "I got just the thing, sugar," she said before walking away.

This had potential to become one of my staples if the food and coffee held up to my mid-level expectations.

"I can't picture you as much of a coffee drinker, Rafe." Wyn smiled while shifting the utensils and napkin in front of her.

"Well, we all need a vice, right? I don't smoke or do drugs. Binge drinking the java of the gods is the next best thing." I winked at her, imagined a blush as her eyelids fluttered closed. "Honestly, I don't really need coffee since I'm such a hyper person by nature. I developed a taste for it when I was younger. My mom would give me some of hers in the mornings before school and on weekends. I guess she hoped it would keep me quiet." I shrugged my shoulders and said, "To some extent, it helped me focus. Most days it still does."

"Hmm. So, now it's just habit?"

"Oh no. I'm addicted to the stuff." Our drinks arrived then. My coffee was piping hot. I poured some cream in and took a long sip. Wyn drank from a tall glass of OJ.

I was in caffeine heaven.

"Your food will be out in a jiffy, folks." Lucy smiled as another table vied for her attention.

"You mentioned your mom?" Wyn took a sip of her drink as she let her not-quite-question lie between us.

"Yeah, my mom was pretty amazing. She died from cancer when I was fourteen." Then I was left all alone with my bastard of a father and brother. I thanked whoever's upstairs every day for Zi and his family. *They were and still are my refuge.*

"I'm so sorry, Rafe. It's hard to lose a parent, especially at that age." Wyn's hand landed on mine from across the table, her voice catching on her last words.

"Yeah, thanks. I still miss her. She was in a lot of pain towards the end. My mom was the one who encouraged me to take that music class at the beginning of middle school." I smiled from the memory. "I was a small, pipsqueak of a kid. Skinny and shy, my mom figured learning an instrument would bring me out of my shell." And keep me out of the house from time to time. She'd been right. *Too bad my dad and Lanni tried to beat me back into that shell after she was gone.*

Taking another sip of my coffee, I glanced over at Wyn and saw so much emotion in her eyes that it damn near broke my heart. She pulled her arm away and resumed fiddling with the napkin in front of her.

Our food arrived then. My stomach decided to growl loudly as Lucy placed two heaping plates of food in front of me. Wyn looked down at her one plate then back at mines. A look of disbelief was there in her big brown eyes.

"I totally got this, sweetheart." I gave her my most confident look and dug in.

# Chapter Seventeen
*Wyn*

Where the hell did he put it all? Rafe ate his food with gusto, an appetite the likes of which I hadn't seen in a long time. I vaguely recalled our date at Rusty's and him scarfing down a bunch of food, but I'd had other stuff on my mind then.

Maybe even now. Without words, we both tucked into our meals. After several minutes, he finished with one plate, turning his attention to the three huge hotcakes and two strips of bacon. I ate much slower while studying him.

Lucy checked back in, refilling our cups and asking after us. "Take your time. We're not putting you out," she said while setting the check close to Rafe's elbow.

"Thank you," left us both at the same time. "Everything was wonderful, ma'am. As always," I added.

Rafe glanced down at his phone, a frustrated look crossing his face. "I have to head back to my apartment soon," he said, almost apologetic. "Band practice in a few hours."

I nodded in understanding, then snatched the check right from under his elbow. "I got it, Rafe. You paid for dinner last night."

"It was my idea to come here, Wyn." His argument was pointless since I already had the check in my hand.

"I don't mind."

Rafe studied me as I retrieved money from my wallet. My body yearned for his touch, wanting to shiver just from his attention, however I held myself almost still.

"Ready?" I peeked up at him, watching him watch me while he leaned against the high-back booth.

*Heat.* There was so much heat in his eyes. And something else. Last night, I realized the enormity… no, the potency of it. All directed at me. It was there now. Front and center.

"Yeah," he coughed. We both stood, and I walked over to the register to settle our bill.

"Thank you," I called to the diner staff as Rafe held the door for me.

"I've been meaning to mention…" Rafe started as we strolled down the busy downtown street. Weekends here were becoming busier since the farmer's market started back up a couple weeks ago. He brushed up against me as we continued walking toward the public lot where we parked Cru. "We're playing a gig tonight at Del Rio's. It'd be great if you could come."

Oh, he wanted to see me again. This all felt unreal. After my freak-out last night, I was sure he would run for the hills, but he'd still been there this morning. And then this unexpected breakfast date. Now, he wanted to see me again. Tonight, no less.

"That's if you're not busy."

"Sounds like fun, Rafe." I smiled, my eyes finding his when I glanced up at him. "Maybe I can get Darcy to come too. She should be back later today."

"Great. I'll leave your names at the door then. I'm glad you can come tonight."

"Me too." And I was. I didn't know what came over me. "I feel safe around you, Rafe." My words seemed to stop him, so I stood on my tiptoes and pressed a quick peck to his stubbled cheek.

That had been my sudden foray into PDA, and I continued to talk about nothing as we strolled down the street. More nervous than I had reason to be. I finally stopped to take a breather. Rafe sidled up next to me, grabbing my hand. I hadn't really noticed him lagging until then.

We turned the corner, reaching the parking lot moments later. Once I started Cru, we were back on the road in no time.

Not sure what compelled me, but I decided to take the back roads home. *I want more time with Rafe*, I admitted to myself. Somewhere deep inside I knew something would go wrong soon because I really liked him. He made me laugh. Smile. With just one thought of him, the muscles in my face hurt. The first couple of times it happened, I realized the simple action had become so rare that I almost had to relearn it.

He brought a lot of good things out in me. Things I thought were lost forever. Rafe didn't know what happened, and the truth might change the way he viewed me. I had to get ahold of myself.

Nothing was written in stone. Especially us.

We were several miles down the road, still a good twenty minutes away from my apartment complex, when a horrible noise came from Cru.

She sputtered then jerked, slowing down even though I still had my foot on the gas. *No, no, no, no. Not now.*

"Shit!" I muttered, almost slamming my hand on the dashboard. Cru couldn't give up on me now.

I pulled over to the side of the two-lane road out of traffic, not that there was any, and pressed on the brake. Cru jerked to a stop, and I put her in park.

"Hey, we're good." Rafe's deep voice washed over me, calm and reassuring.

I dropped my head to the steering wheel. The sound of the horn blaring scared us both enough that we jumped at the same time. *Asshole.*

"Pop the hood, sweetheart. Let me take a look. I'm no mechanic but…" he didn't finish his sentence, already out of the car and tapping Cru's white hood. I found the release and watched in a daze as the open hood hid him from my view.

I rolled down the window and called out to him, "I'll call for a tow truck while you do that." Dejection laced my voice. The sad noise from her like a last breath. I knew this was practically it for Cru. I'd babied her for as long as possible.

While my call connected, my heart broke.

The inside of the car became stifling, even with the window open, so I got out and walked toward the trunk, leaning against it.

"Yes, hi." I gave the operator my insurance information and explained the situation. *Basically, I'm screwed.*

Rafe came around just as I murmured a goodbye, thanking the person for their help. I slipped my insurance card and phone in my front pocket.

"I'm so sorry about this, Rafe." My eyes stayed downcast, defeated. Rafe walked up to me, his shoes coming into view, sidling right up to mine. I peeked up at him.

"This isn't your fault, sweetheart."

"Yeah, I know. You need to get home, though. Maybe you can call an Uber, not spend your entire day stranded on the side of the road with me. I should be fine until the tow truck gets here." At least the person said they'd get one over here within the hour. That wasn't a long time to wait by myself.

"Hey." A hand came up under my chin, the rough pad of his thumb caressed the skin just under my bottom lip. My breath stuttered from his light touch. "Stranded with you sounds like the perfect day, Wyn. And I'm not leaving you here. I'm with you every step until I walk you back to your apartment door. Okay?"

I nodded.

"Good." He smirked, his thin upper lip spreading into a sincere smile. "Plus, I already texted the guys and asked if we could push practice back a couple hours. Colt got back to me quick, so there's no rush."

"Okay." Still, I felt bad about him pushing back the band's practice just because my life crumbled around me. His hand came up to my cheek. I rested against him, taking the solace he offered. "And thanks, Rafe."

"My pleasure." My skin prickled, every cell in my body shivering as he delivered the simple statement in that sexy voice of his. Rafe meant every single, breathtaking word. I believed him now. But I still thought the sentiments were wasted on me.

We chatted about random stuff while we waited, leaning against the trunk since neither of us wanted to sit in the car. Before too long, I noticed a tow truck about a half a mile up the road and sighed.

This was all happening. Not a merely simple chat on a quiet, overcast Saturday afternoon. I might just have to say goodbye to my baby.

I made the call less than an hour ago. Time passed quickly without my noticing.

On the bright side, the weather was being agreeable. The sky remained overcast most of the morning and early afternoon, the last of the spring rains kept at bay. Several times in the last hour the sun attempted to break through the fluffy clouds.

Summer was only a few weeks away.

The truck stopped up ahead, pulling off to the side then backing up to a hairsbreadth away from Cru.

"Hey there, folks." The portly driver called as he hopped down and walked toward us. He introduced himself then got Cru hitched up to his rig in a short amount of time. Rafe reminded me to grab my important documents from the glove compartment just in case. Fred, the tow truck driver, let us ride up front with him. After a short ride, we turned into a driveway leading to R&L Auto Repair shop.

The two initials hung over the main glass door, almost falling into each other. A few cars littered the parking lot, only one car occupied one of the two bays.

A young-looking guy came out of the empty bay with the top half of the coveralls tied at his waist, head down, wiping his hands with a soiled rag. The friendly face brought a small smile to my lips.

"What's Cru done now, Wyn?" he asked me, tossing a glance our way.

"Hi, Rudy. She broke down on us." I shrugged, hearing the slight sadness in my voice. He'd understand.

"Damn, hun. I'm sorry. I'd give you a hug but…" he chuckled, gesturing to his oil streaked T-shirt.

Rafe stood next to me, his shoulder brushing against mine. I felt him stiffen after Rudy's innocent welcome.

I've brought Cru to Rudy and Oscar's place for the last four years, since moving to the area. They took care of Cru so much that I considered them good friends now. I mean, I saw them often enough.

Fred unhitched her close to the open bay, shaking Rudy's hand when he finished.

"I'll look at her for ya. See what I can do." He popped the hood then walked around the front to duck under it.

"Thanks, Rudy. I really appreciate it." I hoped he'd work his magic again. *He kept her running for this long.* "We actually have to get back. Okay if we leave you to it?"

"Yeah, yeah." He waved distractedly. His mind was already at work on Cru. "I'll call you with the verdict later today or Monday." As I inched closer to Rudy, Rafe stepped away. He mentioned requesting an Uber while we rode the few miles to the garage with Fred.

"A car will be here in a couple minutes." He whispered close to my ear. I hummed. Rafe extended his hand, and I reached for it without a second thought.

"Tell Oscar I said hi," I called as a dark sedan pulled up.

"Will do, Wyn. Talk to you soon."

"Thanks again, Rudy. You're the best." His head came up from under the hood and sent me a wink.

"You doing okay, sweetheart?" Rafe asked the question several minutes after we pulled out of the garage's small parking lot. The driver paid close attention to the road and his GPS, my apartment complex just a short, ten-minute drive away now.

"I'm okay. I've had Cru for about eight years. It's just hard. I knew this day was coming sooner rather than later but…"

"I'm sorry, Wyn. Your mechanic any good?"

"Rudy? Yeah, he's amazing. I trust him."

He nodded, turning his face toward the window on his side.

"So, Rudy…" Rafe's deep voice almost boomed in the uneasy silence. "He seems nice. How long have you been going to his garage?"

"Since it opened a few years ago. They do good work there. Rudy has Cru purring like a kitten most of the time. I hope him and Oscar can work one of their miracles again."

"I didn't see anyone else there," he murmured. *Am I hearing something in his voice?*

He'd been quiet and just a little distant since we left the garage. I was probably imagining it. And he was right. After Fred took the car off the hitch, he went off on another call. Other than Rudy, me and Rafe, the place had seemed almost deserted. But that didn't mean Oscar wasn't nearby.

I really liked both of them. They'd always been dependable and honest with me. Always warning me that they couldn't work miracles and then they did. I appreciated it. Plus, those two guys were hot. Even though I didn't feel like smiling, I did at the thought.

*Could Rafe be jealous?* I asked myself, almost scoffing at the idea because it seemed so unlikely.

I was a regular at their place. More than a customer to them, I was a friend. We'd hung out some, but not for a long time. My fault. But neither one of them had any interest in me. I was more than sure of that.

I glanced over at Rafe again and noticed he still looked elsewhere. I didn't like it one bit, especially after having his intense focus on me, filling me up with warmth. Right now, there was a slight chill in my bones.

I'd put us both out of our misery.

"Oscar is his partner. Half the time he works on cars with Rudy and the rest of the time he handles the office." My eyes stayed on Rafe. "They're a great couple." His gaze cut to mine with the last statement.

I watched as my words finally filtered through to him.

"O-oh." He stretched the vowel out for a long moment. "Great. That's great." A genuine smile graced my lips.

"Yeah." *So, I did see a little more green in his eyes there.* I stopped myself from chuckling. It was close though.

The driver turned into my complex a minute later. We thanked him then exited his car. No words passed between us as we took the flight of stairs up to my apartment.

Stopping at the front door, I turned to Rafe. He took two small steps and boom; he was right there in my personal space. I knew he'd kiss me.

I wanted him to, yet he waited several moments. Maybe he needed a cue from me. I didn't know for sure.

His hand came up to my chin, lifting my face. His gaze stole mine, holding me hostage with those green orbs. I couldn't look away even if I wanted to. He had my full attention.

Our bodies inching closer, he brought his lips to mine. I hummed. *Finally.* He tasted of maple syrup and bacon. And the slight bitterness of the coffee he drank earlier. It all mingled together into something amazing. Like Rafe. Strong, dark, and sweet.

He nibbled on my bottom lip for a long minute, my body responding to him in an unsettling way. In a good way.

My hands found his torso, clinging to him. Rafe's arms came around my back and pulled me in closer.

*God, he turns me upside down.*

Trapped between us, I clenched my hands on his shirt, riding the waves of his kisses, needing an anchor.

We kissed for what felt like hours but was more likely a few minutes. Then he stepped back abruptly. I pushed up on my tiptoes at some point and now rocked back on my heels. He leaned toward me again and laid his forehead against mine.

Our ragged breaths mixed in the small space between us. I opened my eyes and watched him wrestle with himself. He leaned away and stared down at me with that intense look again. I unclenched my hands and let them fall.

"I'll see you tonight, sweetheart." I nodded, unlocking my door, and waved goodbye.

Once inside my apartment, I practically collapsed against the door, closed my eyes and took a deep breath as his footfalls faded.

Rafe had the capacity to ruin me. In a whole other way.

He made me feel crazy and amazing. Crazy amazing things. All at the same time.

*Damn him.*

# Chapter Eighteen
*Rafe*

When I kissed Wyn, the world around me felt fucking amazing. The nonstop busyness in my head calmed and slowed down when she was near. If I didn't have to book it to practice, I'd have stayed right there with her.

I'd taste those plump lips and make her breathless, keeping Wyn in my arms where she belonged.

I had to stop thinking that shit right now or the only place I was headed was back to her apartment. I had a hard-enough time getting my act together this morning when I still lay in her bed. Time to refocus. Seeing her tonight would come soon enough.

Still, my latent caveman wanted to pound his chest after the garage deal.

One look at that fucking pretty boy Rudy and I saw green. He had a familiarity with Wyn I didn't like one damn bit. I simmered, almost boiling the whole time we were there. I couldn't explain it. Nothing quite like that had ever come over me before.

I only calmed down when she told me about his partner. By then, I just felt like a jealous fool.

But Wyn was mine.

I needed to get a grip. She seemed closer, yet still not fully within my reach. Like she'd spook at any moment. And that wasn't what I wanted.

Back at my place, I parked my truck and jogged up the stairs to my studio apartment. I had less than an hour to shower and head to practice.

Against my better judgment, I pulled my phone out of my pocket. The digital numbers floating around my screen warned me I had zero time to waste. A shower and grabbing my gear should've been on my immediate to-do list. However, so was calling Zi. My best friend always told it to me straight.

And a quick chat with him would do me some good.

I toed off my boots while holding the phone to my ear. The incessant ring-back tone kept on for long seconds. I was just about to hang up and try again later when he finally picked up, sounding out of breath.

"Yo?" His gravelly baritone came over the line.

Straight to the point I rushed out, "I met a girl, Zi." Sounding like a preteen with his first crush, I owned the fluttering excitement rushing through me. Everything going on with me and Wyn was good. Telling my best friend had been my first thought. *He's my brother from another mother.*

"Whoa, goofball. Start from the beginning. My ass lives vicariously through you now." He chuckled. "One sec, bruh." I heard grunting and some shuffling.

"No, ya don't. You will find someone when you least expect, Zi." Just like I did. Zi sighed over the line, muttering his disbelief. "Did I catch you at a bad time?"

"I finished up my work out a second before you called. Now stop stalling and tell me about your girl."

And I did. I started with how we met, my stare game across the dark stage. He cracked up at the story of my pool lesson and flirting fails from the first date, finding them way too funny. Although he laughed at my expense, looking back I got how funny it all sounded, so I finally joined him.

"Man. It's bizarre, ya know? I've never been able to talk to a girl the way I talk with Wyn. I told her about my dad and Lanni." *My mom.*

"Shit. She sounds special, bruh. Different from some of these other girls you dated before."

So true. This immediate comfort level had never happened with anyone else. All of the intrinsic parts of ourselves attracting us to one another. Not the surface bullshit like looks alone, but the deeper, darker fundamentals.

Nodding my agreement, I realized he couldn't see me. "I think she might be." My eyes caught the red digital numbers on the microwave. I needed to wrap this up. "Zi, I'll catch up with you later. Need to get my ass in the shower and book it to practice."

"Before you go… you hear from Chloe?" Zi's calm voice barely hid his undercurrent of worry, but I knew him too well. Concern for his baby sister was ever-present. Innate. To tell the truth, I was concerned too. She was always in the back of my mind.

"No, Zi. Not for a few weeks. You know I'll call you soon as I do." When she called, I always wanted her to stay on the line long enough to patch her family through. Any time I brought it up, though, she rushed off with one empty excuse or another.

Chloe loved them. She was also afraid *for them*. That much was evident in her goodbye letter.

I knew she'd ring me soon. Faith. *Hope*. Whatever you called it. That word came to mind more and more these days. I had more of the elusive feeling these last few months. On the flip side, I felt like I had a lot more to lose.

Zi had lost a fuck ton of shit in the past seven months. And every time he asked about his sister and I had no information for him, he lost her all over again.

It messed me up just hearing the sadness in his voice. The situation sucked on all sides. My second family was hurting, and I could do shit-all about it.

"Yeah, I know Rafe. Just needed to ask, ya feel me?"

"Yeah."

"Now, get your musty ass washed and to practice. I'm guessing you'll be seeing your girl soon."

"Haha. Wyn said she'd come to our show tonight."

"Good deal. Holla back and let me know what's up with this new band of yours. You've been all hush-hush and shit about them."

"Sorry, man. I'll call you in a couple days. I wanna know what's going on with you. Your parents."

"Same shit, different channel. I won't bore you with the details. Talk soon, bruh."

"Bye."

Yesterday and today played in my mind as I rushed through the shower and getting dressed.

Now, I had five minutes for a fifteen-minute drive across town. I pushed it to the very back of my mind and focused on the road.

The band deserved my full attention for the next several hours.

# Chapter Nineteen
*Wyn*

I texted Darcy, letting her know Cru was at the shop and asking if she'd reserve a rental car at the airport. The plan had been for me to pick her up, but that was impossible now. Her four-hour flight left around ten this morning west coast time, so I expected her home closer to six o'clock this evening.

My phone stayed in the kitchen, far enough away, yet still within easy reach if someone called or messaged me. I stopped myself several times from dialing Rudy at the garage. Worry about the fate of my car was driving me crazy.

If it wasn't Cru, my thoughts went straight to Rafe. Those first moments of waking up in his arms this morning came flooding back.

*Rafe's sleep-rumpled hair. Long and almost wavy, several strands fell across the side of my face and neck. I wanted to run my fingers through it again and stay right there, cocooned in his embrace. Comfortable. He held me so tight and safe in his arms.*

*Warm breaths whispered over my skin; his face tucked into the side of my neck. I tingled all over. In places where I thought I was broken. Ruined for good. But I needed to get up and do something. Anything. Not just bask in this secure feeling I found with him. I couldn't repeat last night, no matter how much I wanted to stay right there.*

*He'd probably sleep for a while longer, I thought, yearning for some solitude. Take stock of what happened last night and how I really felt about it. Right off the bat, I didn't feel dirty or used. Rafe's arms wrapped around me meant security, feelings so incredibly new for me. I for sure slept better than I have in a year, but I couldn't get used to this yet. A wildcard, I was still unsure of what he really saw in me. What he wanted from me.*

*It took a couple tries before I wrestled myself free without disturbing him. Most of our clothes stayed on last night which came as a surprise. I grabbed a T-shirt and shorts from my dresser. Before leaving the room, I took one longer look at Rafe. He turned over, sprawled out and face down on the mattress. A smile formed on my lips. Time for tea and contemplation, my grandmother liked to say.*

*He gave me a lot to think about.*

Darcy opened the front door, barreling through and propping her carry-on luggage against the entry wall. *How long have I been daydreaming?* I didn't even hear all the commotion outside. She tossed her purse and keys on the coffee table and sat down across from me on the couch. A couple hours had passed by while sitting in the same spot on the loveseat, reminiscing about this morning and Rafe.

Without preamble Darcy asked about Cru, "So, the heck happened this morning? Is it the end of the deathtrap?"

The look I gave her let her know to tread lightly. I didn't want to hear all the reasons I should've gotten a new car five years ago. Although I still held hope she'd run a while longer, these might be her last days. "Sorry, Wyn. So, tell me what happened," she urged.

"Well, Rafe and I were coming back here for his car after we had breakfast and—"

"Wait. Rewind!" Darcy almost fell off the couch, she popped up so quickly, barely catching herself on the coffee table and scattering her keys and some papers I had lying around. "I need you to back up a little more because, Wyn, I thought I heard you say you had to come back here to pick up Rafe's car."

"We decided to take my car for breakfast. He'd never been to Paula's before." I shrugged my shoulder, not seeing the big deal.

"So Rafe came back this morning after your date? You two must've had a great time."

"Oh, uh yeah. The date with Rafe was good. He stayed the night."

"You hussy!" Darcy smiled from ear to ear. She leaned closer, poking my side and snickering as she sat back on the couch.

"No, it isn't like that." It was and it wasn't, I guessed. But I couldn't really explain to Dar because she didn't know the whole story.

"We didn't go all the way," I shared instead. "We talked. I'm surprised how easy it is to talk to him, Dar. It's nice." The oversimplification was the only way to describe everything. Rafe laid on the charm, but he could also be himself with me. *Authentic*. He really listened, at the same time knowing what I could handle even when words failed me.

"Wyn, I'm so happy for you. I'm glad you like Rafe so much. Who'd have thunk it, huh? The two of us dating hunky guys." We both chuckled. "Well, I don't know about my situation now with this new project coming up…"

I tucked my leg under me and got comfortable. I wanted to hear about California. "What about your trip, Dar? Were the facilities amazing?"

Thoroughly distracted, she told me about the new job prospect in California. "Yes, it was more than amazing, if there's such a thing. I want to go. I think it'll be good for me."

Neither of us knew what the future held. Rafe? Darcy and Colt? It was all up in the air and landing was spotty. For now, I held on to the hope and excitement shining in Darcy's eyes, and I knew some of that hope was there in my own.

We arrived at Del Rio's ten minutes before the opening act hit the stage. Darcy navigated the rental car through the busy streets of downtown, quiet the entire ride. As we parked, she mentioned not being too gung-ho about pushing to the front. I agreed. She must've been nervous seeing Colt after deciding about California.

We got into the bar with no problem since Rafe left our names at the door. A spot opened up at one end of the L-shaped bar, so we took it, choosing to stay in the background tonight. Still, we came here to cheer them on, even though we had a lot on our minds.

Like an alternate universe, I was the one talking Darcy into coming out tonight. I found the change in our positions a little ironic. She was excited for me, but I also supported her decision to go to California. She just had to find time to tell Colt.

The main goal for coming out was to support the band, even if we were both confused, wary, excited, and everything in between.

The lights dimmed, signaling the first act. The crowd blurred around me while Darcy ordered a cocktail for her and water for me. I volunteered to be the sober one tonight. Plus, we had the rental car to worry about which was sleek and purred like a damn kitten. I hated and loved it on sight, missing Cru all the same.

Del Rio's had a nice, big crowd tonight. I knew more people planned to arrive closer to Country Blue's scheduled start time in an hour. I was glad we got here when we did and snagged this spot at the bar. It had a nice, clear view of the stage. Circumstances might change as more people arrived and volleyed for a spot closer to the stage, but I was happy for now.

A lone guy strummed his first note as the lights came up on stage. Armed with an acoustic guitar and keyboard off to the side, he stood alone. Some people in the crowd whooped, making him chuckle as he started his first song.

Del Rio's was a great venue for acts and concertgoers, alike. Those looking for an intimate night of music. There were some pub tables and chairs placed in the center of the dining area. When we arrived, staff were already removing them to accommodate the standing room only crowd. Some high-back booths sat against the wall, opposite the other side of the bar. People choosing to sit on that side had to watch the show from monitors hanging over the bar counter.

It was a nice and small venue; however, weirdly configured for musical acts, I thought.

The half hour for the opener flew by quickly. He was really good once he settled into himself. His melodic voice floated over the crowd, a hint of a soulful twang. And a surprising contrast to Colt's voice.

Lights dimmed once again while men dressed in black flooded the small stage, setting up for the next act. *Our guys.*

Heightened anticipation reverberated in the incongruous space, growing among the crowd. Staff removed the remaining tables and chairs to make a dance floor. The size of the crowd doubled in a matter of minutes as the low murmuring of voices turned into a loud rumbling in my ears. Throngs of people jostled each other for temporary real estate at the bar, yet Darcy and I stayed resolute in our spot. Everyone revved up for the show ahead.

Twenty minutes passed at a snail's pace.

Darcy remained contemplative next to me. Too quiet. Only a few huffs and murmurs between us. An unusual phenomenon. We had a lot on our minds, and it was showing.

The lights flickered. The guys walked onstage. Berto perched on his stool and rolled drumsticks around his fingers. Although his face was obscured, I knew he wore a grin. A boyish charm all wrapped up in a compact but handsome package. My eyes swung over to Doug next. He plugged his guitar into an amp, fiddling with the chords. A pick trapped between his lips, he smirked around it as some woman screamed his name. Colt stood brooding at the microphone with his head down, hands wrapped around the mic stand. Darcy perked up beside me for the first time tonight, watching him with sharp eyes.

I did my own bit of watching. Rafe looked hot tonight. He always did. A quick glance out at the crowd, his eyes finally zoned in on his bass, his almost black hair falling into his face. Seconds later his gaze returned, sweeping the first few rows of people. I didn't remember Rafe looking at the crowd so much the last time I saw them play. He'd mostly kept his eyes focused on his instrument or the band.

*Was he looking for me in the sea of people?* I wondered.

The thought made me smile. My decision to come had been a good one, I decided. *Giving me and Rafe a chance.* I'd spent enough time fearing my own shadow and blaming myself. Rafe helped me come back to life again. Something I hadn't had the capacity for after last year. Nerves and fear still gripped me, yet the excitement remained. I needed this. To give us a shot. To be normal again. Maybe find some happiness.

Suddenly Berto tapped his sticks and the introduction to their first song played. I didn't know this one. The guys seemed so different, yet when they were together like this, they were of one mind and goal: putting on an awesome show. From the roar of the crowd, they were off to a great start. I settled in to listen and enjoy myself.

My worries and fears took a backseat for now.

They rocked tonight. Beyond just a solid performance. They were in sync, feeding off one another. Rafe was... electric. His kinetic energy floated over, filling me with excitement and hopefulness. That man on stage wanted me. And I wanted him. I craved this new thing with Rafe so damn bad I hurt with it.

Next time I looked up, an hour and some change had passed. Their set had ended, and they were leaving the stage. I was equal parts anxious and eager to see Rafe close up after last night and this morning's adventure. *How would it be between us?* Hours since we last saw and spoke to one another, the situation might've changed for him. Worry consumed me now. I felt a hard poke in my side. "Ow! What?" *Darcy and her bony-assed fingers.*

"The jig is up. The guys are coming this way," she whispered harshly. Darcy took a gulp of her second drink as I turned slightly. True to her word, I saw Rafe in all his rock-star swagger coming my way. Suddenly, I was the thirsty one.

Once the guys exited the stage, the crowd quickly dispersed. Some people flooded the bar to close out tabs and head home. Other concertgoers stuck around to see what the DJ played. Music pumped from the house speakers seconds after the lights came up.

Stragglers waited around, hoping to chat up the band for a few minutes. The guys packed away a bunch of their stuff. They left most of it on the stage in favor of getting a drink and hanging out, I guessed.

Excited fans tried stopping them, but Rafe and Colt's destination was clear. Both gazes locked and loaded on the bar. On us. Doug and Berto trailed behind them, chatting up a small circle of people still by the stage. Those two soaked up the attention. My gaze found Rafe again, much closer than he was before. *Damn, he moves fast.* In a second, he stood in front of me, looking down, a satisfied grin forming on his lips. The lips I kissed several hours ago. That I wanted to kiss again.

"Hey." I got my wish when he bent down and pressed a quick peck on my lips. I caught the surprised and happy look on Colt and Darcy's faces in the periphery. *They weren't the only ones!*

"Hi, Rafe. You were amazing tonight… I mean the band was amazing."

"Thanks." He walked around and stood behind me. Warm air flowed across my ear before he whispered, "That means a lot coming from you." Rafe's arms circled me, his large hands settling on my stomach, and pulled my back flush against him.

Like last night, I felt safe in his arms.

"Do you want anything, Wyn?" I asked for a refill on my water while the others ordered drinks from one of the two harried bartenders trying to keep up with the crowd. As soon as the drinks arrived, Colt whisked Darcy off to the other side of the club. I thought I heard him say something about seeing an unexpected guest but couldn't be sure. It was still quite loud with the music playing and groups of people milling around.

Rafe squeezed me then let go. His warmth and woodsy scent surrounded me. "I'll be right back. Drank a ton of water onstage," he shared. He made his way to the men's room at the other side of the club. *I can do this… be with him*, I coached myself. He's been great so far, not pressuring me or pushing me for answers about my strange behavior.

Suddenly feeling awkward standing at the bar by myself, I scanned near the stage area, searching for Darcy and Colt. They'd crossed to the other side of the venue a few minutes ago. Now, I saw them near the entrance and tried catching their attention. I finished my water and took a few steps toward them, freezing in my tracks seconds later.

*Boom, boom, boom* filled my ears. The air in the club pounded, pushing me down, strangling me. Blood rushed to my head, making me dizzy. Chills slithered up and down my spine. My limbs couldn't move. I choked from the unforgiving panic seizing my body. My nightmare, my monster thrust me back into the darkness again without his grimy hands being anywhere near me. Clear across the room.

Nick Ferrara.

This wasn't possible. The words spun around in my head on repeat. This had to be one of my nightmares because I'd felt so safe only moments ago. All the happiness and safety I had wrapped up in Rafe's arms, it was gone now.

*He can't be here right now. He just can't.*

His obnoxiously loud laugh split the air and penetrated through the dense fog in my head. My body and brain unfroze. Self-preservation told me to run and not look back. I wasn't ready to see Nick. Hell, I never wanted to see that bastard again. The wounds I'd stitched together these last few weeks with Rafe opened again. Longer and wider. More jagged. His unexpected appearance took a blade to them and sliced me right open.

I had to get out of here before Rafe or Darcy saw me. I cracked into little, tiny pieces the longer I stood around. No chance of gluing myself back together, shredded beyond repair. They'd know something was wrong if they got a good look at me now. I'd hid this from Dar for too long, and now it all came crashing down around me.

My entire body went cold; my face incapable of hiding my complete unraveling. Just seeing him brought the night back to the surface in hi-def. *Why did I kid myself?* I wasn't meant to feel safe and happy. Rafe was the best dream, but I lived in a constant nightmare.

I'd never be whole again after what Nick did. Those memories followed me, scarring me anew with fresh wounds every day. Not so easily stitched back together.

This past year was proof I was damaged goods.

One foot moved then the other. I was shaking so damn hard. Before I knew it, I was at the back entrance and heading to the small public parking lot. I sucked in air, bursting through the exit door, feeling chased. Although I knew no one followed, my heart raced anyway, flooding my ears with a cacophony of noise. No one witnessed my escape or else I wouldn't have made it outside as fast as I did.

Tears fell just as I touched the handle of our rental car. Thank God Darcy gave me the keys after we parked. I took a deep breath, wiping my eyes to get a grip. I had to drive home safely, not jump a curb or god forbid hit someone because I was bawling my eyes out behind the wheel. Before I put the key in the ignition, the passenger door opened. Darcy got in and slammed the door.

"Wyn, what's wrong? Was it Rafe?" I had to look pretty out of it for her to think Rafe did this to me. My hands braced the wheel, the key forgotten in the ignition as my whole body shook. "What the hell, Wyn? Talk to me." I tried for a deep breath and sighed with reluctance. She wouldn't let me drive away without explaining anyway.

"Did I do something to make you mad?" Before I stopped her from thinking this was in any way because of her, she kept talking. "I'm sorry I've been consumed by Colton the whole night. You know we still haven't seen each other much since I've been back, but there's no excuse... and with California hovering over me—" She huffed. "I'm a sucky friend, right?"

"What? No. This has nothing to do with Rafe or you or Colt." I released a deep sigh. All this negative energy coursed through me, crawling up my spine and trying to burrow its way in. It messed with me big time, seeing him again.

Opening pandora's box wasn't in my plans, not tonight when everything had been going so well, but I knew Darcy wouldn't let this go. I hit the automatic locks, shutting us in and shutting out anyone else who came looking. "I didn't know Nick was coming... I thought he was touring with his new band," I stalled. A quiver shook my voice just from uttering his name.

"Nick? Colt said they ran into him at the music festival a few weeks back. He mentioned inviting him tonight but didn't think he'd be in town. I guess it was a slim possibility he'd show." I saw the confusion on her face.

"I wish you'd told me." Tonight… thinking I could be normal with Rafe had been a huge mistake on my part. Sighing, I told her, "I would've made up an excuse not to come if I'd known." Safer to stay my butt at home, cocooned on the couch while crying myself to sleep. It was the only plan now.

"What? Why, because of Nick? That makes no sense. Tell me what's going on, Wyn." The crease between her brows appeared when she crinkled her forehead. She wondered at what I wasn't saying, her thoughts traveling a mile a minute.

*How can I tell her this now? Here?* "I never told you what all happened that night we hung out with the band in one of their hotel rooms. After you and Colt went to sleep in the bedroom. Nick and I, we stayed on the sofa bed and did more than kiss." *He did much more.* Her face scrunched even more with confusion. I needed to keep going. Get it all out. Say the words once and for all.

"I'm broken, Dar." *Ruined.* It was anyone's guess why Rafe pursued me. I kept running hot and cold with him. I peeked over at Darcy. "And so far, Rafe's so patient with my weirdness. He's been really good to me." *For me.* "When I tell him to stop, he does. And he took care of me and held me last night. I know he wanted more, but he didn't push, didn't just take from me."

"Wyn?" Although I wouldn't look at her, not yet, I could hear the emotion in her voice. She grabbed my right hand and clutched it against her chest. I felt the deep, shuddering breath she took. "What happened?"

"Well, you saw us cuddling earlier that night. I was a bit uncomfortable. Not because I didn't like him. You know my history; I've never had many guys show interest in me. I wanted to do what I didn't do as a teenager, make out for a few minutes with a guy who found me attractive. I guess Nick took it as an open invitation for more."

The floodgates were open now. I had to let some of it out before the darkness suffocated me for good. "I should've stopped him before he got the wrong idea. I should've stopped it from the beginning, but then my shirt was up, and he was kissing me all over. It didn't feel good or bad, not then."

"Don't you dare blame yourself for what happened!" I heard the quiet fury in her voice, and it made me pause. I blamed myself, every damn day. "You don't have to go into too much detail… just tell me whatever you can."

"I told him no several times, Dar. I did. I didn't want to go all the way." *Not with him, I'd only just met him.* Colt, Doug and Berto sang his praises the whole night, especially when he'd shown interest in me. How great of a guy he was. How honorable he was. It just shows how much I should've trusted my gut, when I first saw the way he strutted through the crowd, like he owned the fucking world.

We were two peas in a pod, Darcy and me. Neither of us made a habit of putting our trust in people easily. Darcy quickly became comfortable with Colt in a way I'd never seen her with other guys. So, I took Colt and his bandmates at their word. My biggest mistake, I guessed. I was old enough to know better, *wasn't I?*

Apparently not.

"He started kissing my neck and shoulders. I liked it. I'm not denying that, but it dovetailed so damn quick. Then my shirt is pushed up and he's fondling me, kissing my chest and stomach." I stopped for a moment. I should've been stronger, I told myself. Should be stronger now but telling my best friend how this past year's been a living hell because of that night was near impossible. It was stupid, not wanting to see her disappointment in me. If she hated me now, it would decimate me.

*My hands found their way to his shoulders and then down to the center of his chest, trying to push him off. Slow him down. He wouldn't budge the lower half of his body, trapping me under him. He grabbed my wrists and pushed them over my head. When both my wrists were in one hand, he squeezed them. I couldn't break his hold. "Mm, I like it when you struggle," he whispered across my cheek. His words scared me. Made me feel powerless.*

*He pushed all the way inside of me and just as I was about to scream, his calloused hand covered my mouth, pushing me further down into the lumpy mattress. I imagined Darcy and Colt slept in the other room, blissfully unaware of how I was being ripped apart from the inside out. Realizing I was just a body to him. Accessible. Disposable.*

*Nick's thrusts became faster and rougher as he neared completion, my cries remained silent. I didn't want them to see me now, not like this. I felt his ragged breath puff against my chin. His teeth scraped me there just as I felt the first jet of spend, him jerking inside me. Unprotected.*

*Oh God. His hand slipped from my mouth and his body fell on top of me. His lips found my cheek as he rolled off me and the bed in one fluid movement. Nick made his way to the bathroom to grab a towel. I heard the wisp of the heavy cotton as it landed on the floor after he wiped me off then himself. His movements were hurried and rough. I pulled my pants back on and shook his hands off as he attempted to help. He grabbed me around my waist and pulled me to his front to cuddle. His head rested on the back of my neck, hot air, and wet lips brushing my skin. I shrunk into myself even more.*

*My head lifted and I noticed the bedside table, seeing the red numbers on the alarm clock. Tears pooling in my eyes made them blur in front of me. So little time had passed since Darcy and Colt went into the bedroom. It felt like I'd been here with Nick for an eternity. The sun had slowly risen in the sky, yet I hadn't noticed until now. I murmured I needed to go. I rolled away from him and sat up. I needed to wake Darcy up and we had to get the hell out of here before I shattered into little, tiny pieces in front of this monster.*

I haven't uttered the words out loud yet to anyone, not even to myself. "He r-raped m-me, Dar." I stuttered, hiccupping as the dreaded admission left my mouth after all these months. "I didn't want to go all the way, but he trapped me u-under him and... I wanted to scream, it hurt so much, but he forced a hand over my mouth." When it was over, I just wanted to get out of there. "I woke you up after he finished with me." My skin crawled just thinking about his hands on me. "And then we left."

The inside of the car was quiet for so long after I finished. My eyes stared into its dark interior. I still hadn't turned the key in the ignition.

"I'm so sorry I wasn't there for you, Wyn. But I'm here now and that rat bastard is gonna pay." Before Darcy shifted to grab the door handle on the passenger side, I stopped her. I couldn't let her go back in there to confront Nick, not with Rafe and Colt there too. The tears streamed down my face again. I muttered "please, don't" while shaking my head, my whole body following. Her arms came around me and pulled me closer. We were both poked by the gear shift, yet neither of us made a move to let go. She shuddered, our tears soaking each other's shoulders.

After a minute I pulled back, turning away. I sniffled and wiped my eyes. "Please, can we just go? Text Colt and tell him I had an emergency. I can't be here, not now," I wheezed. Not anywhere he is. *Not ever, if I had anything to say about it. He torments me and doesn't even fucking know it.* And Rafe, what'll he think about my disappearing act?

It was too much to deal with. And I no longer had the energy to pretend I was remotely okay. I dropped my head to the steering wheel and hiccupped. Wrung dry.

"Yeah, Wyn. Let's go home. I'll text Colt so he doesn't worry. Tell him to let Rafe know you aren't feeling well, okay?" Her confirmation and suggestion swept some of the worry off my shoulders. No more explaining to anyone else. *Not for tonight, at least.* A moment's reprieve and I grabbed at it.

Starting the car, I checked my mirrors then backed out of the parking space. I still couldn't look at Darcy although I knew she threw glances my way. Worried for me, she quickly tapped out the text to Colt. No questions asked; it was how our relationship worked. We dropped everything for each other. Once we were home, I'd feel better, safer.

At least I hoped.

# Chapter Twenty
*Wyn*

Both screens lit up in the dark room as our phones continued to vibrate with more messages. I left mine on the coffee table, turning off the sound while Darcy's sat on the arm of the couch.

We put on a movie, neither of us paying much attention to it. The jokes didn't hit their mark this time. No laughs filled the cool air of the living room. Darcy paused the movie to go to the kitchen then came back to the couch. Her eyes were on me, but I was numb. So damn exhausted and numb. There was nothing anyone could do about it.

"I knew something had happened, Wyn. Not the when or the what. You've been acting withdrawn for a few months now. I didn't question it like I should have." *Like your best friend should have*, hearing the words she didn't voice. "You needed me, and I wasn't there."

"I wasn't ready, Dar. I still don't think I am, but I really like Rafe. I know he's different. I know he's not N-Nick and I can't give him a chance. Give *us* a fighting chance if I keep all of this inside me like I've been doing," voice hoarse from the endless crying jag after my confession at the club and when we got home. I just wanted to stay here on this couch, not saying or doing much. Darcy understood and stayed with me.

I didn't dare tell her the other reason I kept what really happened all those months ago to myself. Her budding relationship with Colt was the only bright spot. She had so much crap heaped on her over the years that she didn't let people in often. Such small things in common ruling our lives. I couldn't let what happened to me railroad this opportunity for her. *One of us deserved some damned happiness for once.* It made little sense for both of us to keep ourselves closed off forever.

"I won't take the job in California next month, Wyn." *Was it just earlier today she told me she'd accept the contract?*

Darcy planned to leave after her fundraiser for an organization she's worked with since high school. The event was a couple weeks away. The California contract seemed short as they wanted her there for the summer and early fall, returning in mid-October.

I threw off the blanket draped around my shoulders and faced her. "Don't you fucking dare, Dar!" I was beyond furious. She blanched from my outburst. I hardly cursed out loud and never at her. This was what I didn't want. Darcy would *not* change her plans because of me, I wasn't having it.

"You will go back to California in a couple of weeks to help those sick and injured sea animals. You will enjoy yourself. And you will keep an open mind about you and Colt. End of story, am I clear?"

The room became deathly still as I watched her. She bobbed her head. Grabbing the remote, I pressed play and burrowed under the blanket once again.

*I won't let Nick's reappearance ruin everything. I won't*, I promised myself. Darcy needed California. A dream come true for her. I just needed some time to think.

The bold-faced lie hovered over me even though I never uttered the words out loud.

# Chapter Twenty-One
*Rafe*

*What the fuck is the world coming to that a guy can't take a piss in peace anymore?* The one time I had somebody waiting for me who I actually wanted to get back to and this drunk dude trapped me in the bathroom.

*Accosted in the damn john*, I shook my head. At least he wasn't belligerent, only wanting to talk music with me.

After a few minutes, he finally left me alone to finish my business. I moved over to the sink to wash my hands and thoughts immediately strayed to Wyn. When I made my way over to her after our set, my eyes traveled up and down her body. She looked phenomenal tonight, but she always looked good to me. Her outfit hugged her generous curves in fantastic ways. I had intimate knowledge of those curves too. Even though we stayed fully clothed, I took my time tracing the lines of her body last night.

Wyn loved pairing long shirts with jeans or leggings. I noticed and approved. And I was in a hurry to wrap my arms around her again. There was also an energy about her tonight. I couldn't put my finger on it exactly. Maybe more of her walls came down since this morning. I hoped that was the case.

In a few, short weeks Wyn's kept my interest and I wanted to learn more. What exactly? I didn't care. Just more because it all felt natural with her. I wasn't a phony or *pansy* and could be myself.

I left the men's room, walking down the short corridor and passing the back entrance. Finally, I returned to the main area and didn't see Wyn standing at the bar or anywhere else.

The huge crowd had dispersed since the band left the stage, so her absence was obvious to me. *Where is she?* "Where the hell did she go?" I asked aloud.

I went to take a piss and then my girl disappears on me? *Can't say that's ever happened before.* Maybe she's out back chatting with Darcy.

Or had I come on too strong just then, made her run away? I thought back to our short conversation and nothing came to mind. No red flags flashed. I had *niente*.

I clocked Berto and Doug on the other side of the bar chatting up the two busty bartenders. Colt stood over by the entrance looking down at his phone. I walked towards him since I hadn't seen Darcy either. He might know what the hell was going on.

"Colt, have you seen Wyn in the last few minutes?"

"Yeah," he answered distractedly. "Darcy watched her head out the back door and went after her a few minutes ago. She looked a little spooked, man. Like the hounds of hell were after her," he added as an afterthought. His phone pinged and I was one second away from following them.

"You didn't go check on them?" An obvious growl entered my voice. His attention remained on his phone, so I turned my back on him with every intention of heading in the girls' direction.

Colt's hand on my shoulder stopped me. "Calm the hell down, Rambo. Of course, I followed behind Darcy. They were still in the parking lot a few minutes ago, sitting in the car. In a deep discussion, I guess." *What the hell happened after I left her at the bar?* "I came back in to give them space, but I just got a text. Darcy says they're on their way home. Wyn's not feeling well."

"What the hell, man?" She seemed fine earlier. Something didn't feel right. None of this gelled or made a lick of sense. Colt even said she seemed spooked. Something happened during the ten minutes I was away from her. And it wasn't any damn illness.

I pulled my phone out and tried calling her. It rang and rang until the voicemail clicked on. Wyn's sexy voice came over the line, instructing me to leave my name and number and she'd return my call as soon as possible.

*Shit.*

I shoved the phone back in my pocket, not bothering to leave a message. She'd see my missed call and ring me back when she could. If not, I'd try again later. And keep trying until I heard from her.

Standing around here guessing what went sour proved worthless. The air in the club stifled me now. The place practically empty compared to when we played only minutes ago. I needed fresh air and answers. Only one was in my immediate future, so I decided I'd cut my losses. No telling when I'd hear from Wyn.

"Hey fellas. Wassup?" Nick walked up out of nowhere holding a tumbler of dark liquor in his hand and a sly look. I was in no fucking mood to deal with his bullshit right now. His appearance was my final cue to get the fuck out of dodge.

I ignored Nick's greeting to the group, looking back at Colt and telling him I needed to head out. Thankfully, we packed most of the equipment up immediately following our set. I grabbed my case from the stage and went back to the entrance. My truck was across the street since I drove myself tonight.

"Catch ya later, Ralph." I stopped myself from turning around and going back to knock him on his ass. He knew my goddamn name. It was just his adolescent way of trying to antagonize me. I wouldn't let him get to me yet visualizing the crunch of my fist hitting his face satisfied the violent impulse. Plus, Colt didn't seem like a guy who'd stand idly by while I kicked his best friend's ass. Even if he was a dickhead.

And I wasn't a violent person by nature, despite my childhood. Nick had me at my tipping point, though, and he'd only said a few words. I didn't need his bullshit or the grief right now.

As the cool night air touched my face, I heard him say, "Yo, what's up his ass?"

Not waiting around to hear Colt's response, I kept walking. Thank God I had some self-control. And bullies and pricks like him didn't faze me *much* anymore.

"Sweetheart, it's me again. I hope you get this message." There's been radio silence since last night. And it slowly killed me. "I'm worried about you. Let me know that you're alright, okay?" Yet another call that'd gone straight to voicemail. I tossed my phone on the bed.

Wyn wasn't answering my calls or texts especially after receiving a vague message from her while I was asleep.

**Not feeling too good. Give me some time pls.**

The text came in around three in the morning. I got back to my apartment just after midnight. To get my mind off worrying, I watched a movie on my laptop, but wasn't too sure when I finally fell asleep. I probably rocked out some time after one.

What had she been doing up so late? And what did Wyn mean by *give her some time*? I dropped back on my futon mattress and immediately felt a pinch. A corner of my phone dug into my lower back, so I shifted and moved it over.

I couldn't just sit around here doing nothing. Driving myself crazy asking the same damn questions and no closer to answers.

Colt set our next practice for tomorrow afternoon. The days were getting longer, and I had too much time to kill. I sent him a text to see if he had time to talk. Maybe he'd heard from Darcy. I was grasping at short straws, but they were all I had.

**You busy? I need to run something by you.**

A few minutes later my phone beeped with his reply. **Nah man. I'm at my place. Stop over if you want.**

**Be there in 20.** If nothing else, I could talk out all this shit gnawing at me concerning Wyn.

I pulled up to Colt's place within fifteen minutes. A little speeding and some rolling stops had me there in record time. Restless and a bit pissed off.

Wyn had me tied up in knots. And with Nick popping up lately, it had me wondering about his angle. Whether he was coming around to take back his place in the band. Or just fuck with me.

Getting answers or punching a wall sounded damn good right now. *Ugh!* Violence wouldn't get me what I really needed. With my luck, I'd be worse off than I was right now. And shit to show for it.

I slammed my truck's door and walked towards Colt's place. The duplex sat in the middle of a small subdivision on the outskirts of town. He seemed to have a sweet deal here. A small backyard to himself. Peace and quiet when he wanted it. And the nearest neighbor sat several yards away.

I'd been over to his place twice with the other guys since joining the band. Apparently, no one lived in the other apartment. A young couple had been renting it from Colt up until they decided to start a family and move elsewhere. Now it sat empty. Colt probably enjoyed it that way since I got the sense he was a loner outside of the band. *There's a story there, but I have other shit to think about.*

"Hey, man. Come on in. I was just hanging out back." He waved me inside then led us through the living room, back into the kitchen. "You want a drink?"

"Nah, I'm good." Colt nodded then opened the door to the backyard. He dropped down on the steps of his back patio. I stood, leaning against the brick even though he had a couple chairs out.

The silence was deafening for a while, neither of us willing to start the conversation. Awkward didn't even cover it. I'd just decided not to bother him with my shit when he turned to me and asked, "What's up, Rafe?"

I pondered his question while taking a seat on a fold-out chair. Maybe talking it all out would give me some fucking perspective.

"Have you heard from Darcy?" I started. "Wyn's not answering my calls or texts, man. I'm tempted to go over to her place..." Stupid, desperate ideas rolled around in my head since last night. I needed to hear her voice. And not her damn voicemail message again.

Alarm bells went off in my head over and over thinking about her disappearing act. And then the cryptic text from earlier this morning.

I ran a hand through my loose hair. Frustration didn't brush the surface for how it made me feel, this distancing. Especially after the other night. We've only known each other a few weeks, but I've enjoyed getting to know her. And after the last couple of days...

Wyn's ghosting and cold shoulder left me at the bottom of a basement in total darkness. And I had no idea how I got thrown down there in the first place. Let alone how I was getting out if she wasn't answering my attempts to contact her.

"I've only gotten a few one-word texts from her since last night." Dammit, now it seemed like we were in the same boat. Without a paddle. Both girls were keeping quiet, pushing us away. "Darcy's been tight lipped about a lot since the beginning. Shit, who am I kidding? She knows fuck-all about me either, but I can't seem to let her go." Colt confessed the last part in a low voice, almost to himself.

He leaned forward on the top step, digging the switchblade out of his back pocket. This situation had us both on edge. "I do know that neither of them has dated very much." The swish and clap signaled him flicking the blade opened and closed.

We were pretty much isolated back here. A fence in his backyard hid us from prying eyes. Nobody but me saw Colt's fidgeting with the dangerous weapon. I've learned since the studio prank that this was one of his tics. Couldn't fault him for this particular one right now either.

I wanted to know what he knew. Needed to know for both mine and Wyn's sakes. Unfortunately, he might be just as clueless as me.

"I'm only somewhat clued-in to Darcy and it's taken a fucking year. But Wyn... I don't know, man. She was definitely more open when we all met last year. Shit, happier even. More so than Darcy if you can believe that. Not closed off like she's been."

*So, whatever happened to her has been recent then,* I thought to myself. His words didn't surprise me much. Not after what she said the other night in bed. And the way she said it, with fear in her voice. It confirmed my thoughts since first meeting her weeks ago. Someone hurt her. "Has Darcy said anything? Maybe about how she's been acting lately."

"No, nothing. Except she's been worried about her. Glad you've gotten her out of her shell a little." Well, that was music to my ears. I wanted her to trust me, confide in me.

And dammit, sometimes I saw just a glimmer of light in her, trying to reignite. Her smiles, her humor snuck up on me, revealing more facets to her personality.

Wyn's unexpected snarkiness surprised and amused me. A sharp barb from her hit the air at the exact right moment. A sweet spot. She kept me on my toes. And I enjoyed every minute except right now. At this very moment, I was a fucking mess.

I saw a change in myself too. Hopeful in a way I hadn't been in years. Probably since I was younger. Before it all went to hell with my dad. "I think Wyn's amazing, man." I raised my head to look over at Colt, so he witnessed whatever was there in my eyes. He nodded like he knew exactly what I meant. All the words in the world couldn't completely describe what I felt. Yet, from his reaction, it probably seemed similar enough to what lay between him and Darcy.

Both of us grew quiet again. How long we'd been sitting here, I didn't know. It looked like one of the last spring storms gathered in the distance. Thick clouds clustered together as the sun hid, tucked behind them until it could shine again.

Colt's blade broke through the silence like a clap of thunder. His next words even more foreboding. "Rafe, someone's hurt both of them. Recently or not. And I can't fucking stand being kept in the dark about it."

I didn't know what warning signs he got from Darcy, but I was glad we were on similar pages. Although some of my observations were clearer now since first meeting her, I wanted something more concrete. Or at least an action plan.

"What the fuck do we do then?" I practically growled.

"We need to let them come to us, yeah?" It was good advice, but *for damn sure* not what I wanted to hear. Not while I was so wired. I wanted my girl to talk to me. Trust me. Shit, I'd settle for her crying on my goddamn shoulder, snot and all. No explanation or talking necessary.

I'd swallow my burning questions because everything else could fucking wait if she'd just let me in.

Getting Colt's two cents helped some. Even so, I still had fuck-all idea what to do about the shit rolling around in my head.

"Thanks, man." I gave Colt a salute and closed his backdoor behind me, finding my own way out. I stood on his front steps and retrieved my phone. Swiping the screen, I punched in my code, my thumbs hovering over the text box.

I didn't know what the right words were. Especially not after talking with Colt. Deep down, though, I knew sending her one last message was necessary before taking a step back.

*Cool my jets.*

Maybe I rushed her, scared her off. Something I promised myself I wouldn't do. The other night at her place got pretty damn intense. It was incredible too. And honest.

Wyn was amazing, just like I'd told Colt earlier. She was also vulnerable in a lot of ways I had no idea about. Not yet.

She obviously craved space right now and I had every intention of giving it to her. But first, I sent off my final text and hoped she knew she could put her trust in me.

# Chapter Twenty-Two
*Wyn*

Sundays used to be my favorite day of the week. But today? Today sucked balls. I didn't have to check a mirror to know how horrible I looked. Seeing my reflection would only make the day suck worse. My eyes remained red and puffy after a night of crying and little sleep. My face ashen, even with my dark complexion.

I felt like crap which meant I probably looked way worse. Death warmed over was an apt phrase right now.

Every time I calmed down enough to sleep, I'd jerk awake before the darkness swallowed me whole. Nick, with his menacing grin, waited for me.

The nightmares came crashing back tenfold, just from seeing him across the room.

Today didn't look any brighter either, especially since all I had to look forward to was a repeat of last night.

I peeked out from under my blanket and noted the time. Just after two in the afternoon. I never slept this late unless sick. By all accounts, the day was almost over.

Darcy wasn't puttering around the apartment—not that I heard—so she was either out or giving me some much-needed space. Either way, I appreciated it. I'd sucked her into my problems enough already.

I waited for my phone screen to light up after tapping it several times. My grandparents usually called or texted after they got home from church.

And then there was Rafe. He'd called several times last night after I panicked and left the club. When his calls went unanswered, he began texting me. I couldn't say at what point he gave up on me last night, but I was sure he did.

I wasn't worth all this trouble. He'd grow tired of me soon enough. Especially after my disappearing act.

If I had any unread messages, they'd have to wait. I needed to put my mask back on. Seeing Nick last night shredded any progress I made these last few weeks. Now I was back at square one.

I tapped the screen again. Nothing happened. *Shoot*, realizing I forgot to charge it.

I threw my blanket off and sat up in bed, feeling grungy. *A shower might do me some good*, I thought. Plugging my phone into the charger, I pulled out some sweatpants, my favorite tee that screamed *I got no plans to go anywhere today* and went to the bathroom.

With the water turned all the way to scorching hot, I got in.

*I was dirty. Scrubbing myself until my skin felt raw, unhinging from the inside out. Dull pain on every inch of my body. Especially between my legs. Now all I felt was constant soreness.*

*A shattering of sorts. This was more than physical pain. I had to hide this from Darcy, from everyone. Once the last of the soap rinsed down my body and swirled around the drain, I broke, unable to hold myself up any longer. Collapsing against the wall and into the tub, I curled into a ball, crying for so long my throat became sore from it.*

*Finally vacating the safety of the bathroom, I saw Darcy sound asleep in her room, her door slightly ajar. I wondered why she never checked on me with how long I took in the bathroom. It was just as well. I stayed in my room and decided not to leave until the next morning. Didn't leave my apartment for a few days except to drive Darcy to the airport.*

*Nothing would ever be the same again.*

*Numb.*

*I just felt numb.*

The memories came like a flash flood, casting a darker shadow over me. I shut off the water and grabbed for my towel. I hadn't realized how long I daydreamed in the shower until I saw all the steam in the enclosed room. Turning on the fan, I toweled off and swept a forearm across the foggy mirror.

*Snuffed out.* That light returning to my eyes for a brief couple of days, showing how happy and hopeful I was for a millisecond, it was gone now.

I wanted the light back.

The fact his mere appearance had this extreme disarming effect on me pissed me off. Froze me right up. Made me more than scared. It had terrified me last night. And today I was back to being a shell of a person like before. I hated it. I hated him for it.

Hated myself.

And the kicker was that Nick had no idea he had this power over me. Power I gave to him. The ability to ruin me again and again.

Back in my room, I pressed the power button on the charging phone then got dressed. I needed a distraction. Something to get me out of my current head space.

My braids fell as I released the messy bun they were in since last night. Damp now from the shower, they cascaded against my mid-back in a heavy, familiar way.

My phone beeped nonstop for several seconds. Figured more than a few messages would be waiting on me to rejoin society. Looking over the notifications, there was a voicemail and text message from my grandparents. They wanted a call-back when I got a chance. I'd try to return their call soon, I promised myself.

The other messages were from Rafe. Texts and voicemails. Running away last night... I just hoped he didn't think it was about him. *But isn't it, in a way?*

Did I want to open those floodgates right now? *Yes, I did.* Gingerly sitting on my mattress, I mentally prepared myself to read and listen to his messages. I started from the beginning.

**Colt told me you left sick? call or text me to let me know you made it home okay.**

I saw his first message last night and shot him off a text about needing time. These next few came earlier today.

**Wyn? I need to know you're alright.**

**Call or text when you get my msgs. Anytime!**

He didn't mask his concern for me and now seeing his worry even as a text made me feel like a colossal bitch. Rafe was being perfectly normal and I was ignoring his messages... ignoring him. After reading the last text he sent a few hours ago, I bawled in my pillow.

*I'm here when you need me sweetheart. I'll be waiting to hear from you.*

Now, it just seemed like the worst possible timing with Rafe. Not for the first time I wished we'd met before that night ever happened. Before Nick. I would've been me, not this broken version of myself who second-guessed his interest, his intentions with me at every turn. And after the other night, I realized I didn't have to.

The sincerity was all there in Rafe's voice, his actions. He made sure of it at every turn. His interest in me was genuine. And I ran cold then hot then cold with him. It was any wonder he wanted to see me again.

But he did. His last message unmistakable.

I needed to gather my thoughts before returning his messages. He deserved that much.

"Hey, Pop Pop."

"Wynter? Love, our baby's on the phone." My granddad called out to my grandma without covering the receiver. His booming voice pierced my eardrum, forcing a smile from me. Without fail, I had the same reaction every time I heard it. "How's my baby girl doing?"

A soft click and my grandma's wispy voice indicated she picked up the other handset. "Hey, sugar."

"Hi, Mama." I could almost see them in my mind's eye. Both smiling from ear to ear. This time of day my grandma would be in the kitchen fixing dinner while granddad watched TV in the living room. It made me miss home so damn bad. I wanted the normalcy of it all. No fear or unexpected surprises popping up, knocking me off my axis and shoving me backwards.

I called the people who've been my parents since I was a preteen about twice a week since leaving home. One call always fell on Sunday after their church service. I couldn't lie to myself, though, because it lightened my mood to hear about the drama. Somebody always acted a fool or transgressed in a way my grandparents deemed *blasphemous*. They were overly judgmental like most church folk and I loved them to absolute pieces.

I finished answering their question with a white lie by saying I was doing fine. "What are y'all up to? How was church?" Subtle colloquialisms snuck into my speech easily. Talking with my midwestern grandparents always brought them out in subtle ways, pulling another tiny smile from me now.

Today, they only had a few stories from church. I ummed and ahhed at appropriate points. The congregation was in the midst of welcoming on a new pastor in a few weeks due to Pastor Tompkins' upcoming retirement. His replacement conducted the sermon today. To hear my grandparents tell it, he still had some work to do. They didn't want to like him yet, knowing in their *heart of hearts* he'd never be as good as Pastor Tompkins. Like I said, church folks through and through.

"That's good," I commented.

"Wynter, you sound tired. You sure you getting enough rest out there, sugar?"

"Yes, Mama. Work's been busy. I told you how swamped spring is for me." It was as good an excuse as any. And one they wouldn't question, I hoped.

"You need to take care of yourself. Don't make me sic Darcy on you. You know I will, young lady. She'll tell me if you aren't taking care." Yeah, she's done it before. "How's she doing anyway?"

I regaled them with some of Darcy's overseas adventures and they were equally interested and confused about what she did. I got a kick out of their puzzlement since it mirrored my own. Again, I realized how much I missed seeing them. We only lived a few hours' drive and I decided right then I'd go visit them soon. I mentioned the prospect and they were all for it.

Darcy probably needed the time away too before her California trip. I hoped I disabused her of canceling the game-changing opportunity last night. If the timing wasn't right, I'd mention it to her when she got back. We both needed some good, old-fashioned spoiling from my grandparents.

"Okay baby, I gotta let you go." My grandma's words broke through my fog. "I'm just getting dinner ready for your grandfather. Call us soon and let us know when you're coming down."

"I will, Mama. Love you both." They've been my guardians, my only parents, for over a decade now and I adored them to pieces.

"We love you too, sweetie. Bye now," my grandpa said and clicked off.

With my phone call to the grandparents done, I felt more ready to contact Rafe, sending him a quick text message.

**Hi Rafe. Thanx for the msgs. Sorry I left w/o saying goodbye last night.**

Not five minutes had passed before my phone rang on the charger. *Rafe.* I couldn't help my smile as his name displayed across the screen. I wanted his picture to pop up too. Maybe I'd make that happen if I got my life together.

My trembling finger swiped before his call jumped to voicemail.

"Hey, sweetheart. How ya feeling?" Hints of concern still echoed in his deep, husky voice and it made me sad. Sad that I didn't deserve it. I wasn't whole enough yet to just dive into whatever this was with him with open arms. No matter how much I wanted to. More than anything.

"Hey." The single word cracked on my lips. Wrecked to my ears, I hoped Rafe didn't notice. "I'm getting better. It all hit me pretty quick, ya know, so I rushed home." The vague comment helped keep my emotions in check.

Rafe didn't need to know Darcy made up my illness, or that fear smacked me right in the face and I couldn't stand being at the club anymore. Not for one more damn minute. He didn't need to know my worst nightmare showed up, messing with the issues I ignored and pushed to the back of my mind. I caught a glimpse of him and my skin crawled. And all I could do in that moment was run.

"No, I get it. And you're feeling better, you said, so that's good."

"Yeah." Awkwardness crept back into our conversation. It hadn't been there the last few times we talked or hung out. I hated that we were back to this.

"So, Wyn. If you're up to it, I wondered if we could go see a movie Tuesday night." I heard the slight hesitation in his voice, like he walked on eggshells around me again. Frustrated, I knew there was no one else to blame but myself for this teeter totter we were on. "Your choice in flick," he added with a low chuckle.

"Sounds fun, Rafe." Decision made.

If I was going to get passed this, I needed to make the effort. Rafe was amazing. I enjoyed spending time with him. He challenged me even when I didn't know it's what I needed.

A relieved sigh came over the line. *Did he think I'd blow him off?*

"Well, you probably want to rest. Feel better, Wyn. And let me know if you have to push our date back." I nodded even though he probably needed a verbal response since he couldn't see me.

"I'll call you tomorrow to see how you are, yeah?" His voice deepened. The words fluttered over my skin like a caress. A touch I desperately craved.

"Yes, okay. Bye, Rafe." Now all I had to do was keep myself together during our date on Tuesday.

*It's gonna be a long two days.*

# Chapter Twenty-Three
*Rafe*

*Fuck. What the hell is wrong with me?* As I got closer to Wyn's place, the hair on my forearms raised, a ghost of a feeling. It had me on edge.

Yesterday when I called, she sounded much better. We agreed to keep our plans for today and I was more than happy about it. The need to see her pulled at me.

Wyn had come to mean more to me than most other girls I'd dated, especially in this short amount of time. No reason for it really. Not one I could explain if asked. Just something about her. She brought out the best in me, I figured.

And now, seeing her tonight had me feeling sappy and nervous in equal measure.

Wyn immediately opened the door following my light knock. She looked the same but different and laying eyes on her after this past weekend set my heart racing. I couldn't explain why I felt the shift except that it was a spark in the air around us.

I pulled at the shirt collar, the cotton sticking to my sweaty neck. After arriving at the theater, Wyn excused herself and headed straight to the ladies' room once I purchased our tickets. The movie started in twenty minutes, so we had plenty of time to stop at the concession stand and find seats before the coming attractions.

Her choice in movie surprised the hell outta me. The newest buddy action film instead of the latest romantic comedy. I still had a lot to learn about my Wyn.

So far though, she fascinated me.

The lights dimmed just as we found seats close to the front. The theater was crowded with couples and large groups. We sat four rows from the screen with almost the entire row to ourselves.

The movie was enjoyable if not predictable. The two main actors were well-known and had good on-screen chemistry. At about the movie's halfway point, after we both snacked on enough popcorn, I leaned back and made myself more comfortable. Wyn had been quiet, totally engrossed in the movie. She let out an occasional chuckle at funny bits, but mostly kept her eyes trained on the screen. I wondered if she did every activity with such focus and figured she just might.

An unexpected explosion happened on-screen and Wyn jumped. I looked over at her and she wore a slight, deprecating smile on her face. When I leaned back, her shoulder found mine over the armrest. And we did this pseudo cuddle thing for the rest of the movie. I felt every one of her laughs, gasps, and all sorts in between. Barely a touch and we connected in a way I hadn't felt before. A simple shoulder-to-shoulder connection, but it was so much more.

*Maybe I'll take her to a horror flick next time.* I pictured her clinging to me, and that imaginary snapshot alone looked damn fine in my head. The fruity scent I associated with Wyn tickled my nose, pulling a groan from me. Like Pavlov's dog, that scent had me thinking back to the night after our last date. Wyn wrapped in my arms, me holding her, touching her. Having her hands on me too. The connection from the other night stuck with me. We both opened up to each other.

I remembered her lips, the sounds she made driving me wild…

*Down, boy!* I quickly stopped those thoughts. They proved dangerous and stupid in our current situation. Now was not the time to pop a woody. Especially in the middle of a crowded movie theater with my girl. A goddamn cliché.

I turned my attention back to the big screen, enjoying how Wyn unconsciously gravitated toward me. So, I stopped reliving the brief yet fantastic memory from last week and focused on right now.

The rest of the film passed quickly after that. In no time, we gathered our trash and left the theater. I glanced down at my phone and noticed it was almost nine. Although it was a work night for Wyn, I tried pressing my luck. I held the door open for her and asked, "Could I interest you in a cone and a leisurely walk, m'lady?" My voice held a haughty air, my attempt at the British accent atrocious. Borderline ridiculous, really. I'd been watching too much *Sherlock* lately.

That was my story and I was sticking to it.

Wyn's giggle my answer. Her low laugh was part innocent and sexy all rolled into one beautiful sound. We passed my truck and walked toward the ice cream parlor. A town favorite. And if you asked anyone, a historical landmark too. The flashing LED open sign welcomed us even though it wasn't quite summer. Yet, the place had a year-round customer base.

The weather had been unseasonably warm, which probably didn't hurt business. It gave us all a false sense of security. Either way, I capitalized on the extra time with Wyn.

A bell jingled overhead while I held the door open for my date, the sweet smell of ice cream and waffle cones teasing us. A teenager behind the counter called out a greeting. Several customers stood in line, waiting for service.

Looking at the variety of flavors through the glass freezer, I rubbed my hands. Wyn peered at the offerings with less excitement. "Do you know what you're getting, sweetheart?"

"Hmm? Oh, yeah." She glanced up at me, nodding. "I always get the same flavors. I'm pretty boring."

"Are you an ice cream purist then? Me, I consider myself a connoisseur of sorts." I winked, rubbing my chin and contemplating the selection. "Ever since I was a young boy, I dreamed of being a taste tester for all of the major companies. Then I started making my own money and realized I could do that, regardless. It just takes more determination on my part." With my flourishing ending, Wyn let out a choked laugh.

I liked learning these new facts about her. But making her laugh or smile got me going, most of all. Around her I could let the silly out, it was so damn comfortable.

*Fun.* A word I hadn't associated with my life in a long while. Or ever. Grinning, I turned back to my serious selection process while she ordered a cup containing one vanilla and chocolate scoop.

Now my turn, I told the server my order and joined Wyn over at the end of the counter to pay. Wordlessly, we left the local business and continued walking in the opposite direction of my car.

"So, any word on Cru?" The question slipped my mind earlier. I knew she still worried about the clunker.

"Well…" she sighed. "I spoke to Rudy and Oscar the other day.

Let's just say I may need to buy a car." She shrugged nonchalantly, but I knew it was a big deal. Maybe even bittersweet for her. *Cru is her baby.*

"Damn, sweetheart. I'm really sorry. There's not much they can do then?" No longer seeing green at the mechanic's name. I definitely felt like an ass after my behavior last week at his shop. Not much I could do about it now though.

Wyn shook her head as we continued walking in relative silence, taking in the not-quite bustling Tuesday night in the downtown area.

"What's bothering you, Rafe? You got quiet there for a few minutes." My eyes found hers as she looked at me, one dainty hand held a spoonful of swirly ice cream to her lips.

I'd been neglecting my own delicious scoops and waffle cone and took a nice mouthful before answering, "Something's been on my mind, I guess. Do you know Nick Ferrara, Blue's first bassist?" I tried for casual. The next moment Wyn tripped, almost tumbling on the pavement.

"Are you okay?" Although she hadn't fallen or dropped her cup, I stopped anyway to make sure. I even glanced down at the sidewalk to make sure no other offending objects got in our way.

I thought I heard her mutter *that wasn't embarrassing at all.* "I tripped on air," Wyn's lips formed a thin, straight line. "What were you saying?" she asked.

"Oh, yeah. I'm probably wigging out for nothing. Just seems like everywhere I look lately, there he is sniffing around." This was the first time I brought him up to anyone. I wasn't sure how she felt about the guy one way or another and I didn't want to seem insecure either. His constant appearance was just another thing weighing on my mind. Random shit I found myself worrying about.

"My place with the band seems secure right now. I just get a bad feeling around the guy, is all." I took another taste of my ice cream. "I know a bully when I see one. You know what I mean?"

"Yeah, I get it." Wyn became quiet then. Maybe the conversation made her uncomfortable. It wasn't my intention to bring down the mood, so my mind worked quickly to get us back to the good time we were having.

"Want to try some?" She looked at me with questioning eyes. In answer, I held the tasty treat in my hand closer to her mouth, giving her enough space to either decline or inch closer for a taste. I hoped for the latter.

"It looks… interesting," she hedged. Decadent might be the word I'd use. And I wasn't only thinking about the cold snack either.

"Oh, definitely. It's also very good. Try some." I chose Donna's Double Dark Chocolate Chunk. I had no clue who the hell Donna was, but the lady sure had good taste in chocolate-y ice cream goodness.

I saw the moment Wyn decided to give it a try, beyond grateful. My hungry eyes followed her every move, wishing I was the damn ice cream right about now. Her pink tongue peeked out from between her lips and slowly came toward me, I meant my ice cream.

"Mm," she hummed, taking a small lick from one side of the cone. And that sound from her got me all riled up. I coughed and turned forward to cover up my growing need for her. Like a damn teenager all over again. I needed better control around Wyn, or I was likely to embarrass myself.

"Good, right?" I turned the cone around, trying to find the exact place her tongue landed. An attempt to get a taste of her again. I lifted my gaze and noticed her sharp nod. Her brown eyes heated, a hint of something amazing hidden just underneath. The look intrigued me.

"We should probably head back, Rafe." It was still a work night for her, so I nodded, the hesitation in her voice not going unnoticed. Maybe like me she wished we could squeeze in another few minutes together. Without words, we turned around and walked back toward the movie theater.

Unfortunately, we got back to her apartment complex too quickly. Hardly any cars on the road this time of night on a weekday.

"So," I stated, prolonging the two-letter word. Desperate for a little more time with her.

"Tonight was great, Rafe." I put the truck in park and unsnapped my seat belt as her words registered.

"Yeah, it was," I agreed, scooting closer to her. A soft glow lit the inside of my truck from the dashboard. Wyn sat primly on the passenger side, looking straight ahead.

Some braids fell from her ponytail since earlier tonight, cascading across her face in a sort of bang. Moving even closer, I pushed them behind her ear and moved to her nape. I pulled her to me, desperately needing a kiss. A taste of her lips in the worst way possible.

She moved closer with little urging from me, my hold only there as a guide. I hoped that meant she wanted this just as much. Her lips pressed against mine, soft and hesitant. I brought my other hand up and rubbed my thumb down her chin, asking to be let in. Lips parting so gently for me, a spark ignited.

I dove in, discovering her addictive taste all over again.

A man starving was what I was. I kept our kiss long and slow. Ice cream still flavored her tongue, the sweet taste shared between us. And I couldn't get enough. Wyn's tongue tangled with mine. I pulled us even closer together with a hungry groan. For better access, one hand cradled her head, angling our mouths for more. A deeper taste. She clung to my clothes, trying to get closer.

"Mm." We finally broke away. I pulled in much-needed oxygen; my lungs deprived. Wyn grinned shyly, touching plump, kiss-swollen lips with the pads of her fingers. Made me want to nibble on them some more. "Haven't done that before," she confessed.

"Huh?" My brain short-circuited from our delicious kiss that I'd ended due only to necessity. I wondered at her curious comment, though.

The dim, interior lighting couldn't hide the mortified look that crossed her face. Her explanation finally came when she said, "Parking and making out." She looked down, fidgeting with the hem of her blouse. "Not an activity I did a lot in my teens... or ever."

I tried reconciling her confession with the way she kissed me, with so much passion, need, and innocence. It made me even more ravenous. Given her nonchalant shrug, she had no idea the effect her words had on me.

"Oh, well I'm happy to continue our make out session. Give you all the practice you care to have. I'm a musician after all. Practice makes perfect is a saying I live by." Waggling my eyebrows, I went for the full effect, not wanting Wyn to be overly self-conscious about her lack of experience. Any of it. Especially since it had me jonesing for her even more.

"Anytime, sweetheart. I'm your man for the job." Your *only* man.

"You're incorrigible, Rafe." Wyn tap-pushed me on the shoulder, shaking her head and smiling. I liked seeing her playful and happy like this.

We walked up to her apartment, our date coming to an eventual end. She asked about our next show and I mentioned our practice on Friday for an upcoming gig.

"You should come to our practice space. I'd love it if you heard some of our new stuff. Get your take on it if you're interested?" Now that I said it, I meant every word. Wyn amazed me the first time we met with her comments about our set. I didn't hear from her before she left the other night. It'd be great to hear her thoughts on the new direction of the band.

"Yeah, okay. That sounds like fun." We got to her door and I stole another kiss before she went inside.

"See you Friday night, Wyn." If I could see this girl more often, like every day, I'd be a happy man. I knew it wasn't possible or a good idea. For right now anyway. She'd probably get sick of my ugly mug if she saw it more than every few days. Still, I planned to wear her down in small doses. It was a difficult process, though, taking my time. Not jumping in headfirst when it felt so right. So necessary. Like nothing's ever felt before in my life.

But this situation called for patience.

*Friday couldn't come soon enough.*

# Chapter Twenty-Four
*Wyn*

He held me in his arms, our lips dancing together again. *So close. Yet not close enough.* An innocent press of lips this time, like all the kisses. I liked the slow start, wanting more. Rafe towered over me, yet his position didn't leave me unsettled. I only wanted to be closer to him.

I stretched a few centimeters, standing on my tiptoes to brush against him. I wasn't ready to say goodnight just yet. The feeling of safety I felt in his arms, it persisted with every kiss and caress. Every word.

I thought it all would've gone away after seeing Nick again, like kindling snuffed out too soon. Instead, my feelings seemed to burn bigger and brighter than before.

With Rafe, I found myself drifting closer, my hands slowly climbed up his back. His shirt in the way of the warm skin I wanted to touch. Hold on to. I didn't know where this longing came from. Why I craved skin-to-skin contact.

My body had a mind of its own, as if someone else held the strings and I was a mere puppet.

He took the kiss deeper, his hands held me tighter around my waist and I clung to him. Staying on this rollercoaster ride for a few moments more. I felt giddy with it. Tonight, like every time with Rafe was unexpected and fun. The sweetness of the ice cream he'd let me sample earlier still on his lips, his tongue. There was more to him than I expected. Hard and sweet. Strong and sensitive. He confused and aroused me.

My hands clutched his thin jacket. It felt too good here with him.

"Are you sure you want to go?" Darcy called from the hallway and jarred me from the memory of the other night. That kiss. I ran my fingertips over my lips, feeling the ghost of him still. The lingering sensation only too real. I'd found comfort in the recent memory. One of the only things holding me together right now.

I needed them to eclipse the shitty memories lurking in the shadows of my mind. And Rafe, he was good for me. I liked him despite all that happened recently. I'd let him in when I didn't have to. When my instincts urged me to question the instant attraction between us. More so at the beginning. That had only been a few, short weeks ago.

He crept in behind my walls, anyway, making me smile and laugh with little effort.

Darcy kept talking while strutting into the living room where I sat daydreaming. "Because we don't have to, Wyn. I totally understand if you aren't up for it. We can make up excuses to the guys and stay home tonight. Order some Chinese food and pig out on ice cream." She laid her proposition on thick, aware that those were two of my favorite food groups in the world.

Too amped to stay home, I'd already promised Rafe and wanted to see the band practice. I knew deep down she wanted to see them too.

"Dar, I'm fine. I want to go tonight. It'll be fun." *How the tides have changed.* Just a few weeks ago I was trying to keep Darcy at home. Admittedly, she did a better job trying to convince me. Usually mentioning Chinese food and ice cream worked an unexplainable magic on me. Just not tonight. And I had enough of talking myself out of experiences that scared me. A bad habit I needed to break. This would be good for both of us.

"Plus, I know you, Dar. Do you really want to miss the chance for a first listen of *Blue's* new stuff?" With those words, I cinched our plans tonight. There was no way in hell she'd miss what was a private concert for us. She tried continuing her negotiation tactics in the car, albeit halfheartedly. However, I didn't fall for them.

We parked up the street from the address Colt sent her earlier.

Maybe some of Darcy's concern came from the conversation she still needed to have with the enigmatic frontman. California weighed heavy on her mind and like me, she most likely had no idea the direction her and Colt headed in. I sympathized with her. Were they developing a strong friendship or more?

It didn't sound like she had an answer to that question yet.

As her best friend for more than a decade now, I knew what she wanted most of all. From what I could see, she yearned for those things with Colt. For her sake, I hoped they talked soon. I hated seeing my best friend unsteady like this when she'd always exuded such strength, no matter what obstacles were in her way.

Rafe expected me there tonight. And I needed to be out and about. Nick could only hurt me, stop me from living my life if I let him. *And I'm done letting him.* I just had to prove it to myself.

When Rafe mentioned Nick the other night, I almost let it ruin our date. Tripping wasn't the worst thing, no matter how embarrassing. But it was like my feet no longer supported me with the simple uttering of his name. I only stumbled, managing not to fall flat on my face. I wanted to scream and rage *Nick's a rapist*, but the misstep halted that first impulse.

Even though I stopped myself from blurting it out, I saw it as a step in the right direction. For so many months, I'd been hiding behind what happened to me. I let fear and self-blame guide how I acted but, at that moment, I'd been angry. At Nick for what he did, and that he was still causing trouble for someone I cared about.

There was no way I could explain what happened to Rafe. I barely got through telling Darcy last weekend. If my dreams reminded me of anything, it was that that night would stay with me forever. But it didn't have to define me. I needed to keep moving. Not stop myself from pursuing new relationships due to fear.

That was no way to live.

Darcy checked her phone for the address Colt sent hours ago. We stood in front of a nondescript building in the middle of a long block, a short walk away from the main downtown drag. The studio shared the sidewalk with a few other storefronts. I heard a thunderous rattle and clank to the left of me. I turned and saw an older gentleman pulling together a security gate. He looked up and waved before shuffling to a dark sedan parked at the corner.

This had to be the place. Numbers, more faded than not, read 1511 Cobalt. Darcy showed me the earlier text from Colt. This was it. The guys had to be here. Somewhere.

No sign or placard relayed any further information about the intimidating building before us. There wasn't even a window to let us peek inside. Every other business on this side of the street had lights out since it was close to seven. The regular business hours had since passed, especially on a Friday night when folks wanted to be home with family or out with friends.

With the sun just setting, downtown crowds had no legitimate reason to come this way. Only a few blocks away, this row of buildings was off the beaten track, perhaps on purpose.

We currently loitered in front of this large one-story building, sandwiched between a shoe repair shop and dry cleaners. The outward appearance of the brick building left us to our imagination about what lay inside. The big, foreboding black-painted door screamed *keep out*; at least it was the vibe to me. The surrounding empty stores provided little to no comfort. "Maybe we should call one of the guys," Dar stammered. "Let them know we're here."

Her idea seemed solid enough to me. I nodded, figuring we were in the right place. Even so, it never hurt to double or triple check. No reason to put ourselves in a dangerous or embarrassing situation.

Dar had her phone out and dialing Colt when the big door opened, swinging wide toward us. She squeak-shrieked. A sound I'd never heard another human being make before. I was no better since the door almost gave me a heart attack. Overall the situation might've been hilarious, especially that god-awful noise from Dar, if my heart wasn't currently hammering a couple hundred beats a minute in my chest.

"Mierda! This door is a fucking hazard." Berto continued cursing in Spanish, exiting the building. He finally noticed us standing there. "Oh shit, did I hit you?" He asked while his eyes tracked us up and down, probably looking for injuries. If that heavy door hit either of us, I was sure we'd be clear across the street in pieces... not standing on the sidewalk about to piss ourselves. "Sorry I scared you, ladies," he apologized sheepishly. "You okay?"

"What'd I tell you about this damn door, ass wipe?" Doug came out after Berto and admonished him. "You have got to be more careful! Hey Darcy, Wyn. This dumbass didn't hit you with the door, did he?"

"What can I say, mano? I don't even know my own strength," he joked, flexing his biceps. Berto went as far as kissing them and I shook my head. These guys were too much and all I could do was chuckle at their antics. Suddenly, I was sad I'd put them at arm's length these last few weeks. They were ridiculously childish, but mostly hilarious, in an annoying brotherly way. I had no reason to remain at a distance with them. Even with the bad egg in their midst.

Colt walked out of the building last, all tall brooding swagger like the up-and-coming rock star everyone saw in him. All his attention on the phone in his hand. Darcy and I composed ourselves as much as we could before he saw us.

He glanced up and said, "Oh, hey. I was just about to call you back." He walked right over to my best friend, bending down considerably and kissing her on the cheek. I saw the telltale blush consume her face; glad I didn't have her fair skin.

Just seeing Colt with her, I hoped it worked out for them sooner rather than later. My friend deserved an abundance of happiness in her life.

He turned to me, "Rafe's still inside, if you wanna go on back." Colt gave me directions to the practice room while Doug and Berto walked down the street toward downtown. From his brief description alone, the place sounded bigger than I expected. The image I had in mind was of them practicing in someone's garage or apartment. Apparently, this place was so much more than that.

A small, empty reception area greeted me as I entered the building. Framed posters and album covers along the walls caught my attention down the long corridor. Some I knew and several I didn't. Either way, the place impressed me. Not at all what I imagined from the outside façade. Now, I knew this was where countless dreams were made.

I got a glimpse of a large recording studio. Passing a second smaller room next door to it, I took a right per the big singer's instructions. I wondered why Rafe stayed behind and not taken a break like the others.

Colt told me there'd be an open door at the very end of the hallway. My rubber soled boots made little noise on the scuffed linoleum floor. Up ahead, a door stood ajar.

*Rafe's in there waiting for me.* About to knock and announce myself, the strum of a guitar made me pause. Then he started singing. And the lyrics sent chills down my spine.

*She keeps running away, running away*
*Her heart's an empty shell*
*She keeps running away, running away*
*Straight to hell*

*There was a girl on the highway*
*But she wasn't going my way*
*She carried her weight in bad choices*
*Cutting through those demons' voices*
*With every turn they've been on her heels*
*Death at heaven's gate on two wheels*
*This tortured soul has been on her own*
*Her whereabouts are still unknown...*

He hadn't sung backup for Colt, at least not that I've heard or seen, but he could with that voice. His rich, husky baritone rolled over me, haunting me. So did the lyrics. Their intrinsic meaning went straight through to my soul, hitting me hard. I knew deep down the song wasn't about me.

*It couldn't be, right?*

We hadn't known each other long and I'd only confided in Darcy a few days ago. But those lyrics resonated with me all the same, seeing myself in them.

My misplaced, naïve trust from a year ago led me to that night and I paid for it every day. The constant nightmares, hiding my internal torment from family and friends. Not to mention my reticence around new people or experiences. Yeah, this song spoke to me even if Rafe didn't intend for it to.

How long I stood in the hallway, amazed and terrified all at once, I had no clue. Rafe hadn't noticed me yet either. I stood off to the side, out of view of the doorway and him. His strumming and singing stopped, then started back up again. He repeated the chorus after a few moments.

Rafe's voice and lyrics stripped me bare. I'd been running for the past several months now. Not really living due to fear and insecurity. I blamed myself for what happened and that's all I let myself deal with. The guilt ate me alive.

I didn't even want to see this great, patient guy right in front of me. We played a game of tug of war. Me constantly pulling away from him while he fought for a chance with me. I needed to reconsider my thinking on this.

Especially with Rafe.

*Why are you running away, running away*
*Mine and your heart beat still*

181

*Keep running away, running away*
*Escape from his hell…*

A cacophony of voices broke through my thoughts, increasing in volume and coming from the front of the building.

*Time's up.* Darcy and the guys would turn the corner in less time than it had taken me to find the room in the first place. I turned back to the door, inching it open and taking my first steps inside. Rafe's eyes found mine as his strumming faded out. Like he'd sensed my presence before I entered the room. I clapped and gathered myself enough to smile.

*Fake it till you make it.*

"Wyn." So much laced in just my name. Surprise, yes, but also much more that I couldn't quite put my finger on. Or didn't want to. No one had ever looked at me or said my name like he did. Just Rafe.

I wished I knew what it all meant. If I was honest with myself, the last thing I wanted to do was get my hopes up. Still, I had to say something instead of just standing there awkwardly staring at him.

*Even hello would be a good start.*

"Wow," I blurted instead. He scratched his scalp, tucking a lock of hair behind an ear.

Rafe rose from his perch on a stool and asked me, "What did you think?" He set the acoustic guitar against the nearest wall, shoving a notebook in the opened backpack at his feet. When he straightened, he started toward me.

"I had no idea you could sing like that," I exclaimed. "Why don't you sing more often? And that song. It was… just wow." My thoughts were all scrambled; I couldn't put my feelings about those lyrics into words. My body felt too heavy from his rendition, but my comments seemed to be the right ones because Rafe wore the most brilliant smile I'd ever seen.

"Yeah?" he probed. "I've been tinkering with it for several weeks now. It's about—" he stopped when the guys came barreling through the doorway. Literally. Doug had Berto in a headlock, the latter struggling to break the hold to no avail.

"Knock it off, dipshits." Colt ushered Darcy in with an arm around her shoulder. "We still got a bunch of shit to cover, so let's get back to work."

"Yes, capitán." Berto saluted snidely, even standing at attention.

"Plus, we have a beautiful audience now," he winked at us before marching over to his drum kit.

Rafe grabbed my hand, tugging me closer and pressing a kiss to my cheek. Before turning away, he asked, "Maybe we can hang out after this?" At my energetic nod, he turned and headed straight for the setup they had at the opposite end of the room. Colt pointed to a small couch behind us, which escaped my notice until now. It appeared lumpy and worn down, pushed up against the wall right next to the door. Although Darcy appeared just as dubious as me, we walked over to it, giving one cushion a try with a hand before sitting down.

The guys became all business quickly, like they picked up right where they left off before their break. Berto got comfortable on his stool and counted them in. They started a song I'd never heard before, already mesmerizing me.

Darcy and I sat side by side on the sketchy couch, witnesses to the true formation of the Country Blue sound. And yes, I fully believed they became a different band with Rafe. Now, after months of just playing with each other, they approached greatness.

It wasn't like they were horrible before. More like guys from a has-been high school band who hadn't found their niche yet, trying hard to be too many things at once. They were far from those vibes now.

The word *authentic* came to mind.

A lot of my feelings probably centered around Rafe. But right now, I was viewing them as a band. A cohesive unit. And together they sounded phenomenal.

This time spent watching them felt intimate in a way. Sacred and private. Like my presence here was forbidden as they practiced in this random room at the very back of an even more random studio space. I felt like an interloper even though I vividly remembered the invitation from Rafe at the end of our date the other night.

Various emotions bombarded me, making me feel prickly and strange in my own skin.

The band poured their blood, sweat, and tears out in this cluttered practice room. They played, refined then regrouped. On repeat.

It was an enlightening experience to see their process. Every one of these men gave it their all at their shows. I witnessed their energy and dedication a few times now. Those shows paled compared to this particular experience right here. It amazed and humbled me that I got this behind-the-scenes look.

Glancing over at Darcy, I knew she understood. The band standing before us had what it took to make it. They were on the cusp of it with this redirect in sound. The music in the room, the lyrics and rhythm in the air vibrated around me. Set me adrift. It was a lot to take in, that I witnessed something wonderful being created, shaped and reshaped right before my eyes. This moment was huge. And I didn't belong.

*Out of place.*

The band continued playing. I listened, appreciating every note and melody. I didn't have words for the feelings coursing through me. The song they played faded out and they went right into a new one. *Fluid.* And I knew right away this one would slice right through and gut me.

The opening notes to the song Rafe sang earlier started. I didn't know the title. Wasn't sure I wanted to.

There was heartiness to it now, the bass and drums accompanying and deepening the sound. I'd know it anywhere, though. It stuck with me on a deep level. Colt's full-toned voice slithered from the microphone and amps, a hidden depth coming through I'd never heard from him. Rafe's voice earlier got to me but this… was too much. Every melody held underlying emotions that were meant to be brought to the surface. And a singer's job was to add their own weight to it, making it bigger and better so that the listener would feel more. Could feel everything. With the full band playing, I got a complete picture of the song.

Yes, the sinister undertone of the lyrics rang throughout. The hint of danger remained, but with Colt's voice, there was also remorse and another emotion I couldn't pinpoint. I closed my eyes long ago, only listening as the memory of Rafe's singing earlier crawled into me and settled again. I shifted uncomfortably on the lumpy couch and looked down at my hands.

Colt's voice made the song different, yet I was still incapable of removing myself, *my past* from those lyrics.

The hairs on my forearms rose, the sensation urging me to look up. And I promptly froze in my seat. Rafe watched me. Green gaze trained on me while he continued to play. He lent his rich voice to the last chorus, no one missing a beat. I wasn't sure if he even realized it.

In our locked stare, Rafe openly shared his emotions, making me speechless. Overwhelmed. The meaning behind his intense gaze wasn't lost on me. I no longer felt out of place. I belonged because he wanted me here. With him.

That was enough for me.

"Ready to get out of here, Wyn?" Rafe stood in front of me, a grim line to his lips, his shins a few inches from my knees. His sudden appearance flustered me. Dazed, I obviously zoned out while they finished up. Rafe's song was their last one to practice. *How embarrassing.* He probably thought I was bored or worse which was the furthest thing from the truth. Needing to disabuse him of that idea immediately, I stood and nodded with eagerness.

I wasn't sure of his plans for tonight. And that worked for me.

Taking his hand, I finally put my trust in him.

# Chapter Twenty-Five
*Rafe*

Berto and Doug finished packing up the gear, throwing it in Doug's van. He had a garage over at his place and kept most of our equipment between practices and gigs. The guys figured out early on their shit was much safer in his van overnight than here.

Wyn and Darcy waited in the corner near the door while we discussed tomorrow night's show. My eyes went to her; it was damn near impossible not to.

Colt made a few more tweaks to the setlist. More than ready to go, I was sure we'd figure out any last-minute changes tomorrow. Thoughts of dancing with Wyn ruled my split focus, replacing all other items on my very short to-do list.

"Hey Rafe, can Darcy and I join?" Colt asked while coming up behind me as I walked a few feet over to the girls. Once I reached Wyn, I immediately caressed the back of her hand before taking it in my own.

God, I wanted to be a selfish prick right now, not liking the idea of another double date scenario. The one last time wasn't bad. It sure didn't start off great either. But that wasn't like me, so I replied, "Sure. I was thinking of checking out Rusty's again. The bartender said they have a DJ and dancing on Friday nights." Not mentioning my plans before now, I watched Wyn for her reaction.

Both girls smiled, Wyn practically beamed while Darcy bounced on her toes. "That sounds like so much fun! We haven't been dancing in forever. Right, Wyn?"

"Yeah, I like Rusty's. I'm down." Wyn turned to me with a shy smile, squeezing my hand. "You trying to impress me with some dance moves, Rafe?"

*Oh, yeah.* "Maybe," was what I actually said.

"We'll see then." That smile of hers gave me some naughty ideas. I forced myself to look away.

I swore as we left the practice room Doug uttered *lucky bastards* to Berto but couldn't be sure.

Taking two cars, Colt left his truck in the studio's back lot while Wyn came with me. We walked to my truck and I heard Colt assuring Darcy about the safety of his car for the next few hours as they strolled toward the girls' rental.

Wyn glanced over her shoulder, worry in her gaze.

"Everything okay, sweetheart?"

"Yes, of course." At my truck, I opened the passenger door for her and helped her in. Until now, I hadn't noticed how quiet *both* women were tonight. I'd come to expect it from Wyn, but Darcy held herself back somewhat too, until I mentioned Rusty's and dancing.

*The subdued vibe tonight, did it have to do with last weekend? Or something else?* I wondered. I'd keep my eyes open regardless, not wanting a repeat. After our date Tuesday, I hoped we were back on solid ground. And I sure as hell didn't want anything getting in the way of tonight's activities if I could help it.

The drive to Rusty's was a quick fifteen minutes. Like usual, Wyn remained quiet next to me. We were two miles away from the bar when I ended our comfortable silence. "What did you think—"

"I loved hearing you guys to—" We started at the same time. Our fumbling over each other definitely broke some of the tension permeating the cab of the truck. One hand let go of the steering wheel as I motioned for her to talk first. We both chuckled.

"Oh, I was just going to say that I enjoyed listening to you guys play tonight. Has Colt, Berto, or Doug heard you sing before? It'd be great if there were backup vocals on some of the songs." Her words almost fell on top of each other. Yeah, I agreed but didn't know if I was exactly ready for that step. It'd be a big commitment on my part. A huge statement even if no one realized except me. Also, there were other issues at hand with her suggestion.

"Colt's the frontman, ya know." I knew early on I could never play that particular role in a band. Too much pressure and limelight for my taste. "I'm happy to stay in the periphery with my bass." *And writing songs hardly anyone knows about.*

"Hmmm." Wyn nodded and I figured she understood that about me. "So, uh, the last song you played. The one you were singing before everyone came back from break... you said you've been working on it for a while. Did you write it yourself?" I nodded as her question trailed off, all low and shy.

"Uh, yeah." Glad for the relative darkness in the truck. "The guys found some of my notes one day while we were practicing. That song, 'Runaway Girl', we're trying it out at tomorrow's gig." I shrugged, shifting uncomfortably in the seat. Why I felt so damn nervous all of a sudden talking about this with Wyn, I didn't know.

*Because you don't want to get your hopes up, idiot! The song could fucking tank tomorrow, for all you know.*

"Well, I doubt my word counts for much, but that's my new favorite song from y'all." Wyn's hand traversed the seat and landed on my thigh. "You're a talented songwriter, Rafe." Her light touch all too-brief. The run-down exterior of Rusty's came into view and shit, I damn near wept. Wyn's hand on me moments ago only added to the hunger pangs I had earlier. I wasn't the best dancer, but someone would catch hell if I didn't get my arms around her in the next few minutes.

The small parking lot was full tonight. Darcy came up right behind us in the sporty red rental. I circled around, continuing my way out of the parking lot and over to the lot at the businesses next door. There were already a few cars parked and no lights on, so I hoped they used it for overflow parking as I wasn't looking to get a ticket.

I found a spot directly under a light post. Darcy rolled up to the slot on my left, exiting the compact car with a grateful smile. We all walked over to Rusty's, the crunch and kick of gravel adding to the murmur of music I heard several feet away.

Two women and a guy stood outside in the cool night. One of them took a puff from what appeared to be an e-cigarette, engaged in a low-toned conversation.

Colt held the door while the girls proceeded us into Rusty's. Before walking fully in the building, the bass of the current song playing transported me right back to my childhood. I remembered the suburban school I went to during middle school and the dances we had.

*Ugh, what awkward memories!*

The girls beelined for the bar and we trailed behind them. Darcy whooped at the people dancing, shaking as she walked by them. Colt's eyes followed her like a hawk. The makeshift dance floor already had some action with a group of friends jumping around, laughing and singing along to the boy band favorite.

Like Colt, I had my own set of curves to look at. Wyn's hips swished as she strutted up to the bar, resting her forearms on the counter and leaning forward. She even bounced on the balls of her feet. *Someone's excited.*

Damn near patting myself on the back, I came up behind her. Tonight was purely self-serving on my part, but I'd take credit for making Wyn happy. *Definitely a bonus.* Standing close, I listened as she ordered a tequila sunrise. I added a beer to the list and pushed a twenty toward the bartender serving us.

Another song came on, this one from our elementary school days. It was a late 90s R&B hit I remembered my older brother listening to on the radio. My younger self had no clue just how sexual this song and many others were back then. Nowadays, songs spelled out every explicit detail.

I still appreciated the ones that held a little mystery. Sensual, but not too explicit.

On the dance floor, around the bar and at some of the booths, clusters of people appeared to be around our age group. Maybe a couple years older. Some of the girls dressed in skimpy outfits like they were at a club downtown instead of the furthest place from it. Besides some outliers, the rest of the patrons had a more laid-back vibe that fit an establishment like Rusty's. More dive bar than upscale nightclub.

Wyn's outfit hugged her abundant curves and I enjoyed the view. She dressed casually yet still looked classy. Her heels giving her a few inches since she reached my chin.

We stood at the bar with our drinks for a few songs. The DJ played another boy band hit and Darcy rushed to the dance floor, immediately shaking and shimmying. I glanced over at Colt with a lot of sympathy. "Dammit," he muttered, taking a last sip of his beer before sliding the bottle on the counter. I watched in amusement for a few minutes as he tried to keep up with her.

"Ready to show me what you got?" I tilted my head to the dance floor. Wyn returned my smile, finishing her drink as well. *Showtime.*

We stepped away from the bar just as the DJ played a slower track.

Stopping next to our friends, I grabbed Wyn's soft hand, whipping her around in a spin. When she faced me again, I laid her hand on my shoulder and held her close. A surprised look crossed her face.

*Yeah, sweetheart. I have a few moves up my sleeve.*

I held her in my arms, pressed against me. Her cheek rested right on my chest and we swayed until the slow jam faded out. With the next selection, the DJ picked up the pace again. Just as I wondered if Wyn had any moves to show me, she spun around. This time, her quick movement surprised the hell outta me. She pushed her ass against my groin, grinding. And drove me crazy.

*God almighty, my need for this girl literally skyrocketed. I'm beyond screwed.*

Wyn didn't miss a beat revving me up with her dance moves. Already exuding *sexy* to me since day one, this was more than that. Wyn moved freely yet controlled all at the same time. This new and assertive sensuality hypnotized me. She took control, and I didn't dare put up a fight.

Very little time passed before my libido practically had a mind of its own around her. The innocence that got my attention in the beginning was still there, hidden behind this level of sensuality shining all around her. Wyn confounded me just as much now as she did weeks ago. *My beautiful enigma.*

She damn near had me mindless and under her spell. I whispered, "You're playing with fire, sweetheart." To my own ears, my voice sounded gravelly and slightly pained. Wyn turned to face me and I immediately noticed her blown pupils. She wasn't unaffected either. Well, good.

We were in a standstill on the dance floor, the other dancers and music all but pushed back to the edge of my consciousness. "Oh no. Don't stop on my account," I grated out between my teeth. It was pure torture. A sweet torture, having her against me, seeing her comfortable enough to let loose. I wanted this sensory bubble of ours to continue shielding us from the outside world. If only for a short while.

Wyn finally smiled. "I'm having fun, Rafe. You make me feel safe here, with you." She lifted her head to kiss me on my chin. "Thanks for suggesting this." She turned around, returning to her unique brand of delicious torture.

With her soft voice filtering over the loud bass, I thought I'd misheard her. Fuck, Wyn's simple words shook me, completely screwing with my equilibrium and making me think I could leap tall buildings and shit. They were equal parts a balm to my soul and a swift kick in the ass.

With Wyn wrapped tight in my arms, I enjoyed everything about this moment. When this woman put her trust in me, not just in words, I felt invincible. Her actions, her openness with me vocalized it as well. And I pledged to myself not to give her any reason to regret placing her trust in me.

I had no plans to pull Wyn off the dancefloor yet. I loved seeing her so carefree. She giggled and whooped when a song she recognized came on. When the DJ played a homage to boy and girl bands worldwide, more sweaty bodies converged onto the dancefloor, including her and Darcy, shimmying and shaking their hearts out. I stepped to the side with Colt and just watched in amusement.

Both girls relished this impromptu night out. It was obvious we all had shit on our minds and dancing proved a great stress release. Colt grunted under his breath and walked off toward the bar, probably needing some strong fortification to keep up with his plucky spitfire. I, on the other hand, just wanted a quick break before going back out there to Wyn. Her energy tonight fascinated me. I needed more of it and her right now.

Her body language was different tonight. Usually cautious and borderline screaming *hands off* at the start of any of our interactions, she was almost soft, open, and more vibrant than I've ever seen her. I hoped this wasn't the last time she'd share this side of herself with me.

*I hope it's just the start.*

Since we got here, I had to adjust myself countless times. I'd be embarrassed if I wasn't so goddamn horny from all the grinding and innocent smiles. Just thinking about it had me ready to get back out there. I'd wait a few more minutes for the DJ to change it up again. Wyn belonged back in my arms.

Depending on the song, she'd alternate between pushing and grinding against me. Or swaying and snuggling. Whatever the music called for, she adjusted, finding the new rhythm and leading me through for a time. But damn, tonight was as close to heaven as I'd ever been.

The DJ finally switched up and played a song that I recognized and wouldn't feel like a spaz dancing to. My feet moved without any conscious thought. Wyn turned toward me, grinning at my approach. A look of anticipation crossed her face. *Fuck, I love that look.*

I stopped in front of my girl, pulling her into my arms. My hands skimmed down her sides, wrapping around to the small of her back. I appreciated all types of music, but reggaeton was a secret pleasure of mine. Her hips swayed to the sexy beat, drawing my attention and my hands, calling to every part of me. A seduction I was sure she wasn't aware of. However, she pulled me in, regardless. My hands on her hips, I guided her the way I wanted. It was my turn to take the lead and she followed easily.

We fit.

*Simple perfection.*

The crowded dance floor faded, the music receding to the very background of my mind. It was just us in this small bubble of our own creation.

Several songs later, *I couldn't be sure how many*, Wyn pulled away and gazed up at me. "You thirsty?" I asked.

She nodded, "Yeah. It got hot in here all of a sudden, I think." It'd been hot and sweaty to me all along, but I kept it to myself. We walked over to the bar and noticed a water cooler and plastic cups at one end. It made sense the bartenders didn't want to fill orders for water the whole night. The money was in the booze. We waited as a woman walking ahead of us helped herself first. Once she finished, I filled cups for us.

Standing to the side, I guzzled mine down in ten seconds flat then refilled it. I looked around while Wyn sipped her water. "Do you think Colt and Darcy left?" They weren't currently on the dance floor from what I saw. Wyn looked adorable searching around for them. I bet she couldn't see a damn thing and definitely not over anybody even with her heels, especially not from our current vantage point.

"With those two and their competitive ways, let's check the back area." Wyn finished her drink and pushed the used cup out of the way.

"Good idea." I reached down and we walked hand in hand in search of our wayward friends.

We found Colt and Darcy in the back engaged in what appeared to be an intense game of pool. From what I could tell, Darcy was winning. I shook my head not at all surprised.

Darcy noticed us first after she made a shot, sinking a solid in a corner pocket. She ran over to Wyn, pausing the game since it was still her turn. They embraced in a long hug, moving over to a corner of the room. They had their heads close together in a whispered conversation. *What's that all about?* I walked over to Colt, "How's it going, man?"

"Thank God I don't have money on this game. Just my pride." A corner of his mouth lifted in a rueful smile. "Otherwise, all's good. Thanks for letting us tag along. I really needed this time with Darcy."

There was no response necessary since I knew exactly what he meant. The last several days seemed particularly weird to me. Sounded like Colt got the same vibes with Darcy. We were chatting about tomorrow night's gig when I felt Wyn's soft palm find mine.

"Hey." She laid her head against my arm. "You ready to go, sweetheart?" She nodded.

We said our goodbyes. I was pretty sure our friends had another game in mind after Darcy won this round. Wyn walked ahead of me as we passed the still growing crowd of dancers. This place would only get busier as the night progressed. Just after eleven and I felt older than my twenty-six years. Damn, I wanted to leave the party, craving some real alone time with Wyn.

Plus, we had the gig tomorrow.

"I thought we'd go to my place to hang out. Maybe watch a movie. Sound okay?" I unlocked the passenger side door and held it open for her.

"Yeah." She nodded and got in. *Well, that was easy.*

I was nervous to let her see my place, but I'd have to get over it pretty damn quick. Now, all I had left to worry about was if I picked up after myself recently.

*Note to self: clean up before inviting your new girlfriend over, doofus!*

# Chapter Twenty-Six
*Wyn*

"Uh, sorry if it's a bit of a mess in here." Rafe pushed his front door open and I walked in. From what I saw so far it looked okay.

*For a bachelor pad?* My imagination could drum up much worse. There weren't any weird or unimaginable smells like in a men's locker room, not that I'd know what a men's locker room smelled like.

His apartment had a warm feel about it. Although I noticed a few items in the entryway just lying around, it was no more or less cluttered than my apartment or bedroom. Rafe ushered me inside, taking off his boots and leaving them by the door.

"You can leave yours on if you want." The entryway flowed immediately into a kitchen and dining room combo, which had hardwood floors. Otherwise, the rest of the studio appeared to have carpet, which made the decision to leave my shoes at the door easier.

His now bare feet made little sound as he walked the few steps into the kitchen. I had a hard time yanking off my boots while standing. "You want a drink, Wyn?"

"Sure. That'd be g-great." I tried yanking off my stubborn left boot to no avail. *I won't let Darcy pick my shoes ever again,* I promised myself. Slightly winded from the unexpected exertion, Rafe was already walking back toward me. With one final pull, I got the damn boot off and pushed up from the front door at my back. He handed me a glass as I tried not to look too embarrassed. I stood up straighter and stepped the rest of the way into his apartment.

Taking a long sip of the water, my body still hadn't fully recovered from all the dancing we did at Rusty's. It felt wonderful letting loose for a change instead of worrying and locking myself away. Having Rafe there was the best part.

*At one point, I thought we'd burn up from all the heat we were generating.*

I smiled to myself, shaking my head. I had better focus on the here and now. My eyes took in as much as they could of Rafe's bachelor pad. The behind-the-scenes glimpse of the bass player and talented songwriter filled me with a kind of renewed energy.

This was a perfect opportunity to learn more about him even though he hadn't been exactly shy with me, all things considered. I mean, it wasn't like pulling teeth with him. He freely shared himself. *Unlike me.* But being here gave me another chance to dismantle the sheltered comfort zone I'd built around myself. I needed to make more of an effort to be open with him.

Rafe's apartment was a nice size studio. From what I saw, he took time to make the place his own with slight manly touches. If I knew nothing about him before today, I'd know instantly he was a dedicated musician.

"Let me give you the abbreviated tour, Wyn." The tone in his voice dripped indifference. I didn't much like it. *Did he think I judged him negatively for his small apartment?* Before the thought even fully formed in my head, I wanted to clear the air.

"Well. So far I don't see any evidence of you being a hoarder so... kudos to you." My gaze caught his and I added with a serious look, "I was really concerned, ya know. I mean, a person can never be too sure nowadays." He chuckled, the rough sound reverberating low and fierce in my belly. His smile stayed in my mind's eye, keeping me warm, as I continued taking in his apartment.

In his main living space, I noticed the large window ahead of me. It almost took up an entire wall, a dark curtain obscuring the view of outside. Only a sliver of light slipped through. Rafe flipped a switch and the floor lamp in the corner turned on, casting the room in soft, white lighting.

A black top desk with white legs sat catty-corner to my left. There were notebooks, legal pads, a laptop, speakers, and headphones strewn about. Above the desk were drilled-in asymmetrical wall shelves with knick-knacks and picture frames. On closer inspection, I saw Rafe in a close embrace with two people: a dark-skinned guy a few inches taller than him and a girl with a slightly lighter complexion. They all had the biggest smiles in the photo, like someone told the funniest joke. Whoever took the picture captured their happy moment to perfection.

I had no clue what came over me, but a need for a closer look drove me. I extended my arm, tiptoed, and reached for the silver frame. My fingers grazed one of the bottom corners, tipping it over. "Oh shit!" One of Rafe's arms wrapped around me, stopping my forward motion and catching the picture frame before it took a nosedive off the shelf, all in a single fluid movement.

"It's all good, Wyn. I got it." His gruff voice reached my right ear and I trembled.

*And you have me too.* Why was I such a klutz around him suddenly? It was damn inconvenient and humiliating.

Rafe handed me the frame, arm still around my waist, his hand covering the left side of my belly. Warmth surrounded me like a campfire on a cool night, he nuzzled his chin into the curve of my neck before standing up straight.

"Chloe and Zion?" I asked, my instincts already telling me the answer. He hummed in the affirmative that I felt more than heard. "She's beautiful. You all look so happy in this picture."

"We took that photo about four years ago before everything went to shit. Chloe's high school graduation party," he nodded at the frame still in my hand. "We had a big party in the backyard for her. A lot of friends and family were there. Pretty sure Pops took this picture. You never found him without that damn camera around his neck on special occasions like this." I heard the happiness in his voice. "It was a really good day."

"Yeah." I muttered. It looked like it. A ridiculous surge of jealousy hit me then.

Rafe coughed, clearing his throat and letting me go. "You still want to watch that movie I promised you?" I turned and reaching up, pecked him on the chin. Realizing that was the second time tonight I found that exact spot. It might be one of my favorites on him.

"Yeah, definitely."

*The pain came swiftly, slamming into every cell of my body. And settling into an excruciating throb. Every part of me hurt. I couldn't breathe from it. From the*

*horror of this moment.*

*How did I get here? How did I let this happen?*

*My throat closed up as he tightened the hand restraining my wrists. Every breath I took suffocated me. When he turned my face to his, I saw the truth about him in that moment. He got off on this... taking my innocence. Ripping me apart and destroying me.*

I jerked awake expecting to see sinister eyes staring into mine. A silent scream right there on my breath. I gulped in air, trying to get my bearings and taking in my surroundings.

A strong arm wrapped around me, tucked against my breastbone. Before I could panic, I heard Rafe's groggy voice, "Okay?" Just hearing his one-word question soothed something inside me. I was with Rafe, not that monster. Knowing that had a significant calming effect. With every breath I forced my body to settle down.

*Rafe was here and we were at his apartment, not back at that hotel room. I was safe.*

This wasn't the first nightmare I had since laying eyes on Nick again. No matter how much I wish it was. I still prayed for a reprieve I knew would never come. Since meeting Rafe, the nightmares had tapered off. Slow but sure. Then last weekend happened, and they returned full force.

My eyelids tightly closed, I tried squeezing those images out of my mind. Wishing Nick never stopped by the club. That I hadn't seen him coming through the damn door after Blue's set like his world was perfect. Meanwhile, I quickly fell to pieces.

Those thoughts were all it took to bring me back to that dark place, where I couldn't move, couldn't cry out for help. Voiceless. It took little effort for these fucked up memories to strip me bare even while I lay safe and secure in Rafe's embrace.

Back at Rusty's, when I told him he made me feel safe, it wasn't a lie. It was a fact I felt deep in my bones. Now, my mental state was questionable. I needed to do something to take my mind off this pain. Imagined or not. The memories still hurt. Still held me captive.

The room was quiet, cast in near darkness. I wasn't sure of the time. The black screen of the laptop was in view, perched in the center of a chair a foot away from the futon. The movie we watched probably ended ages ago.

Over my shoulder, I saw Rafe sleeping undisturbed. He'd tied his hair back with a band before we both got comfortable on the mattress earlier. A few locks lay in front of his eyes creating shadows on his face. I shifted in Rafe's embrace, attempting to find a slightly different position.

His closeness and warmth put me at ease. I remembered our dancing earlier tonight and smiled just thinking about how he made me feel. That I could do anything in his arms and be utterly safe with him. I wanted those feelings again. I needed those other memories gone—the dark impression of unwanted hands all over me—washed away somehow.

Before I fully thought through my plans, I turned around in his arms, my eyes at his chest. Looking up at him, he slept with such peace. With this unhindered view, I looked my fill even though it was too dark to see him completely. With a mind of their own, my fingers caressed his sculpted face, shifting his dark strands, before I talked myself out of the action.

I was tracing the slight hump at the bridge of his nose when his eyes blinked open. "Babe, you okay?" Vestiges of sleep riddled his every word. Throaty and sexy. I secretly loved it when he used pet names for me. Rafe surprised me on so many levels.

"Yeah." I moistened my lips and swept them over his chin in a clumsy kiss. Wriggling my way a few inches up his body, our gazes were now level. I suddenly craved one of his all-consuming kisses. The complete solace I found in his embrace. I snaked my arm around, traveling across his long torso and lingering on his back.

"Wyn?" There was a question in his tone—in the way he said my name—but I ignored it. I touched my lips to his, closed my eyes and waited for him to take over.

And waited some more. He remained still as seconds ticked by and so did I, our lips touching yet frozen. Absolute silence. In a stalemate, I leaned back, murmured "please" and pressed my lips back to his. I felt like such a fool. Then Rafe groaned, finally responding to my desperate attempt at seduction.

He finally took control. *Oh, thank God.* His firm lips and tongue consumed mine, pushing out every thought and worry except for this time with him.

"Damn, sweetheart. What's gotten into you?" The deep, scratchy timbre of his voice made him sound even sexier. Although I should regret waking him up from his sound sleep, I didn't. Rafe's panted breaths tickled my nose as his eyes searched mine, asking another question. Before I answered, he dove back in, taking my lips again in a hungry kiss. I was ravenous too, opening myself up to him, sucking on his tongue. An active and enthusiastic participant in this.

He grabbed my waist, squeezing my rolls as he continued the sensuous attack on every corner and crevice of my mouth. I loved the way Rafe kissed me, like I was a five-course meal and he hadn't eaten in days.

At first, the attention and need from him made me anxious. Now, I didn't want to hold back anymore. Life was too short to let fear rule my actions all the time.

I wanted to continue our lip lock but needed oxygen more. Gulping in air, I caught my bearings and studied him again, drifting my eyes lower. The shirt he wore earlier lay unbuttoned now, hanging open and revealed his olive skin. His chest rose and fell with short pants. Defined pecs and tight abs hid under a smattering of dark chest hair I hadn't taken notice of before now.

*What the hell was this Italian rock god bassist doing with me?* I peeked down at my body in the relative darkness knowing I'd see the same perpetually curvy girl I've always been. I hoped he didn't focus on the stretch marks or any of my other problem areas.

Rafe swooped in, surprising me with a nip to my bottom lip. His message was clear. *Get out of your head, Wyn.* He brought me back with his playfulness and I parted my lips again. Anticipation zipped through my body.

He pecked and teased every inch of my face except my lips. Where I wanted him most. The silliness from him made me giggle. I caught his face as he finished kissing my nose. Extending my neck, I took an opening to catch his bottom lip, nipping on him for a change.

I never thought I'd enjoy doing this. That we could be both silly and sensuous while exploring one another. This was the epitome of my carnal fantasies, being here with Rafe. The anxiety waking me up minutes ago still weighed on me, yet not as much. It was easy to let myself enjoy this time. Our tongues teased and played, vying for more of each other. I was desperate, but I had no idea what for exactly.

We continued kissing as Rafe nudged one denim-clad leg between my thighs, settling in and making me squirm with the new sensation. A sense of being trapped under his weight and broad shoulders overwhelmed me, so I gently pushed him off. He went willingly enough, lying on his back. He lay there for only a moment before pushing himself up, probably to question me. I made a quick decision, climbing on top of him.

"This okay?" I stuttered into the near darkness.

*I've lost my mind.* I shifted, trying to find a more comfortable position so all my weight didn't squish him. Wiggling a little more, Rafe's hands stilled my movements and squeezed my waist. "Sweetheart, you're killing me." From his tone, I knew his words weren't meant to be offensive.

My constant squirming had me more aware of the virile man beneath me.

Taking a deep breath, I averted my eyes from his face and slowly moved down his long, lean body. My deep breaths fortified me. I felt emboldened. In control for the time being, I didn't plan on wasting this opportunity.

The near darkness of the room shrouded me in thrilling anticipation. Moonlight peeked in from the large curtain, casting cool waves of light in the open space. Not enough for me to see all of him or him me, yet I felt fearless in this half-darkness with Rafe. Brave in my own skin again.

I didn't know what came over me, but I needed some carefree fun in my life. Trapped in the clutches of those memories trying to drag me to the depths of hell, he broke through the pain like a saving grace. This man empowered me.

My nose led the way, flicking my tongue out to taste his skin. Heat came off him in waves. My chills from earlier had little chance while he was around, holding me. A faint hint of saltiness clung to his skin. Rafe smelled amazing too. The cologne he wore lingered around his neck and shirt, a citrusy undertone. I liked it on him. His underlying, natural scent appealed to me, assaulting my hyper aware senses.

Masculine and woodsy, it made me want to feast on him.

I continued my slow descent by tracing his chest and torso, nipping and licking to my heart's content. Although I had no clue what I was doing, from the pants and groans I figured he liked my touch.

"Wyn?" He groaned my name.

Now at the front snap of his jeans, the pronounced bulge of his hardness pressed against the denim. I peeked up the length of his body. "Sweetheart, are you sure? We don't have to do anything tonight." I knew he meant those words. Whatever we did, how far we went tonight would be my decision. Rafe wouldn't take my consent for granted. He showed me with each caring deed and every word out of his mouth.

This part of Rafe's anatomy ensnared me, holding all my attention and captivating me. Drawing me in. I popped the button open on his pants; my fingers immediately moved to the zipper. My hands clutched the opening of his jeans. "I want to." I held his gaze for several breaths, wanting him to see the truth in them. I wanted this, with him. Right now. *For longer than that*, if I was honest with myself. Even if the fact scared me too.

The room became so quiet. Easing down his zipper, the snick-snick-snick of the teeth echoed throughout the open floor plan, the noise reaching my ears like surround sound. With his boxer briefs and impressive bulge underneath, I wrestled with the articles of clothing, pulling them down slightly.

My fingers wrapped around his hardness. I remembered him being big, his girth scaring me several days ago at my apartment. Although fear remained, I wouldn't allow my anxiety to overshadow this moment. Here with Rafe would be my true first time because it was *my choice*. My decision.

I cared about him. If the situation got too overwhelming, I knew it'd take a single word from me for him to stop. I felt good about taking this next step, trusting him this way.

That realization comforted me. My eyes tracked the length of his body and I caught him studying me, waiting even as I held a vulnerable part of him in my hand. It didn't warrant any concern considering what I must look like gazing off into space. My epiphanies could wait. I had important matters to attend to.

With sure fingers, I took a firmer grip and stroked him. Rafe's quick inhale and rippling torso let me know I had his attention. I wanted more though. I craved a taste.

His texture intrigued me. Hard steel over velvet, I found it to be a contradiction. Much like the man himself. All outward appearances made me doubt his sincerity, his interest in me. But Rafe was a great guy. A rock star Adonis who was also a sweet and sensitive man all rolled into one. *But why me?* The question came to mind again.

Instead of mulling it over, I watched him take heavy breaths, his stomach muscles rippling as I stroked him. I slid my hand from base to tip and Rafe's eyelids fluttered, closing tight. I couldn't think of anything else but pleasing him even more. A bead of liquid pebbled at the tip and without thinking I swooped down, swiping it with the tip of my tongue.

"Fuck!" His exclamation was guttural, almost pained. I peeked up at him again as his musky flavor coated my tongue. *Was I doing this right?* Insecurity reared its ugly head again. With all the grunting and growling coming from him, I figured everything was stellar on his end, but I didn't know. This was my first attempt at a blowjob. What I didn't have in technique, I hoped to make up for in other ways.

"Come up here, babe." Urgency strained his voice. A husky growl penetrated through my worried haze, completely demolishing the walls I'd erected all those months ago. I had freedom with him that oddly excited me. I was never the girl who took chances and I wanted to be… here with Rafe. I slinked up his body, his hands only helping me the last few inches until my mouth was mere centimeters away from his.

"You amaze me, Wyn. So damn much." *Oh.* No one had ever called me, Wynter Simmons, amazing. I'd always been just me. *Ordinary.*

About to come up with a witty comment, most likely dorky in nature and delivery, Rafe claimed my lips in a bruising kiss. This was so much better than anything I could think of to say in the moment.

I pushed up from his hungry claim on my lips, hands spanning his toned pecs. His perpetual heat warmed me everywhere our skin touched. It was now or never. "Maybe you should, um, get protection."

*This is really happening.*

Rafe ruined me for anyone else. I knew that fact deep down in my soul. His touch knocked down my defenses and helped me rebuild the parts of myself that had been missing for far too long.

*It's my choice this time.*

Rafe was my choice.

And it made all the difference.

# Chapter Twenty-Seven
*Rafe*

The sureness in her voice made me hard even more than her blatant words. *Maybe you should get protection.* Fuck me sideways, I thought this was all a dream. A damn good one. One for the history books of most realistic wet dreams, but a wonderful fantasy, nonetheless.

Wyn's lips were so damn inviting. Close. I couldn't resist the temptation, so I flipped us around and had her underneath me in seconds. "Are you sure?" A question that needed asking. My suspicions about her past had me overly cautious, especially now.

I wouldn't take advantage of her in any way. Not if I could help it. If I hurt Wyn, I'd have to kick my own ass into next week. I'd do it too, so struck stupid by this woman.

Leaning down, we were a hairsbreadth away from one another. I waited for her response. Wyn's eyes lowered, closed in anticipation of my kiss. But I wouldn't let her innocent and tempting look distract me from the question.

I traced along her collarbone, sliding my index finger up to her chin. Not letting her hide from me. Not when we were like this. "Wyn, you sure?"

"Yes." Her response seemed rushed, so I studied her expression with laser focus, trying to see if she harbored any hesitation, doubt, or fear. Whatever happened, there'd be zero regrets on my part. I wanted Wyn with every fiber of my being and needed to know that she was as sure about what she wanted. I expelled a relieved sigh, my tense muscles relaxing as I saw the truth in her eyes.

The old saying about a person's eyes being a window to their soul? The adage described Wyn at this very moment. And what she showed set me at ease. I saw a glimmer of fear. A *whole lot* of desire shined through too. She called to me with her eyes, a yearning in them clear as day.

Wyn hadn't always been an open book to me, yet she now gave me the clearest view behind the wall. Brick by brick she'd slowly let me in. Despite the worries about last week, our time together recently had been amazing. Tonight at Rusty's was no exception.

"Okay," I finally said. She beamed, her lips forming the sweetest smile. It would've knocked me off my feet if I were standing. Craving a taste of her beautiful smile, I brushed my lips against hers with a quick peck before scanning the area around us for my wallet.

*Time to find a damn condom.* This proved particularly difficult with my apartment blanketed in near darkness except for the sprinkle of moonlight coming through my curtain. How the hell was I supposed to find the small square if I didn't want to move from my current position over Wyn?

Tugging the collar of my open shirt, Wyn took me by surprise pulling me flush against her, initiating another kiss. *I love when she takes charge like this, showing me in the most basic way possible that she wants me too.* I got a fantastic sort of high from it.

The remaining blood from my head rushed straight to my groin, making me lightheaded. Wyn wiped out the rest of my brain power with that one innocent, lingering kiss. I was *so* screwed.

I pushed myself up and slightly away, squinting in the dark. I scanned around my bed almost frantic, wanting my hands and attention back where they belonged. On Wyn. My fingers suddenly grazed over something smooth at the corner of my sheet. *Eureka!* My brown leather wallet that I never kept too far away from me.

I pulled the object closer and flipped it open, wanting to shout like a damn *Price is Right* contestant. I decided against it, instead going in for another taste of Wyn's delectable lips. This time around, I wanted to see all of her and needed complete concentration to make it a reality. One last peck on her kiss-swollen lips, I set my focus on the rest of the bountiful curves underneath me.

An image of what she wore imprinted in my mind's eye since earlier in the evening. Now, I wanted her clothes gone. No more barriers between us. I recalled a long, loose-fitted red dress. She wore it with dark leggings and the boots she left near the front door. I roamed my hands down her body, searching for where it ended just below her knees.

I slid the light fabric up, catching her gaze every few seconds to make sure we were still on the same page. And I saw heat in her eyes, sure my own gaze reflected that same intensity. Wyn sat up as the bunched material in my hands reached her round butt, helping me roll it the rest of the way up and off. I worked on the black leggings she wore like a second skin next, working them down her legs and removing them quickly.

Suddenly, I saw a blur of hands. She smacked them against her body, shielding all the good parts from my view. My first thought was that she wanted to hide her interesting underwear choices. One forearm covered a sexy dark-colored bra cupping her buxom breasts so perfectly while the other hand lay over the apex of polka dot boy shorts. Now wasn't the time to let her hide from me, especially if we were taking this next step.

I rolled completely off and away from her, stripping my clothes off in under thirty seconds. Earlier I stopped her at the start of what would've been a five second blow job because lasting with her delectable mouth on me was an improbability. Didn't mean I hadn't planned on doing a bit of tasting and teasing myself. And I needed to uncover all of her sexy bits to do just that.

I enjoyed foreplay and knew revving Wyn up would become a favorite pastime of mine. So, she had no reason to hide. I loved her body and it was about time I let her know it. "You're so damn sexy, sweetheart."

"Oh." Wyn's eyes got huge as her arms fell away, dropping to her sides. Her hands fidgeted on the wrinkled sheets. I kissed her again, intending to settle down her nerves and get us back on track. My index finger traced the right bra strap, inching it off the shoulder.

The act of undressing Wyn proved downright heavenly. Every inch I revealed drew my eyes, like a dog panting for the biggest bone. I wouldn't get enough of looking at her, but I had other more salacious activities planned.

My eyes took in her soft, voluptuous curves. Inches of dark brown skin lay under me. I took my time looking at and touching her, skin so damn soft. One strap hung off to the side and I focused on skimming the other down. Wyn gave me a lingering look as she curved her back, making room to unhook her bra and pulling the cups away to reveal her nipples. *That's my girl.*

Wyn's lust for me was the strongest fucking aphrodisiac. Sharing my honest thoughts with her gave her the confidence she needed. And I'd do anything to keep this momentum going. Her body had curves galore and she was beautiful.

Struck stupid, her body left me spellbound. Wyn's dark areolas drew my gaze and I zeroed in on her pert nipples. My finger circled around an areola, watching her nipple pebble. I pinched the distended nerve gently and heard her breathy gasp. *Shit, she's so damn responsive.*

Holding myself back would be impossible, especially with the way she reeled me in. The touch of her lips all those minutes ago while I was half-asleep and drowsy perked me up. And her soft, almost desperate *please* wrenched a reaction out of me so strong, going backward was no longer an option.

Her breasts reminded me of the sweetest dark chocolate. I stole a taste of her pebbled nipples, one after the other, not at all surprised they were just as scrumptious as I thought they'd be.

The temperature ratcheted up as the heat built between our bodies. I moved downward, kissing my way past her tummy, taking a few precious seconds to swipe above the elastic band of her polka dot boy shorts.

This woman could drive me wild with little to no effort.

My tongue traced the small indents the band made on the uncovered skin as I slid off the very last scrap of clothing she wore. Dark, springy curls covered the vee between her thighs. I pulled the cottony material the rest of the way down her shapely legs, letting it fall somewhere behind me. Reversing my descent, Wyn's intoxicating scent stopped me in my tracks. Her fragrant arousal enticed me, beckoning me like the mating call it was. I barely passed chemistry but was pretty sure we had some strong pheromones passing between us right about now.

Fuck, I wished for more hours before the sun came up. To prolong this late-night, sensuous bubble we were in. I wanted to take my time with Wyn because she drove me to distraction. Heading straight to the main event was holding more and more appeal as the seconds ticked by. I hungered for it. For her. Having her welcome me into her body, taking every inch of me. The image alone drove me wild. I knew the experience would be even better.

Equal parts innocence and sensuality, Wyn appealed to me like no other woman ever had. And every ounce of hope in me prayed this was real and not a dream. *Next go around I'll take my time*, I promised myself.

I crawled up her body, my lips hovered over hers, needing to be closer as my patience snapped like a tightly wound string on my bass. Her soft gasps and quiet mewls fluttered to my ears as I opened and thrust a finger between her slick folds. She squeezed against the intrusion and I imagined how snug she'd feel after I finished readying her. Her dilated pupils and inner muscles massaging my digits told me she was close.

"Fucking tight, Wyn. You're gonna feel so damn good around me." Too heavy for my body, I dropped my head against the curve of her shoulder. I needed to pace myself and not fuck this up.

"Rafe," my whispered name from her lips held so much wonder and yearning. I suited up, ready to explode. I wasn't even inside of her yet. After a deep breath, I lined myself up to her entrance.

I couldn't wait any longer, pushing into her warm cavern without delay. Wyn's loud sob echoed through the quiet, dark room. I froze. She was tight and I wondered again about her past experience. "Wyn. Oh God, did I hurt you?" She was shaking so hard beneath me. "Talk to me, sweetheart."

I was just about to pull out when she said, "N-no. Just full." Her short nails dug into my back. The shaking hadn't ceased. "So full. I can't... Rafe, please." Her plea wrenched my heart. *Please God, don't let me fuck this up.*

"Shh, it's okay, baby." Wyn's eyelids closed, her face scrunched up. I stroked her cheek and rubbed my fingertip against the wrinkle between her eyebrows.

"Breathe for me, sweetheart. It's you and me here. Just us." A long moment passed before Wyn opened her eyes and exhaled long and slow. *That's it.*

She blinked her eyes one last time, staring into mine. She licked her lips then and I couldn't resist. I kissed her with all that I had while keeping my lower half utterly still. This time, the nails digging in my back were clawing at me, begging me to move. So I did. And I couldn't hold back, not with the way her body pulled an insatiable hunger from me. Like a man possessed.

The first signs of her orgasm, her inner walls working me so well, triggered my own. With one final stroke, I let go and held her tightly in my arms. *Jesus Christ, that was beyond amazing.* Electricity thrummed through my body while I spilled into the condom.

After another minute, I moved us to our sides, so that I didn't squish her. I rolled away to handle the condom in the bathroom then rushed back to bed. Back to Wyn. I returned to the main room and found her facing the wall, her back to me. She'd scooted all the way up, leaving plenty of room. That wouldn't do at all. I climbed back in bed, drawing her to me and holding on tight.

I pulled the sheet at the foot of the mattress over our cooling bodies, Wyn unconsciously snuggling closer. She was down for the count and I hoped her sleep remained peaceful for the next few hours. "I've got you, sweetheart. I won't hurt you." Never. It was a declaration. A truth I promised to keep. Wyn was mine to care for, take care of. And I was hers even if she didn't know it yet. I kissed some of the braids draped over her ear, mouthing *I love you* as I closed my eyes and fell asleep.

Wyn was safe and sound in my arms. And it meant life was damn good.

A whisper of noise infiltrated the most perfect date with Wyn, something that didn't belong. We were having a picnic while I played a song for her. Her understated yet sultry voice joined mine at the chorus. Damn, we sounded good together.

The rustling increased and the dream slowly faded away. Wakefulness intruded as I felt the bed's slight movement. Wyn no longer encircled in my arms. After our activities last night, I inhaled deeply, smelling her faint scent all around me.

That was a great smell to wake up to. It was only the second time we'd slept together, but she was no longer in bed. Where had she gone then? Before panicking, I heard the muffled noise again. I rolled my head toward the sound and blinked my eyes opened. Wyn sat at the very edge of the mattress, struggling to get dressed with short, jerky motions.

A thin ray of sunshine peeked in from the gap in the curtain, showing Wyn already wore her dark purple bra and polka dot boy shorts. She was so damn adorable. And sexy. I wouldn't mind waking up to this particular view all the time.

She was shoving her feet into her leggings when I spoke. "Good morning, sweetheart. What time is it?" My voice came out rough, like sandpaper. Looking around for my phone, I found it in the front pocket of my discarded jeans. It was almost eleven in the morning. Wow. Still a bit too early for me, even if we had slept for a long time. *We also stayed up quite late last night and it was well worth it.*

"I, um, I have to get home." She kept her back to me as she put on her red wine dress.

"Oh, okay. I guess we both needed the shut-eye, huh?" My comment received no reaction from her. "Sure I can't persuade you to take a shower here? It'll be even better if we take one together, save on my water bill," I teased.

Still no response from Wyn. "No?" *Well, it was worth a shot.* "Let me throw some clothes on and I'll drive you home."

"Thank you, Rafe," she whispered. I hugged her from behind, kissing her exposed neck then rolled off the bed to find a pair of clean jeans and a T-shirt.

"Of course, sweetheart."

Like always, Wyn remained characteristically quiet on the short ride to her apartment complex, but I noticed she wrung her hands throughout the fifteen-minute drive. *What was up with that?*

"Any fun plans today?"

She shook her head no. "Well, if you're game, we have the show tonight. I can leave your name at the door again." We turned into her complex parking lot. Besides the few words in my apartment a while ago, Wyn hadn't said a peep. I tried not to worry about it. Maybe she needed some space after last night. *But hopefully not too much.*

It was just as much a surprise to me. Maybe it scared her a little too.

Now second-guessing myself, I slid out of my truck and walked Wyn up to her second-floor apartment. She stopped at her front door. My instincts went haywire then. Something was definitely wrong. Wyn held her arms tight against her chest, crossed. The international sign for closed off.

"Can we maybe go inside for a few minutes?" A quiet storm now brewed behind her brown eyes. I hoped whatever it was, I could get a handle on it before it blew up in my face.

Her stride appeared determined as she marched into the living room, dropping her purse on the large coffee table. I met Wyn staring daggers at me as I turned away from the door. "I don't know how to take you sometimes, Rafe."

*Wait, what?* This direct verbal attack confused the hell out of me.

"What's that supposed to mean?" My Italian heritage boiled up to the surface. I forced down a quick response rooted in frustration and anger, not wanting to fuel hers. "I've treated you with the utmost respect, Wyn. Just like my grandparents taught me. What's going on?" I implored. Losing her wasn't an option, not without a goddamned fight. I put invisible armor on and strode toward her.

"What do you see in me anyway, huh? I'm not the type of girl who gets this." She looked at me then down at herself.

Wyn teetered on the edge of a breaking point. Her whole body—even her voice—shook with it. *God*, I had no idea what to say or do to calm her down, but I needed to bring her away from the edge. For both our sakes. I inched closer.

"I don't know what you want from me, Rafe." Frustration and despair laced her words. She hunched her shoulders inward, almost in defeat. Anger I pushed down only moments ago reignited like a grease fire doused with water. Wyn's had one foot out the door since we started seeing each other. Like she waited for me to fuck up and hurt her. I knew going slow was what was necessary, but it felt like every time I got one step closer, she took one giant fucking leap back. Pushing me away. Sabotaging us.

And I'd had enough.

Times like last night made it all worthwhile. I connected with her in such a natural way. We took care of each other. And she felt safe enough to fall asleep in my arms. We connected with one another on a deeper level. That's what I wanted her to fight for. *If she even wants to.*

"Wyn, I want you to trust me." I pushed my hair behind my ears, getting the loose strands out of the way. I wished I hadn't forgotten a band at home. "I want you to stop second-guessing us." *Me*, the word floated between us unsaid.

"I don't know if I can!" I thought the request sounded simple, but maybe it wasn't. Wyn turned away from me and I closed my eyes. Taking a deep breath, I needed to try a different tactic.

"Talk to me, Wyn." I couldn't fix this if she wouldn't talk to me. I walked up behind her, turning her toward me and lifting her chin to see her beautiful brown eyes. The ones that were so desolate now, I couldn't take it. "I'm right here, sweetheart." Slouched down, I settled my forehead against hers, our breaths slowing together. Synchronized. "Please, talk to me." I grazed her plump bottom lip. Her small gasp gave me an irresistible opening, so I took it, claiming her mouth like I'd done several times now.

When we were this close, it was magic. Pure magic.

*How can she have doubts about this?*

Wyn's chest nudged against my midsection, requesting space. Fuck me, pulling away proved hard though. Her forehead and a dainty hand rested on my chest. "I'm scared, Rafe." Her whispered words reached my ears and pulled at my heart in the quiet apartment.

"You don't think I'm scared too? Believe me when I tell you I've never felt this way about anyone before." Yeah, going slow had its moments, but not when I wanted her so damn bad and was willing to fight for it. I've been a goner ever since our gazes collided in the dark bar several weeks ago. "Yeah it's scary, but good too."

"It's not the same." She shook her head against my chest. *What wasn't I getting here?* She wouldn't even look up at me. "I'm damaged goods."

"No, I don't believe that. Not for a fucking minute." I leaned away, needing to see her eyes, make her believe my words. "You're perfect for me."

These last few weeks bubbled down to this. Wyn teased me with her contradictions. She'd push me away with lukewarm silence then pull me in with that playful spark in her eyes. It drove me crazy. I also didn't want to lose any of it. I craved the highs and the lows. Long as it was with her.

My hands moved to her warm cheeks. "You can't deny this thing between us. I know you want this." I whispered before claiming her lips again.

The next moment Wyn's hands pushed against my chest, shoving me away hard. Moisture welled in her eyes; her face stricken. I caught myself from losing my balance and started back toward her.

"I said no." Wyn's panicked tone finally pierced through my desperation. "You keep pushing and pushing and pushing." *Wait, what?*

"Wyn. Sweetheart? I don't underst—" Before finishing my sentence, she shook her head fiercely. A few loose braids whipped around her neck.

"Please go." My forward motion stopped with those two words. What had I done in the last minute in a half? I started toward her again. Wyn flinched, taking a step back.

She moved away from me like I was someone who'd hurt her. The thought stopped me dead in my tracks. Her response was like a puck shot in the groin. It fucking hurt. More than I wanted to admit, but so did seeing the sea of turbulent emotions in her eyes. I saw fear in them, most of all, and it broke my heart.

"Wyn, did I hurt you? Scare you? Tell me what I did wrong, babe." My voice cracked. I was at my wit's end. Not knowing what to do or say to get her to talk to me, I just stood there waiting. For something. Any sign that she'd open up to me.

"Please just go, Rafe. I-I-I don't think I can do this right now." Wyn waved her hand between us. Her words stuttered and jumbled together, yet their meaning was as crisp as the sound of a nail being hammered into a fucking coffin.

Crystal clear and final.

"I'm not the bastard who hurt you." Her breath hitched at my comment. "I wish you'd see that, Wyn. Wish you'd trust me even a little." I stopped at the door, hand on the knob, banging my head against the solid wood. Hoping it'd knock some sense into me. Help me change these last few minutes all around. I raised my voice so she'd hear what I couldn't leave unsaid. "Sweetheart, I hope you trust someone with what's going on with you. What's making you close yourself off. Call me when you're ready, Wyn. I'll wait however long you need me to."

I left the apartment, stopping the door from slamming behind me. More baffled than angry. Uncertain, I knew deep down most of what just happened in there wasn't entirely about me. Something was going on with her and she refused to talk to me. I wasn't even sure if Darcy was in the loop. Whatever it was ate away at her. Made her push me away.

I fucking hated it.

Thoughts on hyperdrive, I barely remembered the couple hundred steps it took me to get back to my truck. I rolled my neck, the anger resurfacing. Furious at myself. At the bastard who hurt my Wyn. One moment I woke up the happiest I'd been in a long time and now...

Everything was a fucking mess.

My chest tightened. Every cell in my body clenched when Wyn pushed me away. Her words, her actions pounded in my head on repeat. Fucking decimating me over and over again.

I hadn't rushed her, *had I?* Steamrolling her to be all-in like I wanted? That tormented look when Wyn shoved at my chest, the image wouldn't leave my mind. It played on repeat and I shook my head. She wouldn't even look me in the eyes, but I saw it. Something terrified her. Or someone. And it fucking gutted me.

Standing up straight, I pushed off the driver's side door and sat there after getting in. I craned my neck toward the back window and stared up at Wyn's apartment for God knew how long. *Dammit!* Tight fists met the leather of my steering wheel before I started the truck and drove away from the woman who unknowingly held my heart in her hands.

Wyn felt like home. Like she was everything I didn't know I needed. And in a matter of minutes, our relationship went to hell.

I'd just lost the best damn thing to ever happen to me.

# Chapter Twenty-Eight
*Wyn*

Dead silence surrounded me as I came back to consciousness. The absolute quiet of my bedroom—in the apartment physically—hurt, along with every single part of me.

*Life sucked big time.* The thought crashed into my mind and stayed there, taking up permanent residence.

The side of my head pounded. A perm rod jammed uncomfortably between my ear, waking me up from a liquor induced coma. After taking out my braids on a whim, I'd installed the torture devices all around my head, wanting a different style. A distraction. Now, my head throbbed with unimaginable pain, but not just from the rods in my hair.

Shitty didn't even describe how I felt right now. There were several reasons for my current state. And the blame fell all on my shoulders.

I'd made a huge mistake. Not just because of the pitiful binge drinking I did alone in my room last night. Not like me at all, the consequences hit like a ton of bricks, pounding my body like I got ran over by a double decker bus.

*I'm not the bastard who hurt you.* Rafe's angry words pierced right through to my chest cavity, hitting its mark with perfect aim. My heart had a huge bullseye and his words never missed. When he said them, in that moment my world stopped. A scratched record in a quiet room, vibrating on the air waves. The vehemence behind them jarred me, but I'd been too scared, angry and hurting to stop my own innate response. I shut down and pulled away. It came second nature to me.

I hadn't looked at myself in the mirror for more days than I could count. Two weeks to be exact since I had the meltdown in front of Rafe. And that was all on me. Yet, those immediate minutes, hours, even days after had those emotions still festering inside of me. Poisoning me against all rational thought.

I was scared. *Still am.*

Even though I knew better than to direct it all at Rafe. Pushing him away was my biggest mistake. Now, every millisecond of those brief minutes in my apartment played on rotation in my head. I tried numbing them last night with alcohol. Thank God I had today and tomorrow to recover before going back to work.

I now recognized his hurt too. I hadn't known what to do with it then. I was even less sure how to deal with it now.

Darcy even avoided me. The first few days I was an irritable bitch towards her. I didn't blame her for staying clear, but now I needed to fix my mistakes. Apologize to my best friend and the guy I didn't even know I needed in my life.

I didn't acknowledge my plan to crash Darcy's gala event tonight until I unconsciously got dressed for it. About half an hour ago. I got a burst of unexpected energy, fiddling with my head wrap. By the time I went to the bathroom to look in the mirror, I realized I desperately needed a shower.

The fight with Rafe all those days ago stayed fresh in my mind. The strong emotions raging inside of me during the argument dulled now. And not just because of the alcohol. I stayed pissy for a few days then self-reflected. After realizing how wrong I handled everything, I drank to forget. That's how last night came to pass.

*Not one of my proudest moments.* That rang true for the last fourteen days.

I hoped there was time to talk to him. Fix this situation with Rafe. Seeing him tonight would decide my fate on that front.

The fellas had a gig at a swanky fundraiser, courtesy of Darcy's ingenuity. At the time, I paid little mind to her story about it. Now, the details came crashing back. The aquarium downtown hosting the event she'd worked with since before she finished her degree. They were unveiling a renovated area to showcase a new species of fish. I hadn't really paid close attention to her activities since she returned home from Scotland, just happy my best friend was back.

About a week ago, Darcy told me the other scheduled entertainment had to cancel. Since she was the one to secure the band months ago, she quickly asked Colt if they'd be interested. From her excited tone that day I got the sense they agreed to do it.

It'd be good exposure for Country Blue. I'd been her plus one at an event before. Anyone could be on the guest list. If nothing else, it was an excellent chance for them to network.

This was a great opportunity for Darcy too. I was pretty sure she played a huge part, and as her best friend, I needed to show my support. I had some major groveling to do on two fronts tonight.

With finishing touches on my makeup and outfit, I went for the classic look with a little black dress I kept in the back of my closet. It hugged and accentuated my curves more than I'd like, but I was taking a chance tonight. Pulling out all the stops.

I shrugged on my faux leather jacket and headed out the door with some hope, a prayer, and more than a little trepidation.

I looked around the complex parking lot and didn't see our rental car. Darcy must've taken it to the event since she had responsibilities there. Plus, she probably thought I'd hide out in the apartment like I'd been doing. I requested an Uber, staying outside to wait so I didn't rethink this outrageous plan. Calling it a plan was a bit of overkill anyway. I had no idea what I was going to say to them. Maybe I'd take my chances and just beg for forgiveness from them both.

The sun slowly set in the distance and I was glad for the longer days. Yes, summer was practically here.

I had to believe there was room for hope. A way to salvage this precious, albeit rocky relationship between me and Rafe.

My Uber driver showed up in under ten minutes. I greeted him, sliding onto the butter soft leather backseat. He already had my destination queued up on his phone's GPS, so I sat back and tried to relax. Glad I didn't have to worry about driving or directions because my nerves were already shot to hell and back.

The aquarium was on the opposite side of town, closer to downtown. The drive would take at least twenty minutes, especially with weekend traffic. My thoughts drifted here and there, trying to figure out what I needed to say to my best friend and *almost* boyfriend. If he wanted to continue calling himself that. I hoped he did. Prayed he'd want to make it official.

Just a few blocks before reaching the aquarium, the driver came to an abrupt stop. *Shoot!* Traffic was bumper to bumper as far as I could see in front of me. There must be a traffic accident or construction up ahead.

I wore comfortable heels and decided to walk the rest of the way. The driver ended the trip early and I thanked him, getting out of the car and mentally preparing myself for the last few blocks. In theory, I knew where to go but pulled up walking directions on my phone anyway.

I walked at a brisk pace for a few minutes, checking my phone to make sure I was still heading in the right direction, when a hard shove knocked me into the side of a building.

A slight twinge ran up my bicep and shoulder from how I landed against the wall. Otherwise I was okay. Just glad I didn't twist my ankle or tear my clothes. A wall of muscle blocked my view of the street. "I'm so sor—" I didn't finish my apology because I noticed the guy hadn't moved yet. I was freaked out and a little pissed off. I got my bearings and looked up. And wished I hadn't.

My eyes found the face of my own personal monster. The person who bumped into me and now held me captive against the side of a building. The guy who raped me.

I froze in place, my heart stuttering then pounding in my chest. I couldn't breathe from it. I was held in some sort of stasis as my mind raced, screaming inside. *No, no, no. Nick shouldn't be here.*

*What is he doing here?*

Neither of us spoke a word yet. I didn't even know if I had words to say. Cry, scream, call for help, I needed to get far away from him. His good looks might fool people, but they no longer fooled me. He was a predator.

*Dangerous and unpredictable.*

Waves of anger wafted from him. His aura wild and malicious like a feral animal. The bad energy rushed me as soon as I registered who blocked my path.

He smiled then, showing off his toothy grin. *How did I ever think him appealing or sexy?* Now, all I saw was his creepiness. It surrounded him like a thick fog. His weight grew heavier against me, forcing me more into the building's brick wall, my curls catching against the rough surface.

He probably smelled my fear. Got off on it.

"Hey, sweets. Just the little bitch I was looking for." The fake endearment crawled against my skin, his words full of menace. I wanted to get as far away as possible, but there was nowhere to go. He had me at his mercy, just like last time.

"You just had to open your big mouth, didn't you? Colt won't even talk to me... hear my side of the story." I stayed quiet. Couldn't speak even if I wanted to. I had no idea what he ranted on about. Hadn't seen or heard from Colt since I kicked Rafe out of my apartment. I had no clue what was happening between them. "And it's all because of you and that ginger bitch friend of yours." I saw one of his large hands in my periphery, clenching into a fist near my cheek. He yelled *fuck* as it barely glanced across my skin, pushing against the wall near my left ear.

A devilish grin crossed his face. My stomach heaved. I wanted to puke when he looked at me like that.

"Ya know, I enjoyed popping your cherry last year. Fuck, plunging into your tight pussy bare. Nngh. Fantastic. I wouldn't mind having another pass at you." He disgusted me. My horrified expression must've given me away because Nick chuckled, the sadistic sonofabitch. "Yeah, I knew you were a virgin. Playing hard to get and shit."

"You wanted it that night. You still do, don't you, baby?" The sick bastard took my silence for acquiescence, pulling his fist away from the wall and squeezing his hand between our bodies. "Yeah, you do." He thrust his bulge against me, visibly excited from the fear I couldn't hide. He had completely lost it.

Nick suddenly stepped back for whatever reason. I saw my chance to get away, to check if someone was on the street who'd seen him crowding me against the building. Making my move, I ducked under the bent arm he rested against the wall, leaving the other side of him open. I felt my jacket scrape against the brick, but I didn't care. I had to get away from him.

I stumbled what must've been a few inches away, losing my footing. My heel got caught on a crack in the sidewalk. "Oh no you don't," Nick grunted behind me. Before I found myself ass first on the ground, he grabbed my forearm and yanked me back toward him. He held me against his front, his thick fingers squeezing where he held my arm.

"Let me go, Nick. You're hurting me." I wrestled against his tight hold.

"I'm not done with you yet, babes." *How did I ever think Rafe could be anything like this sociopathic rapist?* If I got out of this situation in one piece, I needed to apologize to him *big time.*

"I'm surprised I never heard about you and Ralphie, that boy scout replacement Colt found." He spat the venom in my ear. "Doesn't surprise me. You and your friend are just a couple of groupie sluts. If it wasn't me you set your sights on that night, then it would've been Doug or Berto." He spit out the accusation with such certainty.

"I'm kinda glad it was me, though." I heard the mirth in his voice. "Spilling into you felt fucking amazing." Nick leaned down further, grinding against my butt. His hot breath ghosted over my exposed ear. "I can't wait for a repeat performance."

He was a monster and I'd be damned if he'd lay his hands on me ever again.

*My legs shook as I moved off the mattress and walked the dozens of steps to the room where my best friend slept with her potential rock star beau. Darcy seemed safe and cared for in Colt's arms. I felt the tears start again. Took a deep breath and forced them back. I had to. I knew if I let them fall right then they wouldn't stop.*

I felt exactly the same right now. He wouldn't see me break down here either. I wouldn't give him the power ever again to hurt me.

*The miles passed quickly on our three-hour drive home. We made it back to our apartment then I immediately left again. I couldn't just sit around there like everything was okay.*

*Lying to Darcy, I told her I wanted to get breakfast so neither of us had to cook. There was little bluster behind her offer to join me, so I left the apartment alone. Drove a few miles to the pharmacy and bought a morning after pill. I couldn't imagine getting pregnant after that. Couldn't bear the thought.*

*My body ached the days following. I pushed myself to ignore the tenderness and threw myself into work. Darcy left for her new project a week later, so I no longer had to keep the tears at bay, especially when the nightmares came, and I woke from cold sweats more often than not.*

The memories of those hours and days after seized me, taking over. Nick kept seething behind me, becoming more agitated.

"That girl from a few weeks back wanted me too. And now I'm the fucking bad guy?" He asked himself. *Nick raped another girl. How many more were there?*

The thought of other girls out there, naïve like me, being hurt by this bastard breathing down my neck. That they went through the same feelings as me this past year and blamed themselves for what happened, like I did. And I couldn't help but blame myself, knowing

I should've done something that night. Or after. But I hid away. Burrowed inside myself and let this darkness fester.

I was ashamed. And I hated thinking that there was someone else out there who he made feel this way.

"Dill is such a fucking asshole. Taking that bitch's word over mine." I thought Nick referred to Dillon Edwards, lead singer of the band he played with. "Shit's ruined now because of you and that conniving cunt. She has her talons in my best friend, turning him against me. She won't get away with it." Had Darcy told Colt what he did to me. Before, I would've been furious if she told him without my knowledge, but now, I realized I made a grave mistake in not telling someone sooner.

"Well, guess I'll have to teach that ginger bitch a lesson. Ruin her life too." I didn't get a chance to listen to him babble on because he let me go, shoving me hard toward the side of the building again.

I flailed my arms out, one of my wrists taking the brunt of my fall. It twinged, shooting a sharp pain up my forearm. *Shit.* At least I kept my face from meeting the brick. Nick probably wanted to hurt me even worse than that. I waited, shaken to my core. The sound of Nick's loud steps against the asphalt disappeared in a matter of seconds. But I still expected another attack. My head whipped back and forth several times before giving it a rest. He'd vanished. A relieved breath whooshed out of me.

His cryptic but no less dangerous threat rang in my mind. *He'd make that ginger bitch pay for ruining his life.* Did he know about the event at the aquarium and was heading there now? I had to get there and warn everyone. The man had lost it. Completely unhinged. And God only knew what he planned.

The idea to call Darcy struck, so I pulled my phone from the small purse slung on my shoulder. Unlocking it with shaky fingers, it took a couple of tries, but my efforts went straight to voicemail. *Her phone must be off or on do-not-disturb.* She put it on one of those settings sometimes when work needed her full attention.

I had to get to the aquarium. Now.

With little thought, my feet moved.

Out of breath, I burst through the main entrance of the aquarium several blocks and minutes later. I didn't really remember the jog here, but my knees sure did, shaking with exertion. My feet would be worse for wear too. Little did I know these short pumps would be more trouble than they were worth.

Adrenaline coursed through my entire system, a nervous energy vibrating along my skin and through my veins. My shoulder and wrist protested my brief stint into sprinting, but I had to get here fast.

Ignoring the beautiful entrance and lobby of the aquarium, I focused on locating my friends in the aquatic labyrinth.

I caught the look of a bored teenager holding a small stack of programs in his hands at the entrance to one of the exhibits. I swiped the elegant, folded paper stock and whipped my head around the dim lobby. I needed to find my friends stat. Warn them about everything.

Nick's violence scarred me a year ago and I did nothing. Said even less. I wouldn't make that mistake again. It was time to stop being a victim.

I survived that night, and I'd survive this one too. There were people counting on me, even if they'd never know it.

# Chapter Twenty-Nine
*Rafe*

Not a single word from Wyn. And it was the longest two weeks of my whole damn life. No word from Wyn. I was still at a loss to what the hell went so wrong the morning after we made love.

Zi's advice continued playing in my mind over and over. I'd called him when I finally got home after driving around for a few hours. The time alone didn't exactly clear my head. My thoughts remained unsettled even after I reached my apartment, every detail about the small space now reminding me of Wyn. My rumpled sheets even smelled of her sweet scent.

Same-day memories of her were so heightened in the small footprint of my studio that I couldn't take it for long without going crazy.

Damn, I couldn't shake the idea of returning to her place to talk to her again. See if I could figure out what went wrong. Instead I called Zi. He answered the phone on the third ring and his tone immediately calmed me down, pulled me back from the edge. His wise words knocked some cold hard perspective into me. Some that I didn't have when everything with Wyn crashed and burned in an instant.

They also got me in line. It was a welcomed change from what I would've gotten from my father or brother. That was why I never considered them viable options. They only called when they wanted something from me anyway. And by the end, all they did was spew their hatred. I didn't have time for that. It was the reason why I hardly ever initiated contact.

I also didn't want to involve Colt or the other guys. They'd probably have my neck if they thought I hurt Wyn.

Plus, Zi and I excelled at the *no bullshit* rule we had since we were kids. And I'd needed the steady sounding board he provided. Especially before I went back to her place, embarrassing myself and making the situation worse.

*Zi? Shit's gone sideways, man. Everything's fucked. You free?*

*Just got home from an appointment with mom. Wassup?*

*I'm sorry, bro. Rest up. Call me later.*

I knew how drained he got after any of his appointments. My girl troubles could wait.

*Nuh-uh. Start from the top, Rafe. What happened?*

I told him how the conversation snowballed quickly once we got back to her place. Like a switch flipped after the fantastic night we had dancing. I kept our late-night activities to myself because that was between me and Wyn.

*Here's what you need to do, Rafe. Let Wyn come to you. She needs space and you have to respect her decision. When she's ready, she'll come find you. I'm sure of it.*

*Something's up with her, Zi. I just want to fix it and get her back.*

*Damn, bruh. You've never been like this with a girl before. Not that I've seen. But what I'm saying is even more important. If you barge in, trying to do that white knight shit and she's not ready, you'll lose her. Point blank.*

*And from what you've told me about her, she might be quiet, but she's also a go-getter. Independent and strong. She knows her own mind. Let her work through what she needs to. Be patient, bruh.*

*My question to you is, is she worth it?*

Hell yes! I yelled on my end.

*That's what I thought,* he chuckled. *Then calm your ass down and wait for her.*

To wait for someone I really wanted was fucking hard as hell. Especially when I wanted to bust down her door and make her trust me.

With music, I always had a new project or band to keep me busy, so it took a while for me to see that I'd been coasting along. Now, I realized I was just biding time until I hooked up with Country Blue.

But this burgeoning relationship with Wyn had me floundering.

I knew that distractions would get me through the worst of this spiral. When thoughts turned to Wyn at the drop of a hat, I tinkered with any beat or instrument I got my hands on. A doozy of one presented itself by midweek.

Colt marched into practice one night with a lot of purpose, explaining we now had a gig at some kind of fancy benefit; Darcy hooked it all up. We had several days to get our act together for it.

Lately we focused on playing our own stuff. Switching gears, we incorporated some covers over the next several days. It was time-consuming work and the best excuse to keep my mind off Wyn.

We also included some of our own stuff in the setlist. *You never knew who'd be in the audience, especially at something like this fancy affair.*

We practiced until our fingers bled. By the time we finished up and went our separate ways for the night, I was beyond tired. Still, not too exhausted to have Wyn on my mind.

And tonight was the night. Our gig at the downtown aquarium. Darcy really was a genius if everything I heard buzzing around this place was true. Not only did she help organize tonight's festivities, she also had an integral part in the exhibit opening today. Some endangered sea turtle and other fish being introduced into the newly installed saltwater tank. Only having a goldfish growing up, I had no idea what the big deal was, but it all sounded interesting enough.

Colt talked with Darcy and one of the other organizers across the room while Berto and Doug chatted with a couple of servers working the event. Always on the prowl those two. I noticed Berto hamming it up. Doug just leaned back and let the other man work his magic.

The air buzzed around us, waiting for the evening to begin. I stood off to the side in a corner, out of the way, but not out of sight. The solo time was necessary to get my mind in gear. I wasn't feeling particularly sociable right now since I was in a weird headspace.

I hoped my best friend's words rang true. It'd already been thirteen days and no word. It occurred to me to ask Darcy about her, but that seemed over-the-top desperate, and I wouldn't be that guy. Not yet, at least.

My momentary hopeful spark dwindled fast. Even after her disappearing act a few weeks ago, she'd gotten back to me within twenty-four hours. We were way past the *I'm sorry, can we go back to how we were* point now.

Wyn said she wanted time. I just hoped she'd take me at my word and know that I was waiting for her to make the first move.

Music and the band kept me going through this rough patch and the guys were none the wiser. Colt probably knew something was wrong, yet he never brought it up.

I appreciated it.

Out of sight was most definitely not out of mind for me, but I had to deal. Too often, I've been staying up late and fiddling around the apartment.

*I won't be able to keep this up much longer.*

I worked on ideas I hadn't messed with in years, rifling through old notebooks for some distraction. Back to mixing and writing because it had always been a good diversion for me. Most of the time it didn't fail me, except for moments like this when I couldn't stop thinking about Wyn while my notebooks were miles away at home.

With our short sound check done hours ago, all I had was time on my hands. Not much to do but stand around for a few more minutes before the doors opened and guests trickled in from the lobby and small exhibit areas.

I supposed the size of the crowd would fluctuate since the entire aquarium was open for browsing during this special event. We'd get a quick break in the middle as there'd be a few announcements and speakers, but otherwise, we'd play for two hours straight.

*It's gonna be a long night.*

I had to get my head out of my ass. This wasn't like our nightclub slots where we played to the young set for sixty minutes then got drinks. This gig was low-key but high stakes all-in-one. It was nice now and then to change it up and challenge ourselves. Put our music and image to the test. This crowd would be a whole other story, not like the rough and tumble or screaming masses we played to at the bars.

It seemed like all of us had some sort of anxiety about tonight. Mine manifested mostly into a heightened awareness. A few minutes until showtime, a thought to shoot a quick text to Wyn, letting her know I was thinking about her, came to mind. Nimble fingers typed quickly over the qwerty keys and my thumb hovered over the send button, yet I hesitated.

A door between Berto and Colt's small groups swung open, the abrupt action caused a slight stir in the large room.

A woman came running in, skidding to a stop as most everyone in the room gawked in her direction.

*Wyn.*

Although she appeared different, I'd know her anywhere. She

225

looked disheveled but still beautiful as I laid eyes on her for the first time in too many days.

*Tonight just got a little more exciting.*

I took in Wyn's rumpled appearance like a breath of fresh air. *Damn, it'd been a long two weeks.* Her hair was different. She replaced her braids with bouncy, lustrous curls sweeping just above her shoulders. She whipped her head back and forth, glancing around the cavernous space. I hoped she searched for me, but knew it was more likely she sought Darcy.

That was fine. I'd get my chance with her, if not now than later. I wasn't ready to give up on her or us just yet. Seeing her again made that fact pretty damn clear to me.

My eyes tracked her up and down from where I stood on the other side of the room, looking my fill for the third time in as many seconds, wishing I stood next to her.

The hairs on my forearms stood to attention underneath the only dress shirt I owned. Something was wrong.

Wyn didn't calm when her eyes landed on Darcy. She seemed even more agitated, scared, and panicked as the seconds ticked by. I felt her fear like it was my own from clear across the room.

Whether she wanted to see me or not, I'd find out what had her so spooked.

Before I made it halfway across the large floor plan, a body cut right in front me and stopped with little care or notice. Still so focused on getting to Wyn, I hadn't seen the guy and rammed into his back. He had a bit more bulk on me, even though we were about the same size. With the impact, I didn't land on my ass, just faltered back a step.

Zero time or patience for this rude shit, I was set to apologize before moving along. The guy still hadn't moved a fucking muscle, just stood in my way like a boulder. I snapped my mouth shut when I recognized who it was.

"Nick? What the hell are you doing here?" I'd reached my limit with this asshat a long time ago. Thoughts of being polite flew right out the window. I hadn't laid eyes on the arrogant fuck in over three weeks and I was beyond thankful.

And now he shows up here. What the ever-loving hell? A fucking nuisance is what he was. Come to think of it, Colt hadn't even spoken his name in as many days. So, why the hell did he decide to show up at this swanky event?

Nick's shoulder twitched when I uttered his name, but it was his only reaction. He seemed a bit off. Looked a little crazed even. Maybe he was high on drugs

His clothes were sloppy when he usually looked put together. *And is that booze I smell on him?* This prick had some nerve coming down here with trouble in mind. None of us had time for his shit today.

I tried catching Colt's eyes, but he focused completely on Darcy. I didn't blame him. But something was off with this whole situation and it made me nervous. Nick turned his head in my direction, finally acknowledging my existence.

"Hey there, Ralphie. How's it going?" Although the man remained steady on his feet, I swore he'd been drinking today. The strong scent of liquor wafted from him in waves of stink, mixed in with heavy cologne. Memories of my father tried to shove their way in, but I resisted. Now wasn't the time.

"Fine." I kept my eyes on him. He wasn't right. On a good day, I didn't like the guy, but my bullshit meter pinged all over the place. "Are you seriously drunk right now?"

"I'm a lot of things, Ralphie, but drunk ain't one of them." He looked over at the small group with Colt and Darcy. I noticed the moment Wyn finally reached them and watched his fists clench. "That fucking bitch! How'd she get here before me?" He muttered to himself. I watched as his eyes zoned in on Wyn. I didn't know what this was, but I wasn't having it. Definitely not tonight.

"Look, man, I don't know what shit you're on, but I think you need to go. Right now."

"I heard through the grapevine you got my sloppy seconds, Ralphie." Nick sneered; a sinister chuckle cracked against my skin as harsh as a whip. His chin pointed in Wyn's direction, beady eyes slithering over her.

*Hell no!*

"Nick, you need to leave. Right. The. Fuck. Now." *He's gonna get his ass beat if he's not careful.* I was never a hothead growing up, but I was my father's son. His genes were part of my DNA. My blood boiled now, itching for a fight with this cocky bastard.

Colt marched toward us. My heated words probably carried

across the echo chamber of the space we were in. But whatever Wyn said to Darcy had fire in his eyes; his long legs carrying him closer to our position. I directed my eyes back to the prick in front of me, not trusting him. He had more trouble in mind than just the nasty words he threw around. He either needed to leave voluntarily or be removed by force.

Colt rarely let emotion show on his face, but from the look I quickly gleaned, he was beyond furious. Whatever made him charge toward us had to be bad. It was good to have backup in situations like this. Nick was slightly broader than me, and I was no fighter, but dammit, Wyn was scared and I just knew it had something to do with him.

I wouldn't mind causing some damage and getting blood on my hands. Especially if it was from knocking Nick Ferrara on his ass. Let him utter one more derogatory word about Wyn…

Colt quickly approached us and grabbed Nick by his collar, propelling him backwards.

*Whoa!* For a guy who hardly showed his emotions, Colt was furious. My hackles rose even more.

"Bro—" Nick started.

"You're no brother of mine, you sick fuck!"

"Listen to me, Colt," Nick sputtered. "You can't believe those bitches over me. I'm your best friend." Now my fists clenched. If Colt didn't handle his so-called friend, I was fixing to knock some teeth to the back of his throat, so the bastard couldn't sling insults anymore.

"I've heard rumors over the last few weeks. Shit I didn't want to believe, man. About one of my best friends. Your new band even contacted me." He paused, inhaling deep. "Then somebody I trust— someone I fucking adore—comes to tell me how you hurt a friend of mine last year." Colt seethed. His fist got tighter around Nick's collar.

I sought out Wyn's gaze, knowing deep down whatever happened between them was not consensual. Her eyes locked on mine. More than devastation, I saw real fear, felt the power of it directed at me more than anything else. Time stood still with that look she gave me.

Gripping Darcy's hand, both women shuffled a few feet closer. Wyn looked away from me, visibly shaken as tears tracked down her cheeks.

*This prick had a fucking death wish.* I moved closer to Colt, craving any chance to take Nick apart. His fingers scratched at Colt's hands on his collar, fear and disgust in his eyes. Colt didn't budge. That wasn't enough for me, though. Not with the look in Wyn's eyes. All the looks I've seen since meeting her came flooding back. Nick put them there and he fucking needed to feel pain for it.

I charged toward him and Colt, the world exploding around me. "You sonofabitch."

*This asshole's going to pay for what he's done to Wyn.*

I brushed past Colt, clutching the fabric on Nick's shoulder, not caring if Colt let him go or not. My left hand clenched into a fist, ready to meet flesh.

"Rafe, don't." The words pierced through my rage. Wyn's plea in that soft voice of hers stopped me cold at the last second. I couldn't look behind me, afraid to see more fear in her eyes. This time directed at me. Because of me. As if I'd ever hurt her.

"Guess I know who the bitch is in your relationship, Ralphie. She didn't want a pansy after having a real man like me." His crooked smile zoned in on a spot directly behind me. At Wyn. "That's alright, baby. I got more of what you need." He sneered.

When my hand dropped from his shoulder, I used all the force behind my weight and shoved him. He landed on his ass in a hard thud. There was more pain to come his way. I'd make damn sure of it.

Steps carried me toward him, but rough hands grabbed at my shoulders before I could reach down and pummel the piece of shit into the ground. Murder was on my mind and the person currently holding me back would get maimed because of it.

"Mano, calm down and let your woman handle this." Berto rushed his stupid advice in my ear as he held me in a bear hug, stopping any forward motion I had planned. Doug stood close to my side, most likely ready to assist in detaining me. I didn't like it one damn bit.

Wyn walked closer while Nick's drunk ass took his time standing up and brushing off invisible dust. No one came to the bastard's aid.

"This is all that bitch's fault over there. Putting those lies in your head, Colt. I'm here to teach her a fucking lesson in manners."

She froze in front of our group, her back a couple feet ahead of us. Darcy stood just behind her shoulder, close to a seething Colt. What the hell were either of them doing? Someone needed to drag his psycho ass out of the building in fucking handcuffs or on a stretcher. *I'd handle the latter if my so-called friends and bandmates let me have a crack at him.*

"You ruined my life, you ginger bitch!" He pulled out a knife, much like Colt's switchblade. A loud gasp rang through the crowd. Before he could take a step toward Wyn or Darcy, uniformed officers rushed in. "Freeze!" One of them yelled. They immediately drew guns after seeing Nick's weapon. *Well, thank Christ for good timing.*

In quick order, Nick did something smart for once and dropped his knife. It clanked on the marble floor with a sharp sound and they had him handcuffed in a matter of seconds. Berto released me, but I didn't immediately go to Wyn like I wanted—like I craved. I wasn't sure if I was welcome, but *goddamn*, I wanted to be.

"Can anyone fill me in on what just happened here?" Two officers walked toward our small group. Only one spoke, asking the question. The girls stood off to the side, but me and the rest of the guys stayed close and clustered around them.

Wyn stepped forward. "Yes officer, that guy raped me almost a year ago." Her words punched me in the gut even though I suspected something all along. Wyn's hand shook as she pointed at Nick. "I believe he's hurt other girls since then. Maybe before too. He found me as I walked here tonight and threatened to hurt my best friend." She clutched Darcy's hand again.

Wyn was so fucking brave. She amazed me. I couldn't wait to hold her in my arms again and tell her how much she meant to me.

*God*, I hope she'd let me.

Almost an hour passed before I saw my chance. I found my courage reserve, walking up to her. "Wyn?" Colt swept Darcy a few feet away and held her tight just like I wanted to do to the woman in front of me.

I needed to know that she was okay, whether she wanted to see me anymore or not.

I prayed to every holy being in that moment. To anyone who would listen, really. The woman in front of me meant everything and I needed her in my life.

*Here goes nothing.*

# Chapter Thirty
### *Wyn*

Nick's been my own personal monster for the past year, nightmares and all. The trauma kept me in a perpetual state of fear, keeping me in his grip for too long.

Now, I realized he was just a guy who preyed on women. I probably wasn't the first girl he hurt. Nevertheless, he had to be stopped. Once and for all. This meant I had to speak up and talk about what happened to me all those months ago. If not for myself then for all the other women he raped or could hurt in the future.

Our immediate group: the fellas, Darcy and I, we already talked with the uniformed officers. They requested that I stop by the police department the next day to give my full statement. I wasn't sure if I'd be ready, but I had several hours to shore up some courage.

Darcy stood next to me as I took that step forward after the police officer handcuffed Nick. I couldn't look behind me when I'd said those dreaded words, released my painful secret out into the ether, almost an hour ago. The guys stood so close behind me and Darcy, I practically absorbed their body heat at our backs. Although their presence gave me an ounce more of courage, it would've been impossible to look Rafe in the eyes then.

"I'm glad it's almost over. That fucktard deserves this and much worse." The words busted out of me, completely unbidden. Two officers escorted Nick out shortly after they arrived. He appeared to be in a stupor then, almost looking furious and equal parts dejected.

*Guess the booze was finally wearing off.* Well good, I thought. His future didn't look at all promising. And it served him right.

"I hope those cops holding him give the rapist-prick a swift kick in the balls before reaching the squad car." I wasn't a vengeful person, but he'd hurt one too many people already. He belonged behind bars and I hoped like hell they lost the key so that he'd rot.

"There's the snarky best friend I know and love," Darcy said, thrusting up her arms in relieved joy. She wrapped her arms around me in a hug I didn't realize I needed. "I missed you so darn much, Wyn." Her quiet words traveled through me, settled in my bones.

"I know, Dar. I know." *I missed me too.* I felt sad and weak all of a sudden, having been in a deep, dark hole this past year. I convinced myself of a job well done with masking my inner turmoil, believing I protected both of us by shielding the truth of that night. But what Nick did continued to haunt me day after day. Enough was enough.

As the adrenaline coursing through my body finally left me, it felt like I'd run a marathon or got hit by a minivan. Wrung out and stripped bare. My body felt heavy with stress and worry. Thoughts about tomorrow's trip to the police station still plagued me. However, Nick was no longer my boogeyman.

He was just a pathetic piece of shit that deserved to be in prison. I believed that now.

A considerable weight lifted off my shoulders tonight. The fear I carried for a year was gone, brought out in the light of day and vanquished. He could no longer torment me from the shadows, the corporeal or subconscious. What he did to me was out there, the crowd tonight heard what he said, the threat of violence he didn't hide.

I took solace in the fact that people knew now. It just angered me to hear he'd hurt some other girl out there. Maybe even more, and I was disappointed in myself. Huge balls of guilt rolled around in my chest and stomach with the new knowledge.

*I could've stopped it from happening to another person if I'd only spoken up sooner.* Told someone. I realized this train of thought wasn't the healthiest or smartest path to let myself go down, but it was there anyway.

Tonight was the absolute end of giving him power. He wasn't hurting me or anyone else ever again. It was time I took my life back.

At some point I'd have to face Rafe and tell him I wanted to be with him. Let him know I wanted to give *us* a real chance this time. I just needed to find the courage to say something—anything—and figure out if he was still interested in me.

Suddenly Colt came over and swept Dar away in his arms.

I hoped she figured out how to tell him about California if she hadn't already. Both of us deserved some happiness in our lives. We only needed to reach for it. I thought Colt could be that for her.

Rafe's deep voice cascaded over me, murmuring my name over my shoulder, scant inches away. Goosebumps pebbled across my skin even though I still wore my now tattered jacket. I took a deep breath before turning around. Not knowing what expression to expect on his handsome face. Regret? Disgust? Pity? Could I handle seeing any of those emotions from him right now? Or ever? I didn't think so.

A shiver ran through me as I fully turned. "Rafe." His name nearly left my mouth as a sob, but I held back the sudden flood of emotions racking my body. Then, he wrapped his arms around me. *Oh God, how I needed this exact thing from him right now.* And he knew it too. He always knew. I welcomed his embrace. So strong and sure. Safe in his arms.

"Hey, sweetheart. How're you holding up?" He whispered the question against my ear, causing another shiver.

"I'm alright." *Or I will be. Soon.*

My hands clutched at his black, button-down jean shirt, breathing him in. He smelled so good. I missed this. "Could we maybe talk later?"

He leaned slightly away from me. I felt his eyes bore into the top of my head because I wouldn't lift my gaze to his. "Wyn," he said, lifting my chin up. I stubbornly kept my eyes closed. "I told you anytime and I meant it."

*God that sounds incredible,* I thought. I had another chance even though I wasn't sure I deserved his understanding.

And now he knew what happened to me.

I finally opened my eyes and got caught in his sharp green orbs. He didn't look at me like a victim.

He stared at me like I belonged to him and he'd do anything for me.

And I did... feel like Rafe's again. And he felt like mine.

*Rafe*

When that bastard lurched toward her with a knife, I blacked out, a weird sort of energy taking over my body.

I'd never been more furious and called to violence before in my life. Not even when my father and older brother pounded on me for shits and giggles. He better be glad the guys held me back and the cops got to him before I could, no telling where I'd be right now.

*Rotting in jail alongside Nick, most likely.*

We made it back to my apartment in record time. I mentioned going there and she'd agreed, not a hint of fear when I asked her to come home with me.

Her agreement humbled me. Made me smile so fucking wide on the inside and out.

*Wyn trusts me.*

It was what I craved from the beginning. Now, I realized it was something I needed to earn. I'd do everything in my power to continue earning the privilege too.

It was just after midnight. The aquarium event postponed due to the impromptu fanfare and violence of the evening. I was beyond grateful for the reprieve. None of us wanted to play for two hours after the bullshit with Nick.

My bandmates probably had all types of questions running through their heads right now. Conflicted emotions about shit that came out today and how it all went down. A tough pill to swallow about a guy they grew up with, I was sure. But it was even worse... when you learn something so horrible about a person you thought you knew. Thought of as a brother.

Monsters sometimes hide in plain sight.

I knew how harsh a reality that was when someone close let you down. Like an absolute betrayal. Shit hurt worse than anything.

My eyes zoned in on Wyn, taking her in. It felt like we'd been talking for hours. Her back to my front, holding her close to my heart. Hopefully I offered her comfort and warmth. I needed it too after tonight and the last two weeks.

Our conversation slowed down only minutes ago. Nervous energy buzzed around Wyn when we first got here. Now, she seemed a hairsbreadth away from bone-deep exhaustion.

"I know now probably isn't the best time and you most likely won't believe me when I say it, but you look fucking amazing tonight, Wyn. I like your new hairstyle." I pulled on one of her soft springy curls, caressing her neck with my fingertips. "And I'm so fucking proud of you too. You were so damn brave tonight."

"My hair will be a hot mess in the morning. I don't have my stuff with me." We cuddled on my flat futon bed. She turned in my arms, wiggling her index finger at me. "That's your only warning, Rafe. You better not run screaming come morning when you see my ratchet bed hair." She giggled.

The light, raspy sound brought a smile to my lips. I adored seeing this side of Wyn. *My woman.*

It hadn't escaped my notice that she completely ignored everything I said except my comment about her hair. I'd work on her later, but not now. Now, I wanted to hold her close and find peace in the fact that she was okay.

Or she would be. And I'd help in any way she needed me to.

"I really like the good." I placed a light kiss on her neck. "I especially like the bad." I nibbled at the slope where her neck and shoulder met in the most delicious spot. She let out a soft moan and just like that I was hard.

I needed to get a grip.

"So, I know I'll love the hot mess." *I'll love it all because it's you.* I didn't say those words aloud. Not yet, but soon.

"We'll see." She beamed, eyelids fluttering. A subdued happiness radiated from her which in turn made me unbelievably happy. These last few months had been a whirlwind for me and a nightmare for Wyn. And tonight's events were beyond crazy and overwhelming. Scrapes and all. Some of us bore more wounds than others, but we made it through.

Wyn made it through and she was stronger for it. I believed that to my core.

I'd show her I mean what I say in the morning—and longer if she let me—when I planned to worship every inch of her. I held her tighter and forced myself to settle down. "Let's get some rest. Nite, babe." Small puffs of air flew into my neck when she turned into me, burrowing deep.

Wyn fell asleep minutes later and I was right where I belonged. Where we both deserved to be.

In each other's arms.

# The End

## Also by Kelly Violet

## ABOUT THE AUTHOR

Kelly Violet is a born-and-raised New Yorker, living in a California world. A voracious romance reader, she published her first novel, Touch Me Softly, in December 2017. You can expect her stories to be angsty and gut-wrenching, fun and flirty, or just downright naughty. Music and dancing are her go-to outlets. If there's a party and dance floor (optional), rest assured that she will be one of the first people to bust a move.

Kelly loves to hear from readers. To learn more about upcoming projects, you can connect with her at www.kellyviolet.com.

Made in the USA
Middletown, DE
20 December 2020